The Siren and the Scientist

Siobhan Muir

Three Lakes Books, LLC

Table of Contents

THE SIREN AND THE SCIENTIST

Book 1 of Sirens, Inc. series

Published by Three Lakes Books

Cover Design: Kris Norris

This book is a work of fiction. Names, characters, places, and incidents are the product of the author's imagination or are used

First Electronic Print, September 2025

Captain Hermione "Wizard" Wilcox has a problem. The FBI has contracted Sirens, Inc. to extract a Dr. Martell from the Broken Pass Research Center before a wannabe paramilitary group abducts him for nefarious purposes. The problem is Hermione is the only one of the team who gets in when the Eagle Militia goes in guns blazing.

Then all hell breaks loose.

Dr. Chester "Venom" Martell spends his days developing anti-venoms that are cheap and plentiful to produce for the population at large. He's trying to save the world and gets to play with snakes and spiders to do it. When the Eagle Militia crashes the gates of the research center, shooting the guards, he figures the world is pretty much over.

Then *she* shows up to rescue him and his colleagues.

Turns out the Eagle Militia wants Chester to work on an antidote to their personal WMD, and they'll do anything, including kill other researchers, to get him to do it. But the only place to make an antidote is *in* the research center occupied by the militia. Wizard and Venom must return to make the antidote before the Eagle Militia catches them. This time they have a team, but it might not be enough to save the day.

Dedication

D edicated to Kris Norris. You fueled the idea that women could be as badass as the men, and like the incredible woman you are, they deserved a story (or six, lol). Thank you for being such a great inspiration, colleague, and friend. Love you.

Acknowledgments

I know I say this every time, but writing a book is never really a one-person job, and writing a series is especially difficult without help. Keeping track of details from previous stories is so much easier when you have help. Not only does it take a great deal of hard work, editing, and research on the part of the author to get things correct, but without my compatriots, there'd be a lot more mistakes.

Great thanks to Susan Sailors for catching all my typos. Huge thanks to Aerin Varhalmi for catching my inconsistencies and reminding me just which building they were supposed to be going to! And great thanks to Kris Norris for designing the cover for the story in the midst of her own writing deadlines. I'm so grateful. Thank you also to the G-man who put up with all my requests in the formatting.

As always, great thanks to my readers for cheering me on. Y'all make my writing worth the detailed effort.

Chapter One

C aptain Hermione "Wizard" Wilcox lifted her coffee cup to hide her grimace as she leaned against the table in the coffee shop in the rinky-dink town of Broken Pass in western Montana. An old 80s love song seeped out of the speakers hidden in the ceiling, reminding her of her ex-husband and all the ways he'd used some of her favorite things to hurt her. *You're emotion in motion, babe.* Yeah, that's because he'd always made her cry, either by belittling her or hitting her. The only way out was to join the Army and work her ass off until she divorced the bastard.

Oh, he'd tried to stop her, but she'd pushed so hard she'd been asked to join a new SpecOps team so secret, the members were hidden. She'd been the first woman they'd asked, but not the last. Now the Sirens were a twelve-member team so secret even Delta Force didn't know. And it always surprised the boys when they came across the Sirens.

But now she was on a mission, pretending to be hiking around southern Montana with her friends.

While we look for white supremacists threatening a research facility.

She set down her glass coffee cup and let the sun paint designs on the wood table. She tilted her head to glance at the two good ole boys she'd been following as her partner, Lieutenant Lisa "Circuits" Dunwoody, settled into the chair beside her.

"Any movement?"

"None yet. You look nice."

Dunwoody scowled. "I hate my hair down." She brushed her long blonde locks over her shoulder. "It gets in the way."

"You can always buzz your head if it gets too annoying." Hermione sipped her coffee.

Dunwoody snorted. "Nah, that's Banshee's thing. She has the whole Sinead O'Connor look locked in." She opened her laptop, keeping the screen faced away from the men they surveilled. Hermione leaned over beside her like two friends looking at the latest hot guy pics on the internet.

"Anything yet?"

"I've cloned their phones so we should at least get to see who's calling and texting." Dunwoody clicked the keys to open her surveillance apps and the screen filled with texts and calls. "Holy shit. These boys like to talk. Petty Officer Gomez was right as usual, I see."

"She didn't overstate the issue, that's for sure. Looks like those boys are starting to mobilize." Hermione shot a look at the two men as they paid their bill and waved to the waitress, who rolled her eyes and made sure to stay out of reach.

Yeah, those guys are definitely charming, not.

"Show time." She tapped the Bluetooth in her ear and sent out an alert to her team. "They're moving. ETA twenty-five mikes. Remember, this is a disable-and-disarm mission. The DOJ wants tangos they can question so use lethal force as a last resort."

A chorus of "roger thats" came back through her earpiece as she and Dunwoody gathered up their cups and the laptop. Hermoine's team could easily subdue the "Eagle Militia" members, but keeping the jackasses alive would take a trick or two. Frankly, she'd rather shoot them and be done with it, but orders were orders. And the FBI didn't want another Waco.

Which is why they hired us.

She straightened her back, feeling her piece hidden under her windbreaker. They'd never see her coming. They moved past the bussing bin and dropped the glass cups in it as they followed the men out the door. They chattered in easy banter about whose turn it was to drive and if they had enough snacks, but they kept their attention on the guys piling into beat-up pickup trucks.

To the casual outsider it looked like they were headed out to go hunting. But instead of relaxed and happy expressions, each man wore tight intensity and excitement. Hermione settled behind the wheel of their SUV and buckled her seat belt.

"Satellite uplink established, Wizard." Dunwoody had the laptop open with a bird's eye view of Broken Pass, Montana on the screen. "No new texts coming yet, but there's an unusually high number of trucks converging on the research campus for a typical small town. They're definitely making their move."

"Any word from the local PD or FBI field office about an uptick in activity?" The FBI hired the Sirens to watch and spring the doctor in case the Eagle Militia made any wrong moves.

"Nothing yet, Wizard." Corporal Ann "Thunder" Ayeshe spoke up on comms from their temporary HQ in the empty strip mall a klick from the research campus. "But the LTCom says we got our orders directly from the Butte office of the FBI. They want us to make sure we get the doc out of that place before the shit hits the fan."

Hermione shook her head. "What is it with this guy, anyway?"

"Dunno. All we know is the Eagle Militia kept mentioning him in the emails with a date and a location. The FBI seems to think it's going to be a kidnapping."

"Why? Isn't he just a research scientist?" She pulled the SUV onto the main drag headed toward the research campus. "What the hell would a domestic terrorist group want with a research geek?"

Dunwoody shook her head. "If the FBI knows, they're not tellin'."

"Okay, so this doctor. What's his specialty? Did they at least tell us that?"

Dunwoody snorted. "Yeah, he's a PhD in neurotoxins and he apparently spends his time studying the world's most deadly venoms from snakes, spiders, insects, and fish."

Hermione shuddered. "Yikes. I think I'd rather take on a nest of terrorists than play with that."

"Same, Wizard."

"So, why does the FBI think the Eagle Militia is after Dr..." She trailed off as she shot a look at Dunwoody's screen. "Dr. Chester Martell? I mean, he deals with venom, but he doesn't make synthetic versions, does he?"

"Not according to the FBI's dossier. Apparently, he makes antivenom, antidotes for all the worst ones out there." Dunwoody shrugged. "Doesn't seem like a very useful guy to kidnap, frankly, unless they have a big problem with poisonous snakes where they're from. Maybe they don't have the funds to buy enough antivenom for their compound? I don't know. But the FBI is convinced Martell is in danger from the Eagle Militia."

Hermione snorted. "*Everyone's* in danger from the Eagle Militia. What's so special about this guy?"

No one had an answer as they followed the old pickup trucks toward the research facility.

Dr. Chester "Venom" Martell, despite his job at the Broken Pass Research Center studying natural poisons, wasn't prone to unease or conspiracy theories. But something about the few beat-up pickup trucks he'd seen on the way to work put him on edge. Montana wasn't a stranger to survivalist and "militia" groups, but usually they kept to themselves on their compounds. This felt more menacing.

"You're just jumping at shadows." He often talked to himself to hear another human voice. In a job where he spent most of his time in a Hazmat suit to keep from dying on a regular basis, human voices were at a premium.

And worrying about beat-up pickup trucks in Broken Pass, Montana, was the same as worrying about sand on the beach. They were a dime a dozen and twice as rusted. But when another one came into view as he pulled through the gate at the lab, unease trickled down Chester's back.

He parked his Toyota Prius in his usual spot and got out, glad he'd brought his jacket. While only September, the gray skies threatened rain that could easily turn to sleet and snow. Montana didn't fool around when it came to winter weather. He wrapped his scarf around his neck and locked his car as he headed into the building.

"Mornin', Doc Venom. How's the research goin'? Inventing new ways to kill people?" Dirk the security guard smirked as he checked Chester's credentials.

"The research into *finding antidotes* is going pretty well, thanks." While Dirk seemed friendly enough, he always had a bit too much glee when asking about deadly substances. Chester took his creds back. "How are the wife and kids?"

"Same old shit, different day." Dirk shrugged and waved him through, his expression still avid. "You be careful with those poisons, now."

Chester nodded and headed for the elevators. Like the extra pickup trucks, Dirk's fascination with toxic substances seemed elevated. Chester pressed the button for Dr. Miller's lab's floor and breathed a sigh of relief as the doors closed. The last thing he needed to do was create an imaginary crisis where there wasn't one.

He still didn't know why Dr. Miller—er, Tamara, had asked him to come by, but he figured he could take the tunnels to his lab after he met with her. His gut churned a little as he thought of her overtures the last few weeks. She always seemed to seek him out at the cafeteria, and he had the sneaking suspicion this visit was another excuse to see him. While she was smart and knowledgeable in her subject of SONAR, she always made him feel a little like a rabbit walking into a wolf's den. The attraction was definitely one-sided, and his gut clenched at the thought of seeing her today.

"I'm sure it's just the chili cheese fries Eliza had made me try at the Redolent Lion Café last night." Talking to himself usually calmed him down, but it didn't work this time.

He shook his head as the doors opened to another guard who had far more intensity than Dirk on his best day. "Good morning. I'm here to see Dr. Tamara Miller."

"Yes sir. Credentials please."

He dug out his badge and handed it to the guard. The man scanned them and noted his expired permissions to be in the building.

"You say you have an appointment with Dr. Miller?"

Chester nodded. "Yes, she's expecting me." Not that he wanted her to.

The guard picked up the phone beside his podium and dialed a number. "Dr. Miller? I have a Dr. Martell here to see you...Yes, ma'am. I'll send him in." He hung up the phone and met Chester's gaze. "Looks like you check out, Dr. Martell. Down the hall, fourth lab on the left."

"Thanks." He didn't waste time as he had animals to check on and analyses to run. Taking time out to see what Tamara wanted chafed at his timeline.

He followed the guard's directions and passed his previous lab space. When he'd first been moved to Building Two, he'd been frustrated and unsettled with the new lab. Nothing was where he wanted it and it took a whole new level of organization. But after a month, he found he preferred the larger, quieter space with windows for natural light and a hibernaculum for animals that needed to sleep all winter.

He'd never realized just how loud this lab building was until he worked in the new building. While his wasn't the only lab there, the other two occupants were conducting DNA sequencing and botany studies to find cures for diseases like cancer and AIDS. He hadn't realized just how much he hated the sound of the SONAR research shaking the walls or the muted booms of gunshots when another lab tested their new battle armor tech.

Necessity is the mother of invention, and there's always someone making better bullets.

He shook his head as he pushed into Dr. Miller's lab. She was one of the specialists, finding ways of making SONAR undetectable to enemy vessels while still making it powerful enough to track them. That was why his lab had been moved. It irritated the animals and had set his research back months. The uncomfortable hum of the sonar machines buzzed in his ear bones, and he grimaced as he looked around for Dr. Miller.

He found her bent over her computer, her white-blonde hair pulled into a severe bun as she frantically typed an email to someone. Tension strung her shoulders so tight he figured they'd chime if he touched them. Not that he wanted to touch her at all. Ever.

"Dr. Miller?"

She bolted upright and looked over her shoulder with a guilty flash in her eyes. He wondered why she looked as if she'd gotten caught with her hand in the cookie jar but waved to ease some of the tightness around her eyes.

"Oh, Dr. Venom." Her eyes squinted behind her glasses and she snorted a little. "You know, your name always reminds me of that comic book character. You know he's considered a bad guy, right?"

She gave him her version of a sultry smile and it only made him uncomfortable. "Are you a bad guy, Dr. Venom?"

"Not last I checked, Dr. Miller. What did you want to see me about?" He didn't want to get distracted from the purpose of this visit. He had animals to feed and tests to run.

Tamara dropped the pseudo-sultry look and went straight to friendly. "How are you liking your new lab? Do you have everything you need?"

He frowned. It was an odd question considering she'd had no hand in moving him. She was just another researcher hired by Broken Pass to work on government research and development projects. Her specialty was the power of SONAR frequencies.

"Yes, everything is fine, though I do need to get back to the animals and make sure their cages are cleaned. Was that all you wanted to know?"

Annoyance filtered through his system at the deviation from his usual routine. He liked things done a certain way, but he made exceptions for when other researchers wanted his expertise. He rarely made social visits and certainly not during regular working hours.

Matching annoyance flashed across her face before she schooled her expression to something bland, though her eyes glittered.

"Well, I hadn't seen you in a while and thought it would be nice to catch up."

Catch up? She'd never been interested in 'catching up' when they worked in the same building before. Why would she want to do so now? He narrowed his eyes.

"I see. Perhaps another time? I really need to get to work as I have a project review due soon and I'm a bit behind." It wasn't true in the slightest, but he didn't like being manipulated into interaction.

She shot a look at the clock on the near wall and another over his shoulder toward the door before she nodded. "Yes, of course. Another time. Call you later?"

"Sure." He dipped his head in acknowledgment and turned to leave, already calculating how much he had to do for that day.

"Dr. Martell."

He turned just enough to look at her. "Yes?"

"I'm sorry I interrupted your day. Forgive me?" And her face shifted into a pleading pout.

What could he say? She'd offered him more manipulation but the social contract required him to accept her apology or look like an asshole.

"Sure." He twitched the corners of his mouth upwards into a perfunctory smile before he swept out of the lab into the hallway. "When dogs dance on two legs and give dissertation talks."

Chester sealed his lips closed over the rest of his words and nodded to other staff members he passed in the hall. There was no way under the sun that he'd spend any more time than he had to with Dr. Miller. Something seemed off about her, particularly today, and he really didn't have time to figure out what it was.

He showed his ID to the guard at the tunnel door and the man checked him through, clearing him to make the trek to his new lab. The campus had spared no expense with the construction of the tunnels. They were well-lit and heated or cooled by the water pipes running their lengths. Each one had been decorated with different mosaics in tiles at about eye-level. This one had the story of evolution starting with amoebas and gradually showing more complexity to arrive at the other end with mammals, birds, lizards, and insects as known in modern times. It was his favorite mosaic, and it soothed his earlier irritation as he traversed the tunnel's length.

He used his badge to get through the door on the other end but stopped to show it to the guard stationed just inside. He was surprised to see Tessa Barton at this post. She usually sat at the front desk to his new building, not stuck down in the tunnel vestibule.

"Good morning, Tessa. I'm surprised to see you here. Are you well today?"

"I am, thank you, Dr. Martell. Credentials, please."

Tessa was far more professional and sharp-eyed than Dirk, and her impassive demeanor always calmed Chester. Still, he tried to discern anything that might be amiss in her expression.

"Is everything okay? You usually are at the front."

"Everything is fine." She scanned his badge and watched the readout intently.

He'd long ago learned she didn't do pleasantries beyond "good morning" or "goodnight," but she surprised him when the machine chirped with acceptance. "Just the luck of the rotation. What brings you in through the tunnels, doc?"

Her willingness to engage in more than greetings surprised him. "Another researcher wanted me to look at something so I took the tunnel over from there." He almost told her about the evolutionary tiled mosaic, but didn't want to overstep the bounds of their limited relationship.

"Have you been in all the tunnels, Dr. Martell?"

Chester shook his head. "No, about three quarters of them. Each one has some fascinating tiled mosaics along their length. This one has the story of evolution."

"Really?" She glanced over his shoulder at the door. "That sounds intriguing. Maybe I'll check it out after shift." She handed him back his badge. "You're cleared for entry. Have a good day, doc."

"Thank you. You, too."

He looped the lanyard over his head and headed up the concrete steps to the main level. He glanced back to find her watching him, her professional expression back in place, but he wondered if she felt bored or abandoned at the tunnel entrance. His badge let him into the labs as he thought back to the pickup trucks and Dr. Miller's odd need to see him. Combined with the extended conversation with Tessa, something seemed off with the whole morning.

He shook his head at the strangeness and shoved it all to the back of his mind. He had research to conduct and animals to tend. He didn't have time to worry about odd human interactions.

Chapter Two

Hermione kept an eye on the good ole boys in their rusted pickup trucks as she headed for the innocuous buildings housing the lab on the northeast edge of Broken Pass. The labs were set back from the main gate by a long driveway across a cleared area housing an employee parking lot and some tasteful landscaping.

Good visibility to see intruders.

The fencing around the compound stood at least eight feet high and had razor wire at the top. It didn't carry electric current, but there were sensors in the ground around the perimeter to announce breaches.

"What the fuck are they doing?" Dunwoody scowled at her laptop as they watched the satellite surveillance showing several of the old pickups converging on the gate.

And not slowing down.

"I dunno, but get the team in position. I think they're gonna breach the gate." Hermione gritted her teeth and accelerated to keep up.

It looked like a hillbilly road race as an old army vehicle left over from the Cold War positioned itself in front of all the others. The paint job resembled something you'd find in a diaper left in the trash. But the old vehicle blew out a plume of black exhaust and rammed through the gate despite the guards firing automatic weapons at it.

"Holy fuck! Be advised, Eagle Militia has broken through the gate at the Broken Pass Research Center. Sirens One and Two pursuing."

"Roger that, Sirens Five and Three holding perimeter." Corporal Roxanne Bailey reported from the vehicles behind them.

"Roger that, Siren Six standing by." Petty Officer Lin Su "Pinpoint" Ki checked in from her sniper nest in the rocks above the facility.

"Siren Four standing by." Petty Officer Jennifer Moriarty's voice came through the radio with a subtle hint of giggling excitement. Hermione rolled her eyes while Dunwoody grinned.

"Siren Seven standing by. Drone in the air for overhead visuals." Airman Marisol Gomez's soft response completed the team's check in.

"Copy that. Eagle Militia firing on guards. Siren One will take out ground forces at facility. Sirens Five and Three, hold perimeter. Don't let anyone out. Let's keep this contained at the lab." Hermione barked the orders as she roared after the armored vehicle heading for the building. "Non-lethal force if possible, but don't let those bastards get out."

"Roger that."

The rest of the hillbilly brigade fanned out to deal with the guards, but she powered through to the facility where the armored vehicle slammed through the front glass doors. Hermione growled and jerked the wheel of their truck, skidding to a stop. She shared a look with Dunwoody before they both headed into the fray.

This is fuckin' insane.

Not only did they have to watch for the homegrown terrorists, they also had to avoid the guards. Her team wasn't dressed like Special Operators, so the guards wouldn't know who they were any more than the good ole boys. And the good ole boys weren't holding back. Already, several of the guards were down and she didn't think they were unconscious.

"Take down as many as you can. I'm headed around the front to keep them from getting inside."

"Roger that." Dunwoody pulled her sidearm, the weapon looking incongruent against her turquoise fingerless gloves.

Shouts and screams of pain sounded around them as they split up. Hermione used the military vehicle to slip inside the building. A few random shots sounded down the hallways, but the lobby was clear. *Shit, where the hell is the front guard?* More than likely, he was down behind the desk.

Someone grabbed her as one of the good ole boys came in behind her. "What the hell are you doin' here?"

She didn't bother to answer as she swung around and punched him in the throat. His eyes bulged and he gurgled as he dropped back. She pulled him into a headlock and eased him to the floor as she cut off his air. She scanned the rest of the room as she released him and the elevators dinged open. The front guard stepped out and looked around with an air of calculation.

Dammit, the bastard's an inside man.

She rose and sprinted toward him, planning to use her momentum to take him down. But he saw her at the last moment, his eyes opening wide as he stepped back into the elevator car. The doors started to close, and she sucked in her gut and turned sideways to slide between the closing doors.

"What the fuck!"

He tried to pull his sidearm, but she slammed her fist into his bicep and an elbow to his gut. He bent at the waist, and she finished him off with a crack to the back of his skull. He crumbled at her feet as the elevator descended.

She leaned against the car's wall and breathed as she tapped her ear. "Sirens, report."

Garbled voices and static filled her ear.

"Dunwoody?"

Only static remained.

Fuck. Given how insulated some of labs were according to the architectural plans they'd seen, there was no way radio waves would make it down there.

This isn't Star Trek where they can beam shit from place to place.

Yanking out zip ties, she secured the guard's hands and feet so she wouldn't have to worry about him coming after her. The elevator came to a stop on the basement floor, and she braced herself for whoever she'd meet. She held her hands up as the doors opened, thinking, *I come in peace.*

No one stood on the other side. She let out a breath she hadn't remembered holding and peeked around the doors to be sure there were no adversaries waiting for her.

Electricity flickered and crackled down the hallway somewhere, but there was no human movement that she could hear. She tapped her ear again, but only static met her comms check. *Sonuvaprick!* For now, she was on her own. Fortunately, her specialty was navigation and direction. Even underground, she knew which direction was north and roughly how much square footage the building covered.

Purloining the guard's sidearm, a very nice Sig Sauer that didn't look standard issue, she checked the magazine and chambered a round. Then used her knuckle to press the L button on the elevator and sent the guard back to his post. If he was the inside man, he wouldn't be useful for a while.

Hermione scanned the corridor, taking in the glass windows of the various labs. None of them looked like the venom lab. She frowned and dug out the map she'd stuffed into her jacket pocket. According to the lab layout, the lab she was looking for should have been the third door down to the right, on the left-hand side.

She shoved the map away and thumbed off the safety on the Sig before making her way down the corridor between the rooms. She peered into each, looking for people, but no one seemed to be anywhere down there. Had they all gotten out ahead of the terrorists' attack?

She frowned. That didn't make sense. No one knew it was coming. Did they?

Unless there's more than one inside man.

She reached the door marked as the venom lab on her map and tested the door. It opened on silent hinges to a room with counters and cabinets, but it was full of boxes and discarded equipment stacked on shelves. A layer of dust covered the nearby surfaces and appeared unused for a while.

What the hell? What had happened to the venom lab?

She switched off the light and closed the door, trying to discern where all the lab personnel had gone. The electricity flickered again, and she heard whispers coming from around the corner. According to her map, that was where the break room and restrooms were located. She moved silently toward the sounds, keeping an eye on where she'd been to make sure no one ambushed her.

Crouching beside the break room door, she took a deep breath and pushed it open.

"Christ on a cracker!" A white male dressed in a lab coat with pimples and thick glasses lurched backwards, his arms windmilling as he lost his balance. An Asian woman in another lab coat with bobbed hair steadied him. "Who the hell are you?"

Hermione tabbed the safety on her weapon and shoved it into the back of her jeans. "Captain Hermione Wilcox, U.S. Army retired. I'm looking for Dr. Chester Martell. Is he in here with you?"

A white woman with pale blonde hair and a nose ring shook her head. "No, he hasn't been here for over a month. He was moved, but we don't know where. Why? What's happened?"

Hermione resisted the urge to grimace. Fuck, the intel they had was well over a month old. How the hell had that happened? She shoved the frustration away and looked for a solution.

"A domestic terrorist group, the Eagle Militia, has attacked the research campus and they're setting up camp here until they get what they want."

"And what do they want?" The guy with the pimples shot a look out the door to the hallway beyond.

"Like me, they're looking for Dr. Martell."

"I told you, we don't know where he is." The blonde swallowed hard and looked nervously at the others. Something about her made Hermione suspect she was hiding something, but at the moment it seemed moot until she found Dr. Martell.

"You must have a directory or a log of lab locations, right?"

The Asian woman nodded. "Yeah, of course, but it's on the computers and everything shut down when the power went out."

Hermione raised her eyebrows. "Don't you know the different buildings of your research campus?"

The lab techs shook their heads, and she wondered how so many smart and observant people could be so unobservant.

"Then a lot more people are gonna get hurt unless you help me find him first." She sighed and grabbed a piece of paper lying on a nearby table. "Anyone got a pen?"

Pimples handed her one from his breast pocket.

"Thanks. From what I saw of the original map, there are a total of six buildings on this campus, spread out like this." She drew an oval-shaped wagon wheel with a central hub representing a fountain and six rectangles for the buildings. "We're here in the main building. The Eagle Militia has occupied the upper floor and bombed or disabled the elevator. You say Dr. Martell's lab has been moved. Anyone have any idea into which building it was moved?"

Everyone shook their heads, but Pimples shot a look at the white blonde. "Didn't he come in this morning to visit you, Dr. Miller? I thought I saw him talking to you."

Hermione swung her gaze to look at Dr. Miller. "He was here this morning talking to you?"

"Uh, well, yes. He might've stopped by."

Hermione didn't care for the hedging. "Since you know him so well, perhaps you know which building they moved his lab into?"

"I didn't say I knew him well, just that he might have been here today."

"Uh-huh, so where did he go from here?"

"I saw him head down the hallway toward the tunnels." The Asian woman pointed toward the end of the building where the venom lab should be.

The sound of a flushing toilet came through the walls and someone walked into the break room. Hermione whirled with the Sig in her hands pointed toward the door.

"Whoa!" The guy in a guard's uniform stopped short and held up his hands. "Who the hell are you?"

"Captain Wilcox, US Army retired. Who are you?" Her weapon never wavered.

"Anderson, Jeff. Guard for Building One, lower level. I need to see some ID."

Hermione nodded and lowered her weapon. "I was undercover when the Eagle Militia hit the front gates, but I'm going for my ID now." She switched the Sig to her non-dominant hand and reached into the inside breast pocket of her windbreaker and pulled out her Sirens, Inc. badge.

Moriarty had made them to look like a shield because most people wouldn't fight against an official-looking badge. They were about as official as a costume tin star, but when she showed it to the guard and the scientists around her, they all relaxed. Except Dr. Miller. Her jaw tightened, and her shoulders grew even more taut.

Interesting.

"Where were you stationed this morning?" She tucked the badge away and shoved her weapon into the back of her waistband.

"I normally sit at the tunnel entrance." He pointed toward the old venom lab. "You said the Eagle Militia hit the front gates. Of the research campus? Why would they do that, Captain?"

She scanned the faces of the assembled scientists. "We got intel that the Eagle Militia was going to hit this research center, and I was sent in to get Dr. Martell out. But I have to find him before they do."

"Dr. Chester Martell?" The guard raised his eyebrows. "He was here this morning and left the building through my entrance at 0735. He took the tunnel to Building 2 so I assume his lab is there."

"He could have a lab in one of the other buildings," Pimples ventured.

The guard shook his head. "Then he would've gone out the entrance beside the elevators or the other end."

"How many tunnels for each building?" The Asian woman frowned as she pointed at the forgotten map on the table, and Hermione raised her eyebrows. How did the scientists know so little about their campus?

"Three per building. Twelve in total. The tunnels beside the elevators lead to the central hub under the fountain in the courtyard. There are six spokes to the buildings from there." Jeff the guard pointed them out on her hand-drawn map. "And each building is connected on either end with tunnels to the next building."

"Show me which way Dr. Martell went." Hermione rotated the map so she could see clearly.

"He took the tunnel to Building Two from this end, which is down the hall toward the storage room." Jeff pointed back the way she'd come. "My guess is his lab's in Building Two."

"How long is the tunnel?" She folded the paper map up and shoved it in the thigh pocket of her high-performance leggings. "And are they heated?"

"The tunnels between buildings are a hundred yards long and the only heat is from the ground insulation and the hot water pipes in the ceiling. They keep the ambient temperature about sixty degrees."

"Any lights along the way?"

"Just service lights."

"They're solar charged, though." The Asian woman found a tentative smile. "It was a big deal when they put them in because they had the newest batteries to keep them going all night."

"Good to know." Hermione nodded as she focused on Jeff. "Are there guards at every entry point?"

He nodded. "There should be. If there's not, something's wrong."

"What kind of weapons have the guards been issued?"

"Each guard has a 9 mm handgun, but they have access to rifles in a lockbox at their stations."

"Semi-automatic or single shot?"

"Semi-automatic."

Hermione whistled. "You aren't fooling around down here, are you?"

"No, ma'am."

"Do the guards have a special frequency to share information between buildings?" She led the guard back out of the break room. Her gut said she didn't want the scientists in the room to know about the guards' protocols, and she definitely wasn't interested in a firefight with them.

"Yeah, channel two." He held up his walkie talkie as he followed her toward the tunnel doors.

"Good to know. What if the radios break down? How do you identify friendlies in the tunnels?"

Jeff shot a look back toward the break room. None of the scientists had followed and his shoulders relaxed.

"Passwords vary, but the one between this building and Building Two is 'Trebuchet'."

Hermione snorted. "Trebuchet? Like the medieval war machine?"

He grinned. "Yes, ma'am. Figured it wouldn't be something we'd say underground unless it was intentional."

Heh, helluva safe word.

"Roger that." She checked all her weapons and gear before she pushed open the tunnel door. "The lights are still on so no one has cut the power. Pay attention to what's coming through the comms and stay safe."

"Yes, ma'am. We will."

"Bring the guard in Building Two up to speed after I'm through the tunnel. I'll have him message you."

"Very good, ma'am. Good luck."

She wanted to say, *no luck involved, just pure skill*. But she didn't need to give away just how capable she was to anyone in this compound.

"Thank you, Anderson."

She waved and let the door shut behind her. The tunnel remained lit all the way down to its far end, and she breathed a sigh of relief. At least she wouldn't be stuck in the dark. She just hoped the terrorists hadn't infiltrated Building Two yet as she set off.

Chapter Three

C hester heard shouts and watched as security ran past his lab just as he finished inputting his latest results from the new batch of antivenom tests. He'd been working on finding a way to make antivenom more universal and therefore less expensive. But his tests showed his latest tweaks wouldn't even mitigate the effects of the King Brown snake venom by itself.

He made a note in his data file and saved it just as the door to the lab burst open and Tessa growled, "Save your work and lock your computers. The research campus is under attack from domestic terrorists."

"What?" He blinked. Had she said 'under attack'?

"Save your work, Dr. Martell, and lock your data in the safe. We have domestic terrorists on campus."

He swallowed hard and hurried to follow orders as she closed the door and headed for the next lab.

Yesterday would've been a good day to do a backup.

Not that he hadn't backed up his work, but his latest tests weren't there.

Not that they were successful.

But the failures were just as valuable as the successes in his business. He clicked on the results and saved them to the stand-alone hard drive before shutting down his laptop and locking it and the drive in the biometric safe at the back of the lab.

Dr.s Ani Madigan and Richard Bridgewater both scrambled to do the same as they all collected their notes and shoved them in locked drawers. At the last moment, they all remembered to lock away their toxic substances in the biohazard refrigeration unit.

"What do we do if they get inside?" Madigan asked as she removed her biohazard suit, stealing looks out at the hallway.

"Don't be ridiculous, Ani. They won't get inside. They'll be put down in a matter of hours. The guards will see to that." Richard flipped off the lights and pulled out his phone as he looked down his nose at their colleague.

"It's Dr. Madigan, *Richy*, and I don't think the guards can stop a hoard of terrorists with automatic weapons." Madigan scowled at the older man.

"You've been watching too many action movies. There isn't a lone hero that can do more than the guards and cops can." Richard's voice held disdain, both for Madigan's correction and her worries, but Chester agreed with her concerns.

"I don't know. Do you remember the insurrection that hit the Capitol building in DC last year? That mob of terrorists overwhelmed the cops and broke in. They didn't even have automatic weapons. They could do that here, and we don't have nearly the security the Capitol building does." Chester sank down out of sight of the front windows. "If Tessa is warning us, there could be a real problem."

"It's probably just an authentic-seeming drill. Nothing to worry about. See? Nothing on the internet about it." Richard held up his phone. "I'm sure the press would've gotten wind of it if it was a real thing."

Before Chester could say anything, shouts and automatic gunfire sounded outside the lab. Richard's eyes widened, and he put down the phone just as the windows exploded from a hail of bullets sprayed along the hallway. More screams and shouts came from outside the lab as more windows shattered. Richard squeaked and scurried for the wall farthest away from the front hall. Chester ducked down behind the central work table and held his breath.

What the hell was going on? Why would homegrown terrorists attack the research campus? It wasn't like they'd just gotten new contracts from the U.S. government and nothing from the DoD that he was aware of.

More gunfire and shouts echoed around them until he ducked his head, slapped his hands over his ears, and closed his eyes. He'd always been a geek and a nerd, someone who wasn't interested in war games or sports. He did like working out because it was a good way to turn his mind off, counting the repetitions that strengthened his body. But he'd never found pleasure in working with weapons or complex machinery. That's why he had a mechanic for his car, a plumber for his pipes, an electrician for the wiring, a carpenter for renovations. When he needed something done, he paid experts.

"Please let it be over soon." He whispered the words like a prayer as the violence continued until a door slammed and silence filled the underground labs.

Chester opened his eyes and shot a look toward Dr. Madigan across the lab.

"Is it over? Are they gone?" She whispered the words across the space.

"I don't know." He rotated his hips and got to his knees, peering over the top of the worktable. "I can't see anything, but the shooting seems to have stopped."

"Do you think anyone was hurt?" Madigan's face blanched white under her tan.

"With that kind of gunfire, your guess is as good as mine. I'm going to go check."

He used the table to push to his feet, but paused and listened for anything coming from outside the lab. He didn't hear anything, but he hoped that meant the guards had stopped the assault and the attackers were dead.

Could mean the guards are dead, too, dumbass.

He swallowed hard and picked his way through the broken glass to the door, trying not to step on any. All the other windows had been shot out, but the door's window miraculously survived. He pressed the handle down and pushed the door open just enough to peek through the crack.

More glass and plaster lay strewn about the hallway and a couple of the fluorescent lights flickered while their covers hung from the ceiling in broken disarray. Chester swallowed hard and pushed the door open to stick his head out. He didn't see much until he heard a groan and realized someone lay in the hallway.

"Oh, my glory, Tessa!" He shoved the door open and ran down the corridor to the guard leaning against the wall with a pinched expression on her face. "Are you hurt? What can I do?"

"Dr. Martell, I need you to find something to use for a tourniquet."

"Shit!" He crouched beside her and tried not to faint at the sight of blood staining her tan uniform pants. He'd taken basic first aid when he was in high school, but most of it drained out of his memory in the face of blood. "What about my belt? Will that work?"

"Yeah, that should be fine." She looked a little gray as he unbuckled the belt.

I probably look like I'm doing something inappropriate.

At least there was no one else in the hallway to see him do it.

Except the door at the far end cracked open and someone poked their head in. A pretty woman with intense green eyes and sharp arching brows. She wore a ballcap with some sports team's logo and she fixed her gaze on him as he yanked his belt free of the loops.

And of course there is someone who just happens to come in right now.

He just hoped she wouldn't shoot him.

He couldn't worry about it now. Tessa needed his help, and he wouldn't let her bleed out all over the floor. He crouched and wrapped the belt around her thigh, and she tugged it higher, closer to her groin.

"Really tight, okay?"

Chester swallowed hard. "Are you sure? It might hurt."

"Yeah. If it's not tight enough, it won't matter if it hurts." Her words slurred, and he scrambled to yank the belt tight.

Tessa moaned and tears flowed from her eyes, but she didn't try to yank her leg away.

"Oh, glory, I'm so sorry." He hated seeing people hurt. It made his stomach queasy and his vision blur.

"It's okay. It's gotta be done." She held the belt tight. "Cinch it there."

He swallowed hard against bile as he locked the belt down, his fingers stained with her blood. *This is so unsanitary.* Tessa eventually leaned back and closed her eyes, tears streaming down her cheeks though she didn't make a sound.

"Tessa, I'm so sorry to bug you, but there's someone coming in through the door at the end of the hall."

Chester swallowed hard as Tessa's eyes jerked open and she raised her pistol to point at the door. Despite the pain she had to be in and her position on the floor beside the wall, she held her weapon steady.

"Freeze! Identify yourself!" How she managed to shout so strongly he'd never know.

One hand appeared open before the rest of the woman in the ballcap stepped into the open hallway. She appeared to be dressed in fashionable hiking clothes he'd seen in outfitter catalogs, complete with daypack. Despite her "afternoon hiker" attire, she moved like a trained soldier, keeping her hands away from her sides. He didn't see a weapon, but he wasn't skilled enough to look for one.

"Easy, ma'am. My name is Captain Hermione Wilcox, U.S . Army retired. The guard from Building One, Jeff Anderson, directed me here." Her sharp gaze latched onto the belt he had cinched around Tessa's leg. "How bad is the damage?"

Tessa shook her head. "Got an ID?"

"Yes, ma'am. Going for it now." She reached into her windbreaker and pulled out a badge.

It looked official to Chester, but Tessa narrowed her eyes. "Dressed a little casual, aren't you, Captain?"

"We weren't trying to advertise our presence here for this op." The captain tucked her badge away.

"We? Who's we?" Tessa sounded tired but her gun never wavered.

"Sirens, Inc." When Tessa frowned, Captain Wilcox grunted with humor. "It's like Blackwater without all the testosterone."

Tessa snorted but didn't crack a smile. "Why are you here?"

"I'm actually here for Dr. Chester Martell, but considering the damage the terrorists are doing, I'm working on a plan to get everyone off campus safely."

Chester blinked. "You're here for me?"

Captain Wilcox's sharp green gaze locked on him. "You're Dr. Martell?"

"Yes." He nodded. "Why are you here for me?"

She took a few steps closer, and Tessa's gun followed her. "Do you mind putting your weapon away? If I was here to kill you, I'd have done it and not bothered to talk."

Tessa's eyes narrowed, but she sighed and holstered the pistol, slumping back against the wall.

Wilcox nodded before returning her gaze to Chester's. "Intel said you were the target of the Eagle Militia's rumored attack. We were moving into position when they initiated the assault on the research campus."

"Oh my gosh, that's where all the gunfire came from." Madigan had ventured out into the hallway with several others. "Did they hit all the buildings?"

"Unclear. They definitely hit this one and Building One."

"They hit all of...them. Managed...to...stop...them here." Tessa's voice grew softer and her eyes closed. "Don't think they bombed upstairs but... no contact with the guards there."

"Tessa?" Chester leaned closer. "Tessa. Tessa!"

But the guard passed out and Chester couldn't think of what to do.

The guard's eyes closed, and Hermione noticed the spreading stain under her ass.

Shit! "How many times was she hit?" Hermione dropped beside the guard and pulled her knife to slice off the woman's sleeve for a bandage. "How many shots did she take, doc?"

Dr. Martell frowned. "I have no idea. I only saw the one wound. She was already on the floor when I got out here."

Sonuvaprick. She wanted to snap at him, but he was probably one of those science geeks who'd never been on a hiking trip much less in combat. She carefully looked for other sources of blood loss, and found another GSW just under the edge of her Kevlar vest.

"Fuck."

Hermione wished her medic Master Airman Beverly "Pockets" Porter was there. Hermione could patch someone up enough to get them to the hospital, but the second gunshot was beyond her expertise. Porter as a Rescue Medic would've had the guard stabilized and hooked up on fluids. All she could do was hope to stop the bleeding.

She turned and scanned the people around them. "You!" She pointed at a young blond woman. "Run to the bathroom and get a thick wad of paper towels." The woman jumped and scampered down the hallway. "Doctor." She pointed at the woman in the white coat with long, black hair braided into a tail. "I need you to find superglue or something similar."

"Superglue?" The doctor frowned.

"Yes, ma'am. Quickly before she loses more blood."

"Oh, okay." The woman ducked back into the closest lab as Dr. Martell shot her a confused look.

"What's the superglue for?"

Hermione gritted her teeth at the seeping wound in the guard's side. "It's to temporarily bind the wound. Can you find some bottled or purified water, Dr. Martell? We'll need to clean the wound tract before we close it. Hurry, please. We're running out of time."

"Uh, yeah. Yeah, give me a sec."

She knew it was a common response, but she didn't know how many seconds the guard had left.

"Here are the paper towels." The blonde tech came back with a large pile of paper clutched in her hands.

"Good. Give me half of them." She held out her bloodied hand and the woman flinched but split the pile. "Go find a First Aid kit and bring it here." She raised her voice as the blonde darted away again. "Need that water, doc!"

"Coming! Coming!" His footsteps sounded on the broken glass of the hallway as he juggled three bottles of water in his hands. He skidded to a stop, almost falling on her. "Sorry. I'm nervous."

"I get it. Open the bottle. We have to clean this." She waited as he managed to open the bottle then took it from him. "Okay, now this isn't going to be fun. If any of you can't handle blood, I need you to stand way back because I don't want to fix someone's head wound if you knock yourselves out."

A few people mumbled and moved away while Martell swallowed hard and took a deep breath.

"Ready?" She shot him a look as the blonde returned with the First Aid kit, then retreated again.

He nodded. "Yeah. I'm good."

"Okay, I'm going to take away the towels and wash the wound." She glanced over his shoulder. "Doctor, do you have the glue?"

"Yes, it's here. Will one tube be enough?" She crouched beside them.

"Let's hope so," Hermione mumbled grimly. "All right, leave the tube here and get out some gauze and medical tape from the First Aid kit. Hold this." The dark-haired doctor held the paper towels, turning redder by the moment. "Shit, I was hoping her blood would clot and slow down by now."

"I think she's on blood thinners for high blood pressure." Martell shot a worried look at the guard's gray complexion.

"Fuckin' awesome. Okay, then we're going to have to do this fast." She pulled on some latex gloves. "When you move the towels away, I'm going to clean her wound then glue it shut as much as possible. We'll put gauze on it and hopefully it'll seal enough for her to survive." She hoped. Blood thinners changed the game, but they didn't have much choice.

"Ready?"

They nodded, and she pulled the towels away. The blood wasn't slowing down, but she ignored it for washing the wound with water and pressing more towels to it. No one said anything for the next few minutes as she worked to get the glue to close the wound then pressed gauze to it. She didn't know who kept handing her what she needed but it always showed up when it was time and they managed to get the guard patched up enough to keep her alive.

I hope. If Porter had been there, she'd have been more confident in her assessment.

"Did it work?" Martell held the guard's hand between his.

"I hope so. She's not bleeding through the gauze and towels, so I count that a win in our favor." Hermione finished wrapping an Ace bandage around the gauze and shot a look at the labs. "Is anyone else hurt? Where are the other guards? There were more than just this one, right?"

The other doctor nodded. "Yes, there are usually three down here and two upstairs." She frowned and looked down the hallway both directions. "I don't see the others."

There was mumbled agreement, and a few people started to search the labs. They eventually found two more guards, one wounded and one out cold. Hermione had the dark-haired doc stay with the guard in the hall while she and Dr. Martell searched out the others. They found minor injuries on some of the techs who'd gotten caught in the crossfire, but most of the people underground were all right.

They brought the unconscious guard into the break room and laid him on the floor with a tech keeping an eye on him and a bottle of water on hand. The other guard had a minor gunshot graze in his shoulder and glass shrapnel in his face from the gunfight. She got some of the techs to help remove the glass and bind his wound while she went looking for others.

They found three dead domestic terrorists who'd tried to break in. She had to admit that the guards hadn't held back. Two of the men had two shots center mass and the third had died of exsanguination from point-blank buckshot to his neck. There wasn't much left of his carotid or jugular vein on that side. They piled the bodies in a janitor's closet and closed the door. Not her worry anymore.

By the time they got back to Tessa, she'd regained consciousness and was drinking water slowly. Hermione crouched beside her and checked the dressing on her wounds.

"How are you doing?"

"Woozy, tired, and dizzy, but other than that, pretty good." The woman's dry humor gave Hermione hope.

"Oh, so you'll be helping me clear the other buildings of tangos, right?"

"Oh yeah, not a problem." Tessa grimaced.

"Do you think the terrorists will keep trying to get in here?" Dr. Martell frowned as he looked at some of the techs starting to clean up the debris.

"I would if my objective hadn't been met. I don't think the invaders thought they'd get much resistance." Hermione nodded at the closet with the bodies. "I'm pretty sure they had an inside man, but it doesn't look like all the guards were in on it."

"How do you know that?" Tessa's eyes narrowed.

"I met a guy who was too relaxed in Building One on the way down. I subdued him but they'll find him soon enough." She looked at the twenty odd people in various states of shock in the hallway. "We have to get everyone out safely, but I can't get a signal."

She swung her gaze around the lab. Broken beakers and test tubes lay strewn around the floor, and the walls had sustained some damage. Some of the debris had been swept into piles. "I'll need to do some reconnoitering to find out where the terrorists are currently located, and if we can get back to the surface."

The guard shook her head. "No need. When any kind of attack happens, the system is programmed to shut down all stairwells and elevator shafts. It goes into lockdown to protect the research and substances."

Hermione frowned. "Would the tunnels get shut down as well?"

Tessa nodded. "Those too."

Hermione exchanged a look with Martell. "The door I came through was unlocked. Is there an override switch to keep just those open?"

Tessa shook her head. "Not that I'm aware of."

"Could the inside man have disabled them?"

"Was this inside man the guard in Building One?"

Hermione nodded. "I assume so. Middle-aged guy, balding, with a minor paunch and an air of superiority."

"That would be Dirk Hepley. I think he's related to the owner of the complex, which is why he gets a lot of the easy shifts. But he's not smart enough to override the system." Tessa shot a look at Martell. "You see him getting chummy with anyone, Dr. Martell?"

The doc blinked behind his wire-rimmed glasses. "No, not that I'm aware of. I mean, Dr. Miller sometimes flirts with him, but then she flirts with everyone." He shrugged.

"Dr. Miller." Hermione searched her memories. "Works in Building One, white blonde hair, glasses, about my height?"

He nodded, his eyebrows up. "Yes, I saw her just this morning. Is she all right?"

Hermione shrugged. "I think so. She didn't look injured when I left Building One."

"Oh, good."

His relief at the other doctor's welfare irked Hermione for some reason.

What the hell is wrong with me? Of course he's worried about his friends.

But it still irritated her like a small stone in her boot. She'd be worried about her own colleagues and teammates, too.

Thinking of which...

"Is there any way to get a signal out? I need to get in contact with my team."

"You have a team? Dressed like that?" The man who spoke was older, with silver hair styled with some sort of hair gel and enough attitude to remind her of her ex-husband and his disdain.

She leveled an impassive look his direction then turned back to Tessa without answering. "If I can get a message out, they'll know where to find me and the rest of you."

"Do you think it's safer to stay here?" Dr. Martell waved at the damaged labs. "They can't get back in here, can they?"

Hermione shared a look with Tessa. "If the system never locked the doors and elevators—"

"Before you arrived, I would've sworn it did, but now..." She shrugged in confusion.

That changed things. If the building wasn't locked against incursions, Hermione would have to get the people there to a safer location, even if her mission consisted of just rescuing one man.

And I'd like my damn team back, thank you.

"Right. Okay. We'll need to do some recon to make sure we're secure."

"What if we're not? What if they can get in again?" The dark-haired doctor's expression turned frantic.

"Let's deal with one catastrophe at a time, okay?" Not that it had ever happened that way on military missions, but these were civilians, and mob panic was worse to deal with than bureaucracy in the armed forces.

"Why are they here? What do they want?" One of the lab techs shot Hermione a fearful look.

She sighed, debating what to say. Telling them about Martell would either make them come together to protect him or it would make them use him as a bargaining chip for their own safety.

"They want Dr. Martell and his research."

Martell gaped. "What? Why?"

"My intel says they want to weaponize it. Use it for biowarfare against the government."

His face blanched white. "But that's not what it's for. The venom I'm studying is already toxic. They don't need my research."

"Maybe they need whatever you're doing to make it more transmittable." She shook her head. "But first, it'd be harder for them to find you if you weren't wearing that." She pointed at his nametag. "Time to go anonymous, doc." She looked around the room and raised her voice. "In fact, all of you should take off your nametags.

Leave them in your desks or workstations. The less the terrorists know about you the better."

"What are we going to do?" A scrawny male tech shot a look at the windows sporting a spider's web of cracks from attempted bullet holes. "If they come down here, we're all gonna die. I can't die, I'm too young and handsome."

That's debatable.

Hermione would rather end up with Dr. Martell than the tech, if push came to shove. And she didn't really go for the science geek types. That was more Dunwoody's kick.

"Are you sure they're just after Martell? What about my recent paper about molds? It was shared in Fungus Today and other renowned scientific journals."

"None of our chatter spoke of that. What is your name?"

The scrawny tech drew himself up to his considerable height. "Dr. Ian Durbin, fungi specialist. Oh god, they're coming for me, I know it."

Hermione turned her head away but the guard met her gaze and rolled her eyes. Hermione bit her lips to keep from smiling. Talk about crazy, this wasn't the time to be cracking jokes or laughing, but the self-absorption of Durbin strained her patience. She moved her gaze to Martell and caught the end of his eye roll.

I'm not the only one who thinks the guy's a prima donna.

"Let's just make sure we get all of us outta here in one piece, copy?"

Chapter Four

I t took Chester a moment to realize Captain Wilcox had asked for an acknowledgment of her statement, and he swallowed hard.

"Yes, ma'am."

She flashed him a quick smile. "I like the sound of that."

He blinked. Had she just made a suggestive statement? He couldn't be sure as she turned her attention back to the elevator doors. "Is there a way to manually lock the tunnel doors?"

"Yeah." Tessa nodded. "Did Bentley survive? He's one of the guards."

"I think so." Wilcox raise her eyebrows. "But I don't know if he's conscious or not."

"He is. Bentley was the guard with the glass in his face." Chester shuddered at the thought of trying to pick all those shards out of the poor guy's skin.

"All right. Can you get him to come into the hallway, Dr. Martell? Since you know who he is."

"Yes, okay. Right." He nodded, not looking forward to seeing the wounds on Bentley's face again. "Be right back." He'd much rather stay with Captain Wilcox with her confidence and competence, especially now that he knew the terrorists were after him.

Why would they want his research? Nothing he did could be used to make toxic venom more toxic.

Chester found Bentley drinking water and holding his arm where a bullet had grazed it. "Can you come into the main hallway? Captain Wilcox needs to speak to you."

The guard raised his eyebrows before hissing with pain. "Who's Captain Wilcox?"

"She's the woman who came through with me while looking for bodies." Jeez, that sounded morbid even while saying it. "She needs to talk to you about the doors having manual locks."

Bentley got up gingerly and frowned. "Why would she need to know that? The system should've locked everything down once the building was attacked."

"The tunnel doors weren't locked. Is there a way to keep the tunnels open when the rest of the doors are locked down?" Chester led him over to where Captain Wilcox spoke with Tessa.

Bentley shook his head. "No, that's not possible. When the doors lock, all of them do."

Chester opened his mouth to point out that Wilcox had made it into the building from the tunnels when the door she'd come through opened and Dr. Miller bolted inside.

"Oh my God, thank goodness you're still here. They're coming! Whoa!" Dr. Miller skidded to a stop when faced with the muzzle of Captain Wilcox's gun. Chester hadn't even seen her move.

"Identify yourself. Who are you and who's coming?" Her voice had gone cold and hard, and her hands never wavered. Chester suddenly understood why she would have a team despite her casual hiking clothing.

It had to be one of the sexiest things he'd seen in a long time.

"It's me, Dr. Tamara Miller. You met me in Building One?" Tamara raised her hands in surrender.

Captain Wilcox nodded but her weapon remained steadily trained on the doctor. "I remember. My question is why are you here alone? Where are the rest of the people from Building One?"

Tamara flinched and shot a guilty look back at the doors as she sidled closer to Chester. "I was coming out of the bathroom when I heard shots and screams. The people from upstairs had found their way to the underground labs and were gathering everyone up. I think they killed one of the guards." She started to cry and leaned into Chester. He caught her out of reflex. "I used the confusion to run down the hallway to the tunnel entrance and came here. I don't know how long we have until they follow me."

Wilcox's eyes narrowed as she took in Tamara's story, but eventually she nodded and put away her weapon. "Then we better get all of you to safety."

Chester swallowed. "How are we going to do that? Won't they follow us?"

"Not if they don't know which way we've gone." Wilcox headed for Tessa. "Come on, Barton. It's time to get going."

But the guard shook her head. "No. Get everyone who can walk down the tunnels to Buildings Three and Four. Four is the least populated right now, and the research going on in Three won't help anyone who wants to do harm."

Captain Wilcox snorted as she wrapped an arm under Tessa's shoulders. "Anything requiring research can be warped for someone's megalomaniacal purposes. But I don't leave anyone behind. I think you'll make it."

Tessa groaned as she got her feet under her. "Not with these wounds. I'll just slow you down."

"It's not really about speed this time. The goal is to get everyone out without injuries or engagement. So up you come. We're leaving now." She brought Tessa closer to Durbin. "Dr. Durbin, Dr. Miller, I need you two to help Tessa."

"What?" Durbin gaped. "I can't carry her."

Wilcox nodded. "I know. You and Miller are going to help her keep her feet so she doesn't strain the glue holding her wounds together. She's going to lean on you."

The skinny man scowled and Tamara looked like she'd rather eat dirt than get close to Tessa's bloody side, but they both came and moved Tessa to lean on their shoulders.

"Listen up, all of you. I need you to leave your cellphones here. Out of your pockets, I know you have them and want to check Twitter, but they're great tracking devices and anyone who can disable the campus systems to unlock the doors can use your phones to find you. Let's not give them the opportunity."

"But we'll need our cellphones to call home when we get out of this." Tamara again shot a nervous look toward the doors to Building One, and Chester wondered if she'd left someone there.

"Don't worry, doctor. We'll make sure you get in touch when we get out. Leave them on the table here as you go." She pointed to a table just inside a broken window.

People grumbled but extracted their phones and left them. The pile grew to a sparkling and brightly colored grouping, and Chester hadn't realized just how many of his colleagues were fans of Pokémon. He dropped his own phone but caught Tamara hesitating, again shooting another look at the doors behind her before reluctantly dropping her phone.

When Wilcox walked by without depositing her phone, Tamara frowned.

"What about your phone, Captain?"

"Mine is masked and a burner. I'll use it to contact reinforcements outside. Let's get moving. You said we were in a time crunch." She turned her attention to herding the techs toward the doors to the next tunnel as she grabbed one of the weapons Tessa had been carrying. "Dr. Martell, I need you to get people moving. Are you Bentley?" She checked the clip in the rifle before she met the other guard's gaze with her piercing green one.

"Yes, ma'am." Even Bentley sensed her leadership qualities despite her clothing choice.

"Do you have the strength to carry a weapon? I'll gather up everyone and get them moving to Building Three. You'll cover our backtrail and keep an eye out for tangos."

"Yes, ma'am. What about Avondale, ma'am? He's out cold in the break room." Bentley used his good arm to grasp the rifle and swung the strap over his shoulder.

"Shit." She scanned the hallway and landed on Chester and Richard. "You two need to go get the guard from the break room and carry him."

Richard puffed up and looked down his nose. "I shall do no such thing."

Wilcox narrowed her eyes for a moment before she nodded. "I understand your trepidation, doctor, but I need your help here. Contrary to every Hollywood adventure movie out there, no one can protect people and fend off attackers alone. A good captain knows how to utilize everyone's strengths. I need a team, and right now, you're it until I can get to my reinforcements outside. Do you think you can follow orders until we get everyone to safety?"

Richard blustered a moment, his mouth opening and closing like a beached fish.

"Can't wait for your decision, doc. I need you to get going. You can file a report on my conduct once we're out of here." She returned her gaze to Chester's. "Each of you drape an arm over your shoulders and carry him that way. He's probably every bit of two hundred pounds of dead weight. You'll need to work together."

That wasn't hard for Chester, but he wondered if Richard would get off his ass to help anyone without being forced.

Of course, Captain Wilcox looks like she could force him.

"Okay, Captain. Come on, Richard. Let's help us all out, right?" Chester strode toward the break room, hoping his pompous colleague would follow because Wilcox was right. He couldn't carry 200 pounds of dead weight for long.

Richard finally stepped up as the crowd headed for the tunnel toward Building Three. Miller wore nervousness on her face as she passed with Tessa and Durbin. Chester's neck itched as he bent to get Avondale's arm over his shoulder.

Damn, this is harder than it looks in movies.

Of course, in movies, the "dead guy" wasn't really dead and would help get into position before filming.

Fortunately, Richard ducked under the unconscious guard's other arm and they lifted him together. They stepped out into the hallway and he caught sight of Captain Wilcox with her head bent close to that of Bentley's and a strange sensation reared up. It felt a little like jealousy and a little like hurt. The sneaky thought of what about me? slid through his awareness and he quashed it fast. He'd known Captain Wilcox maybe an hour and he was already worried that she gave her attention to a guard?

There is something seriously wrong with me. He shot a look back down the hallway to the other tunnel as she swept past and nodded to them.

"Good. Let's go, people. Bentley, watch our six. I'm taking point."

Chester had heard those terms before but he never understood them until Wilcox showed what they meant. She led them down the tunnel toward Building Three, making sure Miller and Durbin were close behind with Tessa. The rest were surprisingly quiet as he and Richard navigated the narrow space while carrying the unconscious guard. Bentley filled in behind them, his gaze sharp and alert despite his injuries.

Chester just hoped they'd make it out. He didn't want to die down in the lab or tunnels. He had cross-country races he still wanted to run, and movies he'd like to see, and finally taking time to find a woman to date. His gaze slid to the shape of Captain Wilcox leading them down the tunnel, the light reflecting off her ballcap and long ponytail.

If they got through this, he'd set aside more time to do more of the hobbies he'd ignored, like the endurance racing and movies, and he'd work up the courage to ask someone out. He just didn't know if he had the courage to ask Captain Wilcox out. *Fortune favors the bold.* But men bolder than him had probably been shot down. And he meant that literally.

What's the best that could happen? She would take him up on the date and they'd have a great time. *And as long as I'm wishing, may I also get a Rivian and a large house with a pool?* Might as well go for broke.

He snorted softly and hauled the unconscious guard after the hot woman leading the way.

Hermione's gut tightened until she saw Bentley come through the doors to Building Two and give a thumbs-up. But she still had to get all these civilians down the tunnel and into Building Three without losing any of them. And then she had to somehow contact her team. She figured Dunwoody would be sending out a signal every few minutes, but so far there was no signal. Hermione could hopefully connect with them soon.

As if the Universe had heard her thought, her phone began vibrating like a sex toy in her pocket. Apparently, she had connection in the tunnels. *Good to know and glad I made them leave their tracking devices in the last building.* Especially Dr. Miller. There was something about the woman that irked Hermione. Maybe it was her fawning over Dr. Martell.

Which is stupid because he's the mission, not a potential date.

Or maybe because she was acting cagey, like she was playing them and giving a performance. Whatever it was, Hermione was glad the doc had left her phone. If anyone could be tracked, it would be Miller. Which begged the question, was Miller another insider, another person trying to get Martell caught? She filed the thought away to be examined later as she slowed at the end of the tunnel.

"Everyone hold up. I'm going to check that it's safe. Wait here."

The people behind her nodded, some blanching white in the sodium lights of the tunnel. She waited to be sure they'd all gotten the message before grasping the handle to the door and pushing it open slowly.

Again, unlocked. Which meant the disabling of the security lockdown systems was campus-wide. She peeked around the door and scanned the hallway on the other side while listening hard. One body lay sprawled in the hallway, but otherwise, nothing moved. There were voices coming from somewhere, but the length of the building lay open.

"Stay here for a minute. I'm going to check if there's a place to take cover." She nodded to the people directly behind her.

"Take cover?" Miller frowned. "Why?"

"Because I don't know who's following us and I don't know who's ahead, so we'll need a place to rest out of sight. Sit tight. I'll be back." She ducked through the door and closed it quietly.

The problem was they couldn't stay in the tunnel, but she didn't want to lead them into an ambush. That was a good way to get dead fast. Checking the body in the hall, she recognized the guards' uniform and the large caliber gunshot wound in the gut. There wasn't anything she could do so she kept moving down the hallway, keeping low in case the voices she'd heard belonged to the tangos.

She paused at one lab window and peeked over the edge. The lab remained dark and empty, though there looked like two more bodies in lab coats on the floor. *Fuck, guess they took care of those researchers.* The lab across the hall sat silent as well so the voices had to be coming from somewhere else.

They rose in volume, and she realized the speakers had entered the hallway. Scrambling to her feet, she ducked into the lab with the dead bodies and dropped down behind the central equipment table just before the speakers, two men, paused in the hallway.

"Dude, how hard it is to find one egghead? It's not like they're common sense-smart or anything." The voice sounded young but angry, cocky, mean.

Or just sexually frustrated. Maybe Rosy Palm and her five sisters weren't givin' him what he needed.

"Aw, don't worry about it none. Louden got 'em locked down. It's only a matter of time, son." The other voice was older and slightly amused before a phone rang. "Yeah?"

There was a long pause. "Which way they comin'?"

Another pause, then, "All right, boss. We'll check it out."

"Aw shit, whatda we hafta do now?" Rosy Palm's boyfriend growled.

"Boss says there may be a bunch of eggheads comin' through the tunnels from Building Two." They started moving toward the tunnel door.

"How does he know that?"

Excellent question.

Hermione slid around the work table. *Or would this be considered an island?* She'd have to do something about the two goons threatening her charges or things would get ugly fast.

"His inside man told him. Apparently went after them but hasn't contacted again."

Hermione scowled at the news of an inside man. Fuckin' fantastic. She'd just have to deal with ferreting them out when she was done with these two. *Though I have my guesses.* She was running out of time.

Sliding out of the lab, she kept her movements quiet as she closed on them. They'd shifted to bitching about how long this siege would take and what they were going to do after.

"Fuck, if Pinkett's there, I'm not going."

"Anywhere with you there, whinin' and bitchin', wouldn't be that fun anyway, so I'm sure you'll get your wish."

She settled into her cold hunter persona and leapt at the younger guy. He turned just at the last second and tried to raise his weapon, but she landed on his back, grabbed his head and twisted sharply to the left. He went boneless under her, and she dropped to the floor to face the older, grizzled tango.

"Who the fuck are you, bitch?"

He wanted to talk? She mentally snorted and tilted her head, watching his body to decide how best to take him down. She'd make an effort to incapacitate him, but she didn't have a problem killing him. As far as she was concerned, he was just another terrorist. It didn't matter if he had light skin or spoke English. The US didn't negotiate with terrorists, or that was the official line. She upheld it to the letter even after she retired.

"I asked you a question."

He raised his rifle and she darted toward him, grabbing the barrel and twisting it against his hands. He snarled as she tore the rifle from his grip and slammed it into his nose.

"Motherfucker!" He staggered backwards with his hands over his face.

Not today, asshole. She reversed the rifle and flipped it over to squeeze a few shots into his knees. He screamed as he went down, and she followed it up with another blow to his nose. He crumpled, and she stepped over him to get to the people in the tunnel.

Chapter Five

"**A**ll right, everyone out. We don't have much time. We're not staying, so head to the far end of the hallway into the next tunnel and wait for us." She held the door open to the researchers. "Hurry. Let's go."

She let them stream past her, but kept her eye on Dr. Miller. There was something off about the woman. Hermione felt it in her gut, and she'd been saved too many times by it to ignore the feeling. Dr. Martell met her gaze and flashed her a quick smile in greeting as he and the pompous ass carried the unconscious guard through the doors. For some reason, his acknowledgment warmed her heart and made her feel all gooey inside.

What the hell is wrong with me? She abhorred feeling soft and gooey on missions.

"Bentley." She barked it more sharply than she meant to as the guard closed on her.

"Yes, ma'am?"

"Other than the electronic locks, is there any way to secure these doors and keep our pursuers from following us? Or at least slow them down?"

"Not really. We could try to jam something in the way of or under the door to make it harder to open. How do you know someone's following us?"

She shot a look at the people flowing down the hallway. "The two hicks I just took out said an inside man has infiltrated our group."

He blanched white. "Which man is it?"

She shook her head as they entered Building Three. "No idea. But don't discount the women. They make better spies than most men. And Dr. Miller just recently joined the party."

He blinked. "You think Dr. Miller is working with the terrorists?"

She shrugged. "I can't rule it out. There's something off about her, but I have no proof, just what I overheard. In any case, let's make sure it's harder to get through these doors to follow us. It'll slow them down and force them to use the fountain tunnels."

"What about these guys?" Bentley pointed at the two bodies on the floor.

"Let's drag them into one of the labs. Use something from the dead one to bind up the other one's wounds. He's just out cold. And take off his pants."

Bentley froze. "Take his pants, ma'am?"

"Yeah, it'll make it harder for him to want to go anywhere. Men are kinda twitchy about not having pants in my experience." She shot him a dry smirk as she hooked her hands under the arms of the corpse.

He laughed nervously. "Remind me not to piss you off, ma'am."

"Copy that."

She grinned as they dragged the bodies into one of the abandoned labs. Bentley shucked the older terrorist's jeans, grimacing when the man's dirty, smiley faced boxers came into view. Hermione wondered when was the last time he'd done laundry.

Probably don't want to know.

While Bentley tried to slow the terrorist's bleeding, she cast about for something that would make opening the doors more difficult. She found the rubber doorstops for the lab doors and collected as many as she could before bringing them to the tunnel door. It wouldn't stop anyone forever, but it would make things difficult and possibly give them more time to get away.

They'd just finished their respective tasks when Dr. Martell trotted down the hallway, his face taut with worry.

"Captain Wilcox."

"Yes, doc?" She finished kicking the doorstops into place and turned.

"We have a problem. I think the tourniquet came loose and Tessa is in and out of consciousness. We tried to tighten it, but I don't think it's doing the job. Moving her seems to make it worse. What do you want to do?"

"Shit." If they couldn't move the guard, they'd have to figure out a way to make this place defensible until they were either rescued or could move again. "Okay, doc, I hear you. Bentley!"

"Yes, ma'am."

"Let's secure the tango and go help Barton. Take their weapons. No point giving them any tools."

"Yes, ma'am."

Bentley found some zip ties in the tango's pocket and they used them to bind his feet, his wrists together, and his hands to one of the utility pipes running to the ceiling. Hermione approved. He wouldn't be going anywhere.

"That should do the trick. Now go stabilize Tessa. You know any first aid?"

"Yes, ma'am. I keep that training up regularly." Bentley nodded as he followed her back out to the hallway where Dr. Martell waited in tense silence.

"Good. Keep her alive. I'm going to search for a place to rest and any weapons to be had. Dr. Martell is coming with me. Hopefully, Avondale will regain consciousness soon."

"Copy that, ma'am."

"Come on, doc. Let's see if we can find a safe place to hole up." She led him down the hallway.

"We're going to stay here? Don't we have people coming after us?"

She nodded as she glanced into a darkened lab. "That's the word. We'll need a place we can defend for a short time until we either take out our pursuers or the cavalry arrives. These labs are pretty sweet for a top-notch facility, but when it comes to providing shelter, they suck."

Martell snorted. "I'll be sure to tell the campus administrators when it's time to remodel."

Hermione shot him a surprised grin. "You do that. Make sure they put in plans for 'potential hostile takeovers' in the future."

He chuckled, and the sound rippled through her with a warmth she didn't expect. Even in the face of terrifying violence and injury, he managed to find some humor to share. Hermione expected that in other soldiers who'd seen combat, but not in civilians used to quiet, relatively safe places.

"Will do." He stopped at a door. "I think this is the break room. Should we check in here?"

She nodded. "It looks like there's only one window. That's a plus."

She pushed open the door. The room inside sat dark and quiet. The vending machines glowed from the back wall showing the usual candy and cheap snack bags. While they weren't her fuel of choice, they'd work to keep everyone less surly when hunger struck.

She flipped the lights on and nodded. The space was bigger than the break rooms in the last two buildings and could hold all the people they had with them. Plus, there was running water, food, and supplies to make a siege more sustainable. A blind had been attached to the one window looking out on the hallway. That would help keep anyone walking through unaware of their presence if they could stay quiet.

"This will do. Let's get the others and sack out here for the time being." She left the door open, glad to see it had at least a knob lock.

"Will we be safe here?" Martell shot a look back down the hallway toward the tunnel door she'd barricaded.

"For the moment, but it's going to take some more work to make it that way. Let's get everyone out of sight first."

He nodded, and they rejoined the group. Dr. Miller watched them come with a flash of contempt that disappeared as they got closer, and Hermione wondered what the hell that was about. Did the doctor have a thing for Martell? Did they have a relationship she wasn't aware of?

And why am I worried about one woman's issues when it comes to Martell?

She shoved the question aside and waved to get everyone's attention.

"All right, people. We're going to rest up in the break room here. There's food, water, and space enough for all of you. Let's get everyone inside." She strode over to where Avondale had been deposited against the wall, the Pompous Ass dropping him when Martell had come to look for Hermione.

Martell followed her and took up Avondale's other arm. Together they managed to get his dead weight up and haul him toward the break room while everyone else made their own way. Avondale groaned and lifted his head, but he couldn't seem to focus his eyes as they brought him inside and sat him on the floor next to the wall.

"What's going on? Who are you?" His voice came out slurred and groggy.

"I'm Captain Wilcox, U.S. Army, and this is Dr. Martell. You're now in Building Three. The doctor will explain the rest to you." She nodded to Martell. "Be back in a bit."

She needed to get in touch with her team, but she couldn't leave everyone unprotected for too long. Unfortunately, she had to be in the tunnels to get any kind of signal, and she couldn't go back the way they'd come, not if the rumors of pursuit were true.

"Bentley, I need you to stay here and make sure everyone gets what they need. I'm going to secure the door to the fountain tunnel and try to contact my team. You good here?"

"Yes, ma'am. What should we do if the doors don't hold?" The guard scanned the room to make sure everyone was there.

"Lock this door and stay quiet. Hopefully the locked door will deter them enough to ignore this room. They don't strike me as having much experience clearing buildings."

"What about you? If the door's locked, how will you get in?" He handed her one of the automatic weapons taken off the tangos.

"Do you know Morse code?" She checked the clip and the chamber.

"Yes, ma'am. Did four years in the Air Force."

"Well, hoorah, Bentley. If I need back in, I'll knock in SOS, three rapid, three slow, three rapid beats. That should come through clearly." She nodded to him as she stepped out into the hallway. "Lock the door behind me and keep watch through the blinds. That'll give you a heads-up who's out here."

"Will do, ma'am."

She nodded as he closed the door and locked it behind her. She took a deep breath and scanned the hallway. She needed to contact her team and figure out which way was the best to get everyone out safely. And who the mole was.

So just a few simple things. She snorted and headed for the tunnel to the fountain hub.

Chester tried not to follow the captain with his gaze as she moved around the room, but it was hard not to watch her. She moved with efficient grace, no extra motions in anything she did. And her quiet strength gave him hope that they'd get out of there alive. She'd said he was the terrorists' target, but why him? He worked with different kinds of venom from the toxic animals of their world, but it wasn't as if the venom was hard to come by. They could catch themselves a rattlesnake and milk it for its venom without him.

Hell, he didn't even have enough venom on hand to make it worth their while. So why were they after him?

"What's going on, Dr. Martell?" The guard with the name tag Avondale looked dazed and in pain. "Why the hell am I on the floor and who are all these people?"

"From what I understand, the entire campus has been taken over by terrorists."

Avondale frowned as he lifted a hand to his head. "Terrorists?"

"That's what I'm told. Apparently, the Eagle Militia has taken over the Broken Pass Research Center because they're looking for someone. These people are from Building Two getting away from the terrorists in Building One."

"I thought you said they attacked all the buildings. I think I remember gunfire in Building Two, too. Is that right?" Avondale rubbed his face.

"Yes. You've been unconscious for a while. We brought you to Building Three to escape."

"Okay. So, who is Captain Wilcox?"

Just her name settled some of the anxiety coursing through Chester. "She was sent in here to rescue us with her team, but she's the only one who made it into the below-ground labs before the Militia took the campus. She's trying to find us a way out now."

"But who is she, Doctor? Do you even know if she's who she says she is?"

Chester took a moment to answer. Did he really know Hermione was who she claimed to be? *Oh, it's Hermione now, is it?* No, he didn't have any proof that could be used as hard data. But everything she'd done to keep him and the others alive, including the guards, told him she wasn't working with the terrorists.

"I saw her badge. But even if I hadn't, Tessa Barton is convinced, and Wilcox has been working to keep us all alive. All those things seem to be enough."

Avondale met his gaze. "Are you sure it wasn't her shooting things?"

"Fairly sure. She's been doing nothing but helping all of us when her mission was to rescue one person. She could've taken them and left the rest of us, but she's making sure everyone has a chance." Why was he defending the captain? He barely knew her, but he definitely didn't want anyone to get the wrong idea about her. "You should talk to Barton. She killed a couple of the terrorists and was there when the captain arrived."

Avondale craned his head to look for Tessa. "Where is she?"

Chester looked around. Where had Durbin and Miller set down the injured guard? He frowned and stood, scanning the break room. It wasn't a large space, but there were so many people, it made it hard to see around them.

"Give me a moment and I'll find where she is."

He rose but before he could take a step, Tamara slipped up beside him and threw herself into his arms. He grunted in surprise and tried to keep from falling over Avondale on the floor.

"Oh, thank goodness you're okay. I was so scared they'd hurt you." She smelled like sour sweat and too much perfume, and he swallowed against bile as she pulled back to look at him. "You are okay, right, Venom? Please tell me no one hurt you."

He narrowed his eyes and tried to get out of her embrace, but the guard and the nearest table blocked his escape. "Yes, I'm fine."

Why the hell was she hugging him? They didn't have that kind of relationship, and he didn't like to be touched.

At least by her. You wouldn't mind Hermione touching you.

He shook his head and scowled at his thoughts, but Tamara shot him a surprised look.

"You're fine or you're not fine? Which do you mean?"

He glanced down and took a step to the side, which forced her to let go of him. "I'm unharmed. Where did you put down Guard Barton?"

"Who?"

"The injured woman you helped carry in here?" He kept scanning the room for Tessa.

"Oh, we put her over by the trash bins." Tamara waved negligently toward the dirtiest spot in the break room.

"What? Seriously? Why?" He pushed past her and wound his way through people and tables. She followed him with a squawk.

"She was bleeding all over everything, and it was gross."

Chester's amazement pushed the anger higher. How was this woman even an adult? "Barton was bleeding because she was shot defending us. Have a little compassion."

He found Tessa where they'd dropped her, and she looked a little gray as she leaned against the wall beside the trash cans. Chester scanned the room for Bentley and nodded to him to bring the big guard over to the wall.

"Help me get her up. We can't leave her near the trash cans."

He crouched on one side, and with Bentley on the other, they got Tessa up. She groaned and Chester grimaced, but they moved her deeper into the room to a cleaner corner.

"Did you fix the tourniquet?"

Bentley nodded. "Yeah, and I think I stopped the bleeding for now, but she's gonna need some real medical help soon."

Fuck.

Real medical help wasn't available that he knew of, and they were on their own.

"Okay, thanks, Bentley."

The guard nodded and went back to his post beside the window of the break room. Chester had seen Hermione talking to the guard before she left and hoped she had a plan. A little flare of enviousness sparked in his chest. He wanted her to talk to him like she did Bentley. He snorted and shook his head.

All I have to do is learn how to accurately fire projectile weapons and take down other people, and I'll have the job.

"What's wrong, Chester?" Tamara's voice intruded in his thoughts, and all his amusement drained away.

"Nothing. Why don't you ask some of the more mechanically-minded researchers to find a way to get into the vending machines so we have some food. I'll keep an eye on Barton here."

She turned her head to look at the other people in the room but not before he caught her disdainful grimace. Disappointment eroded some of his professional rapport with her.

"Or, stay here and keep an eye on Barton to make sure she's hanging on while I go see about the vending machines." He rose to his full height. "If there's any problems, talk to Bentley. He'll be able to help. Okay? Good."

She opened her mouth to protest, but he'd already turned away. Not that he wanted to leave Tessa in Tamara's less-than-capable hands, but if he didn't get away from her, he might say something out of anger and disgust that he couldn't take back.

Like she's a selfish, entitled bitch who shouldn't have followed us?

Yeah, that wouldn't have helped the situation even if it made him feel a little better.

But he focused on finding a couple of the engineering researchers to help him with the vending machines. Better than worrying about Tessa or Hermione.

Chapter Six

Hermione listened hard as she moved down the hallway toward the elevators. She didn't hear any sounds indicating someone else had entered the building, at least from this level. And she hadn't checked the ground floor. Bentley had given her the zip ties out of the second tango's pockets, and she hoped she could use them to secure doors if need be. That the terrorists had zip ties froze her blood. There was only one reason to carry them in this kind of operation and that was to take hostages and keep them restrained.

Unease and anger filtered through her. The thought of these researchers bound and incapacitated made her sick to her stomach. Especially Chester Martell. She'd do her damnedest to keep him safe, and not just because it was her mission.

You like him.

The voice of the cartoon dragon from the kid's movie about a Chinese warrior, her favorite of all the princesses, echoed in the back her mind. And like the warrior woman, she scoffed.

I think it's more accurate to say I respect him.

Uh-huh, sure, Wilcox. Keep telling yourself that.

She ignored the snarky voice and moved down the hall to the elevator bay. She didn't know if they worked but the power remained on so in all likelihood, the elevators remained functional. Another way in for the tangos.

And a quick way up to the surface level.

But there were cameras in the cars and she didn't know where the feeds went. Some central security room? Individual to each building or campus wide? Her gaze slid to the upper corners of the hallway. Other cameras pointed at the hall and guard's desk near the elevators. The problem was she had no idea who could be watching.

Shit, that means anyone who was looking could've seen me take down the tangos and everyone going into the break room.

There was no help for it now, but she could disable the cameras by disconnecting them. Pulling her knife, she reached up and cut the wires she could see before ducking through the door to the hub tunnel. She sheathed the knife and pulled out her phone, relieved she still had bars and battery life. She needed her team and to let them know she was still alive.

This tunnel had seasonal murals as far as she could tell with everything from plants and animals from North America in their seasonal garb. Her end of the tunnel depicted winter and a bobcat trotted across a snowy landscape with a rabbit in its jaws. She hoped she was more of the bobcat than the rabbit in her current scenario.

She dialed Dunwoody's cell and hoped she was somewhere she could receive the call.

"Dunwoody."

"Glad I caught you, Circuits. This is Siren One. Give me a SitRep above ground at the research labs." Hermione let her gaze trail along the pipes in the tunnel, searching for cameras along the ceiling.

"Captain! Where are you? Are you okay? Do you need backup? What's going on?"

"I'm in the tunnels outside Building Three. That's the only way I can get a cell connection. Where are you?"

"After you disappeared into the main building, I took down a few of the tangos still fighting the front gate guards until the explosion. That's when you disappeared off comms. I wasn't sure you'd made it so I headed back to the truck and took it across the landscaping toward our sniper's nest, behind the building directly across the green space." Dunwoody paused to speak to someone on the other end. "Porter wants to know if you're injured, Wizard."

"Nope, managed to avoid shrapnel and bullets this time, but besides the package, I have fifteen other civilians with me down here and one is badly injured."

"Can you get them all to my location, Captain?" That was Porter's voice. Dunwoody must have put her on speaker.

"That's my objective at this point. But after getting blown to hell and ending up underground, I'm a little turned around. I'm not sure where you are in relationship to me."

"Copy that. Do you know which building you're in?" Dunwoody was back.

"The civilians are in the underground break room of Building Three. I'm in the tunnels outside." Hermione paused and pulled the phone away from her ear. Had she heard something down the length of this tunnel? There wasn't any place to hide along the wall, especially with her bright hiking attire, but anyone else would be just as visible to her.

"Roger that. The whole complex is like a wagon wheel with a fountain at the hub over an atrium. It looks like the tunnels mirror the paved paths on the surface." The rustling sound of paper came through the phone. "You say you're in Building Three? We're directly north of Building Four so if you can move the civilians there, we can get to you and provide cover fire."

"Roger that. What about the surface around Building Four? Has there been any movement from the tangos?" Hermione kept her gaze trained on the other end of the tunnel.

"We haven't seen anyone in or out for a couple of hours, but there has been movement to Buildings One, Two, and Six."

"Roger that. But not Three or Four?"

"Nope. At least not above ground."

"Copy that. We haven't seen anyone else down here except a couple of tangos I took out in Building Three an hour ago. But there's a rumor of pursuit and a mole in the group, and we have injuries." She took a moment to glance down at her feet. "Circuits, I need you to do some digging. Do a background check on a Dr. Tamara Miller, Caucasian woman with white blonde hair. She said she got away from the tangos in Building One to warn us that they were coming, but there's something off about her. Text me the intel when you have it."

"Roger that, Captain. ETA to Building Four?"

Hermione hesitated. "Not sure. It'll depend on the injuries and whether we can move the victims quickly. I'll have to confirm. I'll text you when I have more intel. No calls get through from the buildings, though a text message might."

"Copy that. We'll keep an eye on the surface and relay any movement to your cell via text, Wizard." Dunwoody's voice sounded distracted, and Hermione could hear her fingers on the keys of her laptop.

"Roger that. Siren One out."

Hermione stuffed her phone into her pocket and stopped for a moment to listen again. Were those voices she heard? Had the researchers come looking for her? She inched closer to the door to the building, listening through it. Whoever they were, they didn't seem to be worried about keeping their voices low. She crossed the tunnel to stand behind the door should it open and waited.

"Where the fuck are Jasper and Dean?" A male voice sounded just beyond the door.

"How the fuck should I know? If they were smart, they would've found the escaped scientists by now." Another male voice threw out the derisive words. "Wait, is that blood?"

"Probably. I heard there was a firefight in Building Two. Might've been one here, too."

"Then where are the fuckin' bodies? Not like the dead can get up and walk."

"Coulda been just a scratch."

"Then where is everyone? Shit. We gotta tell Max what we seen. They gotta be around here somewhere. You check the tunnel to the hub. I'm gonna run upstairs to see if they went that way."

Hermione pulled her knife as she plastered herself to the wall. She held her breath as the door was pushed open into her tunnel. The hick on the other side stared down the hallway for a few seconds, listening like she'd done earlier. She flexed her hand around the hilt of her Ka-Bar and waited to see if he'd look around the door.

But the guy decided there was no one there and closed it. Hermione let her breath out softly, and her heart slowed down from a gallop. *Crisis one averted.* Now all she had to do was make sure they didn't find the people in the break room.

She cracked the door open and listened for the hicks. Had they both gone upstairs? She almost stepped out into the hallway when footsteps echoed from her left and she slipped back into the tunnel.

Guess not.

"Carl, didja see anything?" That had been the guy who searched the ground level.

"Nah, nothing. I was checkin' some of the labs but there's no one. You see anything upstairs?"

"Nope. It's empty, too."

"Think we should check the tunnel to the next building?"

There was a short period of silence as the first guy thought about it and Hermione waited with them, her mind setting up options for whichever path they took. Either they'd miss the people she was protecting or they'd be dead.

Your choice, assholes.

"Nah, Max has some guys comin' through there. Let's head back up to the surface and radio in. No point in reinventing the wheel here."

"What do wheels have to do with it? Let's just get back and see if Max has found his guy yet."

Their voices faded as the door to the stairs closed noisily behind them. She tugged open the tunnel door and listened to make sure they hadn't changed their minds to come back down. She waited a couple of minutes before slipping into the hallway and hurrying all the way down to the other tunnel entrance, cutting the security camera lines as she went.

No point in reminding the bastards that we're all here.

Once all the cameras had been severed, she paused to hear if anyone noticed they were no longer getting the feeds. They didn't seem to be too on the ball, but she suspected their time being safe was limited.

Hermione returned to the break room and knocked using the Morse code. The blind on the window moved a bit before the door opened and she slipped inside.

"Any problems, Captain?" Bentley closed and locked the door before turning to face her.

"No, but I'm sure you saw the tangos from Building Four come by?"

"Yeah, just in time. Got everyone quiet before they tried the door. Was afraid I'd have to take them out." He grimaced as he shot a look at the other people around them. "Did you take them out?"

She shook her head. "No, but like you, it was a close thing. They took the stairs up to the ground floor, but they said their leader was sending men through the tunnel from Building Two. I don't know how much time we have until we get more company. It might be a good idea to get moving. How are Barton and Avondale doing?"

Bentley grimaced. "Avondale seems to be coming around enough to move on his own. But Barton isn't doing so great. She's gonna have to be carried."

Fuck. Not the best news, but not surprising either.

"Any ideas about our other problem?"

"The mole, ma'am?"

She nodded as she let her gaze slide over the researchers in the break room. All of them seemed subdued, though she was pleased to see Dr. Miller was nowhere near Dr. Martell.

That's messed up, Wilcox. It was, and she shouldn't care if Miller and Martell were a thing, but the relief at their separation was real.

"Have you seen anyone acting shifty or watchful or nervous while I was gone?"

Bentley snorted. "I wish those adjectives would make someone seem guilty, but in this situation, everyone is hypervigilant, nervous, and twitchy."

"Yeah, I figured it would be a long-shot, but did anyone seem more nervous than normal? Everyone's spooked, but was anyone uneasy above and beyond?"

He shook his head. "Not that I could tell. Durbin and that woman doctor dumped Barton near the trash cans and Martell helped move her into a cleaner corner, but that's all that happened while you were gone."

Disdain dumped into Hermione's system at the entitled researchers' dismissal of the injured guard, and she had to tamp it down before it showed on her face. She shouldn't care. She wasn't here to care other than to get these people safely out of the situation.

Oh yeah, Wilcox. Doin' a bang-up job of that not-caring stuff.

"Okay, then we should take advantage of the lull between tangos and move everyone to Building Four. From there, we'll meet up with my team and the corpsman we have. That's the best chance for Barton."

"Yes, ma'am."

Hermione nodded and pointed at a poster hung on the wall above the trash. "Is that a map of the campus?"

Bentley nodded. "Yes, ma'am. It shows all the underground tunnels."

"Fucking fantastic." She moved to the poster and studied the lock on the poster frame.

Plexiglass with a lock. Easy.

Hermione shoved her Ka-Bar into the gap between the frame and the locking mechanism and twisted. The frame popped open, and she was able to take down the map of the campus inside. She sheathed the knife and brought the poster to the closest table. Bentley joined her and to her surprise, so did Martell. She tried to ignore her burst of pleasure.

Focus, Wilcox.

"Okay, from what I can tell, we're here in Building Three and there are tangos coming in from Building Two." She traced the lines on the map. "My plan is to get everyone into Building Four where my team can meet us and help evacuate off campus."

"What about Barton? I don't think she can take much more movement." Dr. Martell looked tired and wary.

"I know, doc. But we don't have much choice. If we can get to Building Four, my team can help us get out of here and take care of her. We just have to get there."

"What did your team say about getting us all out?" Durbin's whine cut across her explanation.

Hermione took a deep breath to keep from barking at him to shut up. "According to the team, the Eagle Militia has camped out in the main building, here, but so far hasn't sent many men through the tunnel system. There's activity in Buildings One,

Two, and Six, but they haven't bothered with this building or Four and Five, at least on the surface. My team is closest to Building Four, directly north of the main building, and they're planning to get us out that way."

The "us" really only included Martell and her. She'd be happy to leave Durbin and Miller behind, but there was no way she could justify it.

Even if it might make my job easier.

The others were technically on their own, but she wouldn't leave anyone to the militia's tender mercies.

"Okay, everyone listen up. We don't have a lot of time so I'm not going to repeat myself." She made sure she met every gaze as she swept hers around the room. "We're going to move to Building Four where the rest of my team should be able to meet us and evacuate everyone off campus. We need to move as quickly and quietly as possible. Avondale."

"Yes, ma'am?" The guard looked a little pale but was steady on his feet.

"I need you to help Guard Barton along with Dr..." She raised her eyebrows at the pompous ass who'd been a dick earlier.

"Dr. Richard Bridgewater."

"Right. Avondale and Bridgewater will carry Barton. Bentley, I need you to make sure everyone gets out of the break room and into the tunnel. You'll cover our sixes, copy?"

"Copy, Captain."

"Good." Hermione nodded. "Dr. Martell, I need you up front with me. Copy?"

"Yes, uh, yes, ma'am." Martell's eyes grew wide behind his glasses and he swallowed hard.

"Right. Let's move. Avondale and Bridgewater, get Barton up, please."

For once, the pompous ass did what he was told without quibble, and everyone else got ready to move. Hermione eyed Dr. Miller, but the woman wasn't showing anything other than anxious excitement. She'd pushed closer to the front of the room, but couldn't get around a couple of the other researchers. Hermione hid her petty satisfaction that Martell would be separated from the other doctor.

"Ready?" At their nods, she pulled the door open and stepped into the hallway.

Chapter Seven

C hester glanced back at the people behind him. Everyone seemed to be keeping up, and there hadn't been any problems leaving Building Three. Bentley had brought up the rear and somehow signaled Captain Wilcox that it was all clear. She'd nodded and hustled them all down the tunnel to Building Four.

Despite the seriousness of the situation, he found himself excited and pleased to be close to Captain Wilcox.

Her name is Hermione, like the character from those kids' books.

And rightly so. When it came to this kind of event, she seemed magical and powerful. Definitely focused like the witch in the story.

It was stupid and bad timing, but he liked being near Hermione. He liked her sleek, intense energy, and her obvious capability. Granted he knew very little about her, but what he did know, he liked, and it made him want to know more.

When they reached the end, Wilcox held up her hand in a fist and everyone slowed down. She leaned forward and pressed her ear against the door, listening for sounds on the other side. The only things Chester could hear were the footsteps and breathing of the people behind him along with his own heartbeat.

After a few moments, she straightened and motioned to Avondale.

"Keep everyone here and quiet. I'm going to recon the lower labs and take out the cameras to give us some cover."

"Give me a moment and I'll come with you. It'll be faster."

Wilcox shook her head. "No, I need you here just in case things go south. It won't take me long, and I can move faster on my own."

Chester had no doubt about that, but he didn't like the idea of her being alone with no one to watch her back.

"You know the adage for survival, Captain. Two is one, one is none. Everyone needs a team." Avondale shot her an earnest look, but Wilcox wasn't buying it.

"Right. You're the team that's going to take care of these people while I secure Building Four. Stay here, keep quiet, and I'll signal when it's safe." She nodded to them and pulled the door open just wide enough to slip through.

Avondale growled when the door closed. "Stupid woman, doesn't know what she's getting into alone."

Chester scowled at the guard. He was older with silver at his temples and a little paunch at his belly from age, but not soft.

"She's not stupid, and she's gotten us this far without your help. She's completely capable of doing this alone. We're the ones slowing her down."

Avondale snorted. "She's a woman. What does she know about combat and stealth missions?"

"Hear, hear," Bridgewater muttered.

Barton grunted painfully. "More than you, Avondale. You let those militia yahoos get the jump on you. That woman you're sneering at saved your ass instead of leaving you out cold on the floor, and she got us this far without your help. So how 'bout you keep your misogyny to yourself and bitch about it after she rescues our asses?"

Chester chuckled to cover his own discomfort. Barton wasn't wrong, but he had this irrational worry that Wilcox would need his help.

Is that because she's a woman? Fuck, I have some of that 'archaic sexism' too. If Wilcox had been male, he wouldn't have been nearly as worried at her capabilities. *That just proves I'm a misogynist along with Avondale.*

The wait was interminable, and his mind filled with all the ways it could go wrong for Wilcox. What if she was hurt and needed help? What if she was lying somewhere bleeding out? What if the terrorists had captured her and were beating her? The anxiousness rose to a screaming pitch and he almost didn't hear the latch on the door click open.

Oh, glory. Is it Wilcox or is it the terrorists?

"All clear. I repeat, all clear. The cameras are disabled, and there are no tangos in the underground labs." The whispers preceded Wilcox poking her head around the door. "Time to move. Get everyone into the break room, third door on the left. Let's go."

Chester grasped the door and held it open. "Get moving, Avondale. Barton needs to rest."

The older guard scowled, but he started moving with Richard's help, and the others followed behind them. Chester stayed at the door and watched everyone who passed, including Tamara. But she stepped out of the flow and flung herself into his arms. He barely caught her with one arm as she squeezed him tightly.

"Oh, thank goodness you're okay. I was afraid something had happened to you when we stopped for so long." She pushed her breasts against his chest, and he stiffened.

"Please let me go, Dr. Miller."

She froze then pushed him back to look at him. "What?"

"I don't like being hugged, and we don't have that kind of relationship, so I need you to stop touching me." Where were these words coming from? He'd never been so forthright with a woman before in his life. But he definitely didn't want to be touched by Tamara Miller anymore.

"Oh. Um, I'm sorry. I didn't realize I'd overstepped." She blushed as if embarrassed, and guilt tugged at Chester. "I won't do it again."

Social protocol dictated that he comfort her or forgive her for her intrusion, but his patience was at its end. *And I only want one woman touching me right now.* Yeah, too bad that woman was here only to rescue and get them all to safety.

"Thank you." He nodded sharply as the last person passed them into the building. "Let's go." He gestured for her to precede him through the door and she went with a hurt look over her shoulder. He gritted his teeth and stepped in after her while Bentley followed.

Wilcox directed everyone into the break room again but stopped him at the door with Bentley.

"Bentley, I need you to see if the weapons have been cleared out of the guards' arsenal and bring whatever remains back so we have some defense."

"Yes, ma'am. Where are you going to be?"

"I'm going up to the ground floor to scout out an escape route and to contact my team again. About the cameras. Do their feeds go to a central security room or is it specific to each building?" She checked her weapons and tugged down her vest to cover the pistol in the back of her pants.

"Each building has its own security feed. The external cameras get directed to Building One, but the internal is just for the local building." Bentley held the break room door open so Chester could enter, but he held his ground. The guard raised an eyebrow while he listened to Wilcox.

"Outside cameras that show the area behind the buildings all the way to the perimeter fence?"

"Yes, ma'am."

"Fuck." She bit her lip and frowned. "Is there a way to disable them, even short term?"

"Not that I know of, ma'am."

"Dammit. They just couldn't make this easy. We're gonna need a distraction to get everyone outta here." Her eyes narrowed and she rubbed her chin. "Okay. Everyone sit tight while I recon the ground floor. Give me your radio. What's a good channel no one else should be listening on?"

Bentley handed it over. "Channels four, seven, and nine are never used, not even for emergencies."

"Right. Switch to channel nine. I'll contact you on that when it's all clear."

"Copy that, ma'am."

She nodded. "All right. Keep everyone inside and quiet, and I'll be back in fifteen mikes unless I radio you." She headed toward the door to the stairs topside.

"Roger that, ma'am." Bentley waved then herded Chester into the break room. "Let's go, Dr. Martell."

Chester wanted to protest, but he didn't see any reason not to follow instructions. Still, his gut said Wilcox needed his expertise this time. There was no rational explanation for it, but the feeling wouldn't leave him alone. Bentley crossed the room to talk to Avondale, presumably to get his radio, and Chester took his momentary distraction to slip back out the door to the hallway.

He didn't bother to quiet his steps as he hurried after Wilcox. The door to the stairs leading up sat closed and he couldn't believe how fast she'd moved. He opened the door and let it close quietly behind him before taking the steps two at a time. He hit the landing and came around the corner, only to stop short with a barrel of a gun held at eye-level in steady hands.

"Oh shit!"

"Dr. Martell? What are you doing here?" Wilcox scowled and lowered her weapon.

"I'm coming with you in case you need backup." Okay, that excuse sounded weak even to him, but it was the only thing he could think of on the fly.

"I don't need backup, doc."

"You heard what Avondale said about one being none. It's always better to have someone watch your back." He tried to sound confident even though he had no experience watching anyone's back.

She glanced at the watch on her wrist and back down the steps before grimacing. "I don't have time to take you back to the break room, so you can come with me if you stay quiet and behind me. Don't make me regret this decision, doc."

He gritted his teeth to keep from grinning. "No, ma'am."

She snorted and shook her head. "Follow my lead. Don't move unless I give the go ahead. Got me?"

"Yes, ma'am."

He could've sworn her mouth twitched with amusement, but she turned away and continued up the stairs before he could be sure. He tried to be as quiet as her, but his footfalls sounded a hundred times louder despite his efforts to be silent. Fortunately, the stairs were in their own room and she held up her hand in a fist just as they reached the door at the top.

She didn't wait to see if he understood. She grasped the handle on the door and tugged it open a crack to peek around the edge of the jamb. Chester couldn't hear or see anything, but he found himself holding his breath and listening hard.

"Okay, all clear. We'll head for the guard's desk and use it as cover until we determine how many hostiles are in the vicinity. Copy?" She glanced back at him.

"Uh, yes, copy." He nodded.

"Let's move."

She held the door open and gestured for him to precede her, her gaze constantly moving around the open foyer of the building. He focused on getting to the guard desk as quickly as possible, hoping there was no one outside the windows who might look inside as they crossed the open floor. Excitement and fear gave speed to his strides, and he made it to the desk before he realized he was moving. His heart thundered in his ears and his breath sawed in his chest worse than when he'd tried sprinting in high school. How in the hell did she keep so calm during this kind of event? Wilcox never flinched and pushed him down behind the edge of the desk before she crouched beside him.

"I'm going to contact my team—" She stopped as her phone chirped with several incoming texts. She pulled it out and swore. "Get under the desk now, doc!" She shoved him hard into the foot well of the desk and scrambled in beside him just as voices entered the foyer.

He scrunched as much as possible, pulling his knees to his chest as she pressed up against him, shoulder to knees, her own knees shoved into his side. They both stilled as the voices drew closer. She raised a finger to her lips and he nodded, holding his breath.

"Holy shit, Max is pretty worked up." A nasal male voice echoed in the entryway atrium.

"Yeah, well, this shoulda been a quick in-n-out and now he can't find the doc." The second male voice had a plugged sound, and the owner promptly sneezed. "Fuckin' allergies. Damn tree giz."

Nasal laughed. "My wife says you should eat local honey so's you don't get all plugged."

They paused just outside of the guard's desk. Chester swallowed hard and shot a look at Wilcox. She didn't meet his gaze, keeping her attention straight up. He realized her leg and shoulder might not be completely under the desk surface and the men on the other side could look down and see her. He turned sideways to allow her the space, but she pressed a hand on his arm to keep him still.

What a terrible time to have broad shoulders.

"So, you think Max's plan is really gonna work?" Nasal grabbed whatever he'd set down on the desk.

"Oh, yeah. He's only lookin' for the doc to make us all safe before he uses it. Fuckin' libtards won't know what hit 'em. Just imagine what you could do. With it in our hands, everyone will hafta take us seriously."

"But it's still fuckin' bad, right? And we don't have the antidote for it yet. How long's he gonna hold out if he can't find the doc?"

"Oh, he'll find him. The guy can't get off the campus now. It's just a matter of time before we flush him out." A radio crackled, and they paused. "Hammond here."

"Head over to Building Three. The cameras seem to be down."

"Copy, sir. Hammond out." There was another pause. "Guess we're goin' over to Building Three and see what's what."

Chester swallowed hard as the voices moved away. What had they meant he wouldn't be able to get off the campus? Did they know about Wilcox's plan to take everyone out on the back side of Building Four? He shot a look at Wilcox and raised his eyebrows. She shook her head and lifted her hand to caution him to wait.

Seconds ticked by as they listened for other voices, but heard nothing. Eventually, she unfolded herself and crouched in the open space of the desk, scanning the area around it. Chester waited until she gave the all-clear and scrambled up beside her, not nearly as graceful.

So much for my athletic abilities.

"What do we do now? Do you know what that guy meant when he said we can't get off campus now?" He peered over the top of the desk but didn't see anything that meant danger or threat.

"We're still going to find a way out of here, doc. My team won't leave us here, and the militia isn't that well organized. I hope to do it when they're not looking, but we'll take what we can get." Wilcox rose and headed for the hallway. "Stick close and when I tell you to stop, stop. We have no idea how many tangos there are in here."

He swallowed hard. He didn't know what a "tango" was, but he understood that they didn't want to meet them. He followed her down the hallway, trying to move as quietly as she did, but she ghosted along the corridor without any noise. *How does she do that?*

He wanted to emulate her, but he felt too big and heavy.

They crept down the hallway, pausing at each door and window to keep out of sight of whoever stood inside. Wilcox periodically checked her phone for texts from her teammates outside and stopped at the corner of where the hall branched off.

"What's down that way?" She pointed to the intersecting hall.

"The loading docks if this building is anything like Building Two." He shot a look behind them. Hopefully, no one would come up on them from that direction.

"That's probably our best bet." She tapped a text into her phone. "The question is if they're guarding the docks or not. Let's go."

They kept moving until new voices made them freeze. There wasn't anywhere to hide in the hallway, but Wilcox darted across the corridor and shoved open the door to a darkened lab. They hurried inside and crouched beside the window, letting the door close behind them. Chester's heart thundered against his breastbone as they peeked over the sill.

The light from the lab opposite them flooded into the hallway, and they could see several people standing around others kneeling on the floor. The people standing were armed to the teeth and had the look of the guys his sister had called "Meal Team Six" from the news. Most wore grungy clothes, had unkempt hair and beards, and more than a few carried guts that rivaled Santa Claus. They looked pathetic on the news, but here in-person, they were ugly and frightening.

They had their backs to the hallway until one of the thugs moved and Chester caught sight of the person who seemed in charge.

"Oh, my glory." Horror and disappointment skittered down into Chester's gut. "That's my cousin, Avery Gentry. What's he doing here?"

Wilcox frowned. "Which one is your cousin?"

"The one with the torn denim vest pointing at the tech."

Her eyes narrowed. "Are you sure?"

"Of course. Why?"

"Because our intel said that guy is Max Louden, the social media voice and financier of the Eagle Militia."

"Wait, you're saying he's part of this crazy, violent separatist group we've heard about on the news?" Chester swallowed hard as he looked back at Avery. "That's insane. Why would he do something like this?"

"No clue, doc. But according to all the shit he's posted on social media and their website, he feels that a demonstration is needed to show the corruption of all our shared values, etc." She scanned the room full of homegrown terrorists with her sharp gaze. "The door we passed. Is that the only way out of that lab?"

He shook his head. "No. There should be one in the main hall, too. This doesn't make sense. What the hell is he doing here?"

"Our intel says he's looking for you specifically. It's why I'm here to get you out."

"But that's ridiculous. Why didn't he contact me directly? This Call-of-Duty BS doesn't get results. Violence isn't the answer."

Wilcox grimaced. "Oh, it gets results, just not necessarily the ones we like. I don't know why he didn't just email you, doc. But with militia groups, violence seems to be their go-to action in my experience."

"How do you know he's here for me? Maybe I can talk him out of this."

Before she could answer, Avery took out a pistol and shot the tech in front of him, point-blank. Chester whimpered and swallowed hard.

"Yeah, no, I think we should find a way outta here without him seeing you, doc."

"What about the others?" He balked as she pulled him back into the hallway. "We can't just leave them to be shot by these...these terrorists."

"Dr. Martell—"

"No, I didn't sign up for this, but I'll be damned before I let my coworkers get killed because these miscreants are after me."

He turned to head back to the foyer when a door ahead of them opened. Wilcox grabbed him and whirled him through another door, pushing him down as she closed it with a soft click. Avery and another man stopped beside their door, talking in urgent voices.

"Where the hell is Dr. Martell?"

"I dunno, Max. The security guy messaged us that he came in this morning, but no one's seen 'im since we took the front building."

"It's not like he's adventurous or a goddamn superhero. He's a geek, and the key to our plan. We need to find him."

Wilcox shot Martell a speaking look before she reached up and turned the lock on the door, hoping the men outside wouldn't notice. Then she braced her body against it and put her finger over her lips. He swallowed hard and nodded.

"Have we searched the whole facility?" Avery's shadow filled the crack under the door and the knob rattled.

"Not yet, boss. But there are a lot of labs down in the basement of these buildings. We haven't been able to get to all of them yet."

"Well, get to them. And find Martell!"

Chester swallowed hard and held his breath. Were they still outside the door? Had they moved on? What the hell did they need him for? Avery had always been quiet at the family gatherings, but his silence had been intense and watchful. He kept to himself despite Aunt Janette's and Uncle Milton's boisterousness.

Isn't that what we always say about serial killers too? 'He was always quiet and kept to himself.'

Chester had had no idea his cousin leaned toward anarchy and overthrowing the government. If Avery had come to Chester and asked for his help in whatever they were planning, he might have heard him out. But watching his quiet cousin whip out a pistol and shoot someone destroyed more than an innocent life. It disintegrated Chester's willingness to even hear him out.

Yeah, fuck that noise.

Wilcox pressed her finger to her lips then pointed to herself and used two fingers from her other hand to point at her eyes. He nodded as she rotated around to face the door, pressing her ear against it. The silence stretched as they waited. Then she grasped the knob and cracked the door open.

Chapter Eight

Hermione settled her heartbeat and listened as she scanned the hallway outside. No one appeared in her field of view, but she couldn't see the intersecting hall behind the door. She listened for footsteps or voices, but nothing sounded in the corridor. She pushed her head through the gap and scanned the view to the reception area.

Max or Avery or whatever his name was and his henchmen had by all appearances left the building, but she didn't trust that they wouldn't pop back up like weeds. She eased back into the room and closed the door.

"No one is outside for the moment, but I have no intel on where anyone could be and I don't want to give our position away for the moment. Let me contact my team and we'll go from there. Copy?"

Martell nodded and swallowed hard as he leaned against the wall. This couldn't be easy on him, though he'd done well over the time they'd been stuck underground. Frankly, she had no idea how he could work down there with no windows and no sunlight. She needed fresh air and open spaces, though she could operate in close-quarters and under the cover of darkness. She just preferred to be in the light.

She dialed her call and waited with her back to the door, grateful it had a lock on it. Hopefully she would see it turn should someone try to get in from the other side.

"Dunwoody."

"It's Siren One. I have some intel for you. Turns out Max Louden is actually Avery Gentry, cousin to Dr. Chester Martell. Do some research on the familial connection. Also, check for outside surveillance cameras. We'll need to disable them to get across the open space to the perimeter fence line."

"Copy that, Captain. Any new injuries?"

"Negative. We've left the main group underground in Building Four to scout the upper floor. Damn near ran into Louden."

"Roger that. You said 'we', Captain. Who's we?"

"Dr. Martell joined me last minute."

Dunwoody whistled through the phone. "Oh shit. Were you wearing the brown pants?"

"It was a close thing." Hermione chuckled. "But we overheard some of his men state that we wouldn't be able to get off campus now. I don't have intel on what it means, just that they seemed pretty confident. Have you seen any increase in patrols?"

"Negative, Captain. The usual so far. No one seems to be taking security very seriously. They might be relying on the security cameras to give them a warning." Dunwoody snorted.

"You've hacked into the system, haven't you?"

Dunwoody chuckled. "Affirmative. I can turn on or off anything I want. If they're not right there, they won't see it coming." Her second hesitated. "Will you be coming out soon now that you have Dr. Martell in pocket?"

Hermione shot a look at the man beside her. He was her primary objective and she had him. All she had to do was make it out of the building and over to the perimeter fence. Ostensibly, she was free and clear to go. She could take the doc and head out, and that would be that.

But the others in the underground break room, they'd be left to defend themselves against Louden's thugs, and he'd proven to be a violent asshole when he didn't get what he wanted. Despite having secured her target, she couldn't leave the others to fend for themselves.

You can't save everyone, Wilcox.

The voice of her former commanding officer echoed through her head from the past. One of her last missions had brought her squad to a school in a war-torn country. The students had been terrified but unable to get out or away. Not without help. She'd begged her CO to let the squad protect the kids as they all moved to the safe zone, but her request had been denied. They had their package and were ordered to move out.

She'd left those kids behind against her better judgment and followed her orders to get the package out. But they'd found out later that the school had been bombed into rubble less than an hour later. No survivors. Hermione never forgot the hollow feeling of having left innocents to die when she could've helped them.

No, I can't save everyone, but I can save a few.

"Negative. There are a few researchers and guards we'll be bringing with us. One has serious injuries. Be advised, there's a rumor we have a mole. I repeat, there's a rumor we've been infiltrated by a mole, but the identity is unknown."

Dr. Martell's eyes widened and he mouthed, *Mole?* She nodded.

"Copy that. ETA for evac?"

She bit her lip and tried to estimate how much time it would take to get the researchers and injured guards out of the building.

"Thirty mikes. But I'll text when we need the cameras diverted."

"Copy that. Team on standby."

"Roger that. Siren One out."

Hermione ended her call and rose, Martell scrambling to his feet beside her.

"Is there really a mole in the group?" He looked a little green.

She nodded as she scoped out the hallway again. "Yeah. I overheard some of the tangos talking about an inside person relaying information to them. I don't know who it is and if I'm lucky, we deprived them of their communication when I asked everyone to leave their cellphones in Building Two. But the guards all have radios and it could be one of them."

"Fuck."

She grinned at his expletive. "You got that right."

"So, what are we going to do?" Chester didn't relish meeting up with the mole when they were just trying to get off the campus in one piece. That seemed like a recipe for disaster.

"We're going to collect the rest of your colleagues and get them out the backdoor of this building." She patted her pockets for her phone and some plastic zip ties. "Let's get moving. We'll be outta here in an hour."

He hoped she was right, though given the problems they encountered while trying to get to Building Four and the likelihood of a mole being in their ranks, he didn't have much faith it would go according to plan.

"Stay close, doc." She darted into the hallway, and he had to follow or be left behind.

Doesn't it make more sense for me to stay here and she get the rest of them upstairs?

"Wait, shouldn't I just stay up here?"

Wilcox shook her head as she kept going. "Nope. If you get captured, my whole mission goes to shit. You need to stay with me while we get the others. There's no way I'm leaving you here for your cousin to collect you. Besides, I'll need your help to carry some of the others. Now, let's go."

He sighed inwardly and followed her careful but quick progress down the hallway to the foyer. No one seemed to be anywhere nearby, and he wondered how long their luck would hold. She pushed open the door to the staircase and listened a few seconds before shoving him through and following him down the stairs. Their footsteps echoed in the concrete stairwell, and he hoped the sounds didn't carry into the main portions of the building, upstairs or down.

Wilcox held up her hand in a fist when they got to the door at the basement. Chester nodded and held his breath as she softly pressed the thumb latch and pulled, cracking it open. They listened for a few moments before she let it close without latching.

"I'm going to scope the hallway out before we head to the break room. Give me two minutes. If I don't come back in that time, stay put until I come for you."

"What if someone comes down the stairs from the ground floor?"

"Then find a place to hide." Wilcox met his gaze. "Two minutes."

"Yes, ma'am." He swallowed hard and hoped she'd be back before then as she ducked through the door.

"One...two...three..." He started counting under his breath as he listened hard for anyone coming down the stairs or outside the door. "Twenty-two...twenty-three...twenty-four..."

Were those voices? He kept the count going in his head as he closed his mouth, trying to keep time and still listen. He didn't hear anything else and had reached about a minute and twenty seconds when the door opened and Wilcox yanked him through.

"Let's go, doc. We don't have a lot of time before Louden realizes that he's losing men faster than he can send them." She herded him down the hall toward the break room.

"Losing men? Did you kill them?"

She shook her head as she pulled out the walkie talkie. "Nope, just incapacitated them, but he's gonna notice when they don't answer their radio summons." She turned on the walkie talkie and listened for a few moments. Only silence came back. "Bentley, come in, over."

"This is Bentley." The reply came back quickly.

"We'll be at your locale in one mike, over."

"Copy that. See you in one."

"Roger that. Out."

She shoved the radio away and hustled them to the break room door and knocked in a complex series of beats. The door opened to Bentley holding a rifle, his face full of relief.

"Good to see you, Captain. Any trouble?"

Wilcox snorted as they slipped inside. "Plenty, but now we have a way out. Let's get these people ready to move. The tangos are checking the buildings systematically, and we don't want to be here when they get to this one."

"Yes, ma'am."

Chester turned to do the same but Wilcox pulled him aside. "How well do you know Dr. Miller?"

He blinked and shot a look toward the blonde woman. "Well enough, I guess. We're not friends, but I've known her a while." He widened his eyes. "Shit, do you think she's the mole?"

Wilcox's expression didn't change and she didn't move her gaze from his face. "That's what my gut is telling me, but I don't have any concrete evidence. I just recommend not saying much around her until we're in the clear."

He swallowed hard and nodded. "Okay, Captain."

She gave him a sharp nod before she headed over to Bentley. He took a deep breath and crouched beside Tessa. Her skin had gone gray and she didn't move much, but she met his gaze and gave him an exhausted smile.

"You getting on good with the Captain, Dr. Martell?"

He snorted despite the rush of pleasure in his chest. "Well enough that she hasn't shot me to keep me here yet."

"Oh, come on, doc. I can see the way you look at her. She's hot shit, no question about it, and she's also got beauty and brains to go with it. Not like Dr. Miller." Tessa shot him a dry look.

"You don't think Dr. Miller is smart?"

Tessa grimaced. "Oh, she's smart enough, but she's obsequious."

"Obsequious?"

"You know, smarmy? Like she's hiding something, or something. There's just something off about her." Tessa shrugged. "And she always seems to be hanging all over you, especially lately."

Before he could reply, Miller appeared at his elbow and brushed his shoulder as she wrapped an arm around his waist in a half-hug, ignoring his earlier admonishment about touching.

"Are you all right, Chester? I almost swallowed my tongue when I realized you hadn't come back with the male guard. I was so worried about you. Where did you go?"

Chester cursed the social contract that required him to interact with her. Tessa was right. Dr. Miller was smarmy and intrusive while Captain Wilcox seemed to talk to everyone around her with a measure of respect. Of course, he hadn't seen her interact with anyone she was attracted to—*and let's be honest, I want her to be attracted to me*—but she didn't strike him as a woman who'd have to chase men.

He didn't want to tell Dr. Miller anything, especially after Wilcox mentioned her suspicions. So, what the hell could he say?

Hermione tried not to react as she watched Dr. Miller wrap her arms around Chester—*Dr. Martell, dammit!*—and forcibly turned her attention to getting everyone organized. But something about the woman's closeness to Martell bugged Hermione.

Maybe because you're attracted to him and you're acting like she's stealing your man?

When it was put like that, it made her want to bitch-slap herself. Still, there was something weird about Miller's interest in Martell, and Chester didn't seem as enamored with the other doctor as she was with him.

Which I really shouldn't care about.

Hermione turned back to helping everyone get to their feet and checking for injuries. They'd need to move relatively fast to get out before the terrorists realized they were there. But she kept an eye on the two doctors, wondering why it bugged her so much. They were just hugging like friends in a rough situation. Why would that seem off?

She finally got the researchers organized with who would be carrying whom, and the guards ready to face the outside world, but something kept pinging her warning system. She narrowed her eyes and scanned the room, wondering what it was she'd missed.

"Are we all ready to move? You need to be as quiet as possible and keep going. This is our one opportunity to get out of here without more injuries. Clear?"

Everyone nodded. Martell moved away from Dr. Miller and her hand got caught in the pocket of his white lab coat. She apologized as annoyance flashed across his face and Hermione narrowed her eyes.

The coats...

If Miller was the mole, there was the possibility she'd put some-thing in Martell's pocket. A tracking device or a bug would help whoever she worked with find Martell later. *The question is how do I get them to remove their coats without alerting Miller?*

"Before we go, I need everyone to take off their doctor's coats." She met their gazes and confusion filtered through their expressions.

"Why?" Dr. Durbin frowned.

"Because the tangos are looking for a doctor, and I'd rather they not have easy targets with people wearing white coats. You kinda stand out. Bring them here and we'll leave them in a pile. I'm sure you'll be able to come back for them later."

The doctors grumbled but complied with her request, handing her the coats. However, she watched Miller's expression and frustration flashed across her face as Martell took his coat off and added it to the pile.

Bingo.

"All right, I'll take point. If I raise my fist like this..." She clenched her fist as she held up near her ear. "That means you all stop and keep quiet. Our goal is to get out of here without alerting the terrorists or having to shoot anyone. Copy?"

Everyone murmured assent and gathered up, ready to move. Hermione nodded and cracked the door open, holding her breath.

If we're lucky, we'll get out of here without new casualties.

But Murphy's Law was strong with military personnel, and she'd long ago accepted that all the planning and luck wouldn't cover everything.

The hallway outside sat empty, but she listened for a few seconds to be sure no one was coming.

"Okay. Let's move out. Head for the elevator bay as quietly as possible. Bentley, you cover our backs."

"Copy that, ma'am."

She nodded and darted into the hallway, checking her watch. Fifteen minutes had elapsed since she'd talked to her team, but that was fifteen minutes for Louden and his thugs to reconverge on Building Four. Her heart settled into a steady, focused rhythm as she moved to the door to the stairs, listening for intruders.

The researchers behind her sounded like a herd of horses, but at least they weren't speaking. Hermione wanted to keep an eye on Miller, but she had enough to occupy her attention. She reached the door to the stairs and cracked it open as the others gathered behind her.

Take Martell and go. Just leave the rest of these people here to fend for themselves.

The efficiency expert in the back of her head made a compelling argument. Could she even get them all to safety? She shot a look back at the guard held up between two people. She'd be signing Tessa's death warrant.

And I can't do that to her. Hell, she couldn't do that to any of them. Not after the mission that left the children dead.

"Everyone ready? I'm gonna scout the top floor to be sure we're clear. Then we'll move. Copy?"

They all nodded.

"Back in three."

She swallowed her unease at leaving them alone with Miller as she stepped into the staircase and let the door close softly behind her. Especially Martell. She trusted Miller just about as far as she could spit a dead sewer rat. *Get a grip, Wilcox.* She shook off the worries as she listened. No one moved on the stairs, and she took them two at a time up to the ground floor.

And this is when shit gets tricky.

Hermione clicked the walkie talkie. "Bentley, come back."

"Bentley here."

"Bring them into the stairwell. All clear. I repeat, all clear. Over."

"Roger that."

Hermione reached the top of the stairs and paused by the door. A few heartbeats later, the lower door opened and footsteps sounded on the stairs. She cracked her door, checking the open floor of the building. Nothing moved or made sound, but she didn't think the break would last for long.

Martell was the first to reach her, and she ignored the little spurt of delight and relief as he stopped behind her.

"Anyone out there?" His whisper warmed her chest, and she ruthlessly squashed the feeling.

"Negative. All clear for now. But we don't have a lot of time." She glanced down at her watch. Four more minutes had passed. She shot a look down the stairs. "Are they all in the stairwell?"

He nodded. "We even managed to get Tessa up the steps, but she's really pale."

Hermione nodded. Her worry spiked, but she shoved it down with her attraction for Martell. "Roger that. As soon as we get out of the building, my team's medic is standing by." She waited for the others to join them and looked over their strained faces. "I know you're all stressed and tired, but we're almost out. We're going to take a right out this door, go to the end of the hallway, then take the cross corridor to the loading docks on the back of the building."

Durbin swallowed hard, his Adam's Apple bobbing in his throat. "Are you going with us?"

"Yeah, I'll be there, but I want you to keep going even if we meet resistance. I'll do my best to keep them occupied while you get out. Understand?"

Durbin blanched a white so pale his freckles stood out like a dalmatian's spots, but he nodded.

"Okay, listen up. We're going to move as fast and as quietly as possible to the loading docks at the back of the building. Don't stop. Just keep going to the docks. Bentley and I will do our best to take care of any tangos in our way, but you have to keep moving. Do you understand?"

There were whispered yeses through the group, and she nodded sharply.

"Good. Let's go."

She checked the corridor again then pushed open the door. "Go, go, go."

The researchers scurried through the door and down the hallway with Avondale pushing them and Bentley watching their six. She jogged with them, listening for anyone else in the building as she tapped her phone.

"Dunwoody."

"Heading for the docks. ETA three mikes."

"Copy that, Captain. No patrols outside in the last ten mikes. Shutting off feed to the outside cameras now."

"Copy that. Be advised, we'll need medical help and escort to the perimeter fence."

"Roger that. Deploying Sirens Three, Four, and Five for the evac. How many in your party?"

"Twelve with one serious injury. Be advised, suspect a Benedict Arnold, but have no confirmation."

"Copy that. Rendezvous five mikes at the back door to the docks."

"Roger that."

Hermione ended the call and shoved the phone into her back pocket. They reached the corner of the hallway when two members of the Eagle Militia appeared in the corridor. The first guy wore a red baseball cap and a dirty t-shirt straining over a belly that would've given the Buddha a run for his money. He went down from a throat-punch and a swept leg before he could raise the alarm. She used her borrowed Sig to smack him in the temple while he gagged on his own tongue. Then she turned to his partner.

The second guy wore overalls but he seemed to have some experience with the weapon in his hands. He was slow to react, standing there a little dumbfounded when his buddy went down.

Definitely part of Meal Team Six.

"Holy fuck, Rosco! What the fuck?"

He finally raised his weapon to fire, but Hermione already had one hand on the rifle and her pistol pointed a few inches from his jowly face.

"Now, I'm gonna give you a choice. Either you put down this rifle and we stash you with your buddy. Or I'm going to shoot you right here, and he's gonna wake up next to a body. Copy?"

Chapter Nine

C hester had never seen anyone move with such grace or skill in all his life. When Wilcox took down the first guy without fanfare or much sound, he shivered with the eeriness of her abilities. Now she held another man, who probably had a good fifty pounds on her, at gunpoint and she never wavered. Her hand held steady and so did her voice and eyes.

"Now, I'm gonna give you a choice. Either you put down this rifle and we stash you with your buddy. Or I'm going to shoot you right here and he's gonna wake up next to a body. Copy?"

At first, Chester wasn't sure the guy would comply. Anger and disdain that a pretty woman in brightly-colored high tech hiking clothes had knocked out his buddy and had him facing a bullet flashed across his face. Chester watched him calculate the likelihood of overpowering Wilcox.

Don't do it, buddy. She's better than you think.

Unfortunately, the guy didn't hear Chester's warning because he snarled and tried to get his rifle up as he squeezed the trigger. Wilcox didn't hesitate. She pulled the weapon closer to her and shot the thug point-blank. His body dropped and the shooting stopped, but Wilcox scowled as people started to cry out.

"Move! We don't have time to hide the bodies. Head for the docks now!"

"I've been shot! Oh my god, I've been shot!" Durbin's voice carried above footsteps as the rest of the techs stampeded toward the door to the docks.

"Sonuvaprick!" Wilcox pulled out her phone. "Dunwoody, be advised. We have a GSW to the arm on another researcher. Target secure but unfriendlies could be incoming." She listened a moment before adding. "Roger that." She stowed the phone again and helped Durbin up. "It's just a graze, which is gonna hurt like a mudfucker but isn't life threatening. Now let's go, Durbin, or you're gonna be as dead as this guy here."

Dr. Durbin whimpered but got to his feet with another researcher's help and lumbered off toward the docks. Wilcox disarmed the two men on the floor and met Chester's gaze.

"Move, Martell. We gotta get outta here now."

He nodded and hurried after the others, coming up behind Tessa and her escorts, his mind still reeling from what he'd just seen. Wilcox was both savage and powerful, and yet she hadn't been wasteful in her actions. Her deadly skill was sexy, and he couldn't help the heat that warmed his chest when he remembered what she'd done.

There's something wrong with me.

How could he admire violence? But the violence had been necessary to protect everyone else, and she'd done it with focus and precision, both of which he admired in people. Granted, her skill set was completely different, but she was definitely a master, and a shiver of excitement shot down his spine as she pushed through the crowd at the docks.

"Bentley, watch our backs while I check to see if my team is in place."

Wilcox ducked through the doors while Chester and the others waited in tense silence. Bentley shot Chester a look as he moved to the back of the crowd facing down the corridor. The two bodies lay in the blood pooling out of the man in overalls. Chester turned away and scanned the closed doors as his heart beat a rapid tattoo against his ribs.

Please hurry before more of Avery's goons come for us.

The doors opened, and Wilcox gestured everyone through. "Let's go, people. The team will escort us across to the perimeter fence. Don't stop. Don't look back. If someone falls, help them up if you can, but keep going."

"What about you? Where will you be?" Dr. Miller might have sounded frightened if not for the narrowing of her eyes.

"Keeping an eye on anyone coming after us. Go now!"

Wilcox braced her back to the doors as they piled through. Chester didn't want to move far from her despite his lack of expertise in defending anyone. Besides, he was a runner and in great shape. If he had to sprint across the field with her, he could do it.

But you can't outrun a bullet, dumbass.

No, but neither could she and he'd rather be there if she went down.

"Dammit, Martell, what the hell are you waiting for? Go!"

"We'll go together. I'm not leaving you here to face them alone."

She snarled. "I'm not alone—the team is here to help. Besides, I'm better equipped to deal with unfriendlies than you. Get your ass moving!"

She shoved him out the door and followed with her pistol in her hand, glancing back over her shoulder. He took off down the stairs to the floor of the loading bay. The others had already reached the outside door and were met by more women dressed like Wilcox, except they held automatic rifles resembling the militia members.

"Is that everyone, Captain?" A tall Black woman caught up with them at the backside of the building.

"Yup. This is the last one of our crew."

"Copy that." She turned and motioned to the other two soldiers. "Move out!"

Then it was a mad dash across the open lawn between the building and the chain-link fence surrounding the campus. Chester wanted to bolt, using his speed and strength to carry him out of harm's way, but he couldn't leave his colleagues vulnerable.

Everyone made it almost all the way across when shouts sounded from behind them. Chester started to look when someone ahead tripped and sprawled on the ground. He darted over to Ani Madigan and pulled her up.

"Dammit, doc, you can't save everyone if you're dead. I'll get Dr. Madigan. I need you to run, now!"

But Chester shook his head and kept his arm around Ani. "Everyone's important. I'll help her and you cover our butts." He steered Ani toward the breach in the fence ahead, getting her to jog. "Are you all right?"

Ani nodded as tears streamed down her cheeks. "Yeah, fine. If Dr. Miller hadn't tripped me, I would've been at the fence already."

Chester frowned. "Miller tripped you? On purpose?"

"Yeah." Ani didn't say anything more as shots rang out and they ducked through the fence line.

Wilcox and the others returned fire as they retreated through the barrier before everyone melted into the cover of the trees. Chester kept helping Ani until they got to the emergency vehicles parked on the forest service road a hundred yards from the fence. One ambulance already shot off down the road toward the Broken Pass Medical Center. He hoped Tessa would be all right as other EMTs converged on the freed hostages.

Chester lost sight of Wilcox as he helped Ani over to another ambulance. Cops, FBI, and medical personnel swarmed the area, checking out the researchers who'd escaped. He kept his head down and declined medical help as he stepped to the side, watching the others get checked out.

His emotions swirled around in a kaleidoscope of feelings. Adrenaline pumped through his veins, and he shook with reaction. Why the hell was Avery after him? Why hadn't he emailed or called? Was Tamara Miller working with him? Had she helped plan this raid? Or had she figured it was safer to help the terrorists? And why had she deliberately tripped Ani Madigan?

The fear he'd felt all throughout his ordeal now rose in anger, and his hands tightened into fists. What the fuck was going on, and what did it have to do with him? He almost stomped over to the man who looked like some sort of field commander, but stopped himself. He didn't want to actually talk to anyone except Captain Wilcox, so he said nothing as he stood beside Ani's ambulance.

"Dr. Martell?"

A white man wearing a dark suit and a stylish tie approached with Captain Wilcox. He stopped and eyed Chester with an impassive expression.

This guy looks like the stereotypical FBI agent.

"Yes?"

"I'm Special Agent in Charge Ray Matthews. I need you to come with me."

Chester's gaze slid to Wilcox's face before returning to Matthews's. "All right."

SAIC Matthews's shoulders loosened as if he'd expected a fight. "Right this way, Dr. Martell."

He followed the agent toward a black SUV that screamed "government vehicle" and wondered if they should just rename them as GUVs, government utility vehicles. He snorted to himself as they climbed in, making Matthews raise an eyebrow.

"Something funny, Doctor?"

Chester shook his head. "Nothing about this situation is funny, Agent Matthews. My colleagues have been terrorized and hurt, and there was gunfire in the labs. That might be an ordinary day for you, but it's not the norm on a research campus."

"I understand." The driver put the GUV into motion.

"I doubt that very much. Where are we going anyway?"

"We're taking you to a mobile command center to debrief you on the events that just transpired."

The GUV pulled out of the forest onto one of the paved roads leading into town and sped down the asphalt away from the research campus. He wanted to look at Captain Wilcox, but she'd said nothing since stepping up with Agent Matthews, and he didn't want her to look at him with the same dead-eyed look of an implacable government official.

They finally arrived at the dilapidated strip mall just west of the King Soopers. Most of the small shops had closed, leaving plenty of places open for a temporary FBI command center. They parked in one of the slanted spaces and left the GUV to enter a storefront with "GOING OUT OF BUSINESS SALE" and "70% OFF" and "EVERYTHING MUST GO!" in bright red and yellow writing on the windows.

Inside, the room was filled with computers, cables, and men and women in the same FBI suits as Agent Matthews. No one paid them much attention as Matthews led them through the throng of agents through a door to a neighboring space with the shades drawn over the windows. A set of folding tables had been set up for a make-shift conference table and several uncomfortable folding chairs stood around it.

"Have a seat, Dr. Martell." Agent Matthews gestured to one chair before sitting down at the end of the table.

Chester almost refused to sit, but it would be churlish. He did, however, pick a different chair than the one Matthews had indicated and the agent's lips pursed with annoyance. Fortunately, Captain Wilcox joined them with another white woman who held a laptop computer in her hands. They sat down across from Chester, ignoring Matthews's scowl.

"All right, Dr. Martell."

Chester doubted anything was "all right" as he raised his eyebrows for the agent to go on. The silence stretched as if the agent waited for him to respond, and Chester bit back a smirk. He'd rarely succumbed to the social pressure to fill silence, and he leaned back in his chair.

Go ahead, Special Agent Matthews. Have at it.

Matthews finally cleared his throat and raised his chin. "Tell me about the nature of your relationship with Max Louden."

Chester shook his head. "I don't have one."

Captain Wilcox shot him a look but said nothing as Matthews frowned.

"You don't have a relationship with Max Louden, the leader of the Eagle Militia?"

"No, I don't know him." That was true. If Avery had become Max Louden, the frontman of the Eagle Militia, Chester definitely didn't know his cousin at all.

"Why do you think he'd be after you?"

"You're making an assumption that he's after me specifically. There are a lot of research scientists in the Broken Pass Research Center. How do you know this Max Louden just wants me?" Okay, he was playing a bit of a game. He'd heard Avery say he wanted Chester, but he wanted Matthews to tell him everything he knew.

Wilcox tilted her head and the other woman resettled in her chair, but neither said anything to gainsay him.

"We've been watching the Eagle Militia for a while and caught chatter that they'd be making a move on the research campus. There were some emails mentioning a Dr. Martell and his research—I assume you're the only one at Broken Pass?"

"Yes, as far as I know."

Matthews nodded. "There seemed to be some familiarity between Louden and you in his communications, at least on his part. The person with whom he was writing seemed to know you as well."

Chester frowned. "Who was the person this Louden was writing to?"

"No names were given, but the personal email address was irishdrumflower at black dot net." Matthews tapped his pad of paper with his pen. "Louden intimated that he had some personal history with you that he could use to secure your cooperation in his scheme. What can you tell me about that?"

It was too late to try to come up with plausible deniability. Chester let his gaze move to Wilcox, and she dipped her chin in a quick nod.

"When Captain Wilcox got us to Building Four, we were almost caught by Louden and one of his lieutenants." Matthews's eyebrows went up but he didn't stop Chester's story. "At first, I had no idea who he was or why he wanted to take over the campus. But we were outside one of the research labs when he shot someone, and I recognized him, though not by the name Louden. I know him as Avery Gentry, my first cousin on my mother's side. I had no idea he'd gotten involved or even commanded the Eagle Militia, and I knew nothing about this raid until this morning. But I did overhear him say he wanted me found. He didn't say for what at the time."

Matthews nodded but before he could speak, a new voice joined them from the computer.

"Sorry for interrupting, but I wanted to let y'all know I'm here. I'm Lieutenant Colonel Grace Burke, commander of Sirens, Inc. I overheard most of that and might have a few questions of my own after you're done, Special Agent Matthews." The other woman sitting beside Wilcox turned the laptop, and the face of a Black woman with elegant braids and a non-nonsense expression filled the screen.

Matthews cleared his throat and sat up straighter. "Yes, ma'am. What else did you overhear, Dr. Martell?"

Chester shook his head. "Nothing useful. He just said he was looking for me and needed to find me to make his plan go forward."

"Did he mention what his plan was?"

"No."

"What does your research consist of, Dr. Martell?" Lt. Colonel Burke spoke up.

"I study toxins and venoms from the deadliest species around the world. The venoms come from reptiles, spiders, insects, and the occasional mammal like the platypus. I try to make antidotes in large quantities to make them affordable to anyone of any income bracket who comes in contact."

Wilcox looked impressed. "Are you saying you're researching how to mass-market antivenom of all the venomous animals in the world?"

Chester nodded. "Yes. There's no reason a person's financial status should preclude them from getting antivenom when they need it."

"Could this research be used to combat a biological weapon of mass destruction?" Matthews sat back in his chair.

Chester shrugged. "I suppose. If I knew what the components of the biological toxin was used, I could create an antidote to combat it, sure." He narrowed his eyes. "Why?"

Matthews tapped his pen again. "Part of the chatter we picked up was about some sort of biological agent they were attempting to use, but they needed you for some reason. Nothing was ever said plainly, but if you could build an antidote, my guess is they needed you before they deployed their weapon."

"Sonuvaprick!" Wilcox snapped. "Are you telling me you sent my team into a situation with the possibility of a biological attack? When the fuck were you going to tell us about this?"

"It was need-to-know, Captain."

"I was in the military, *Agent* Matthews. I know how that works, but you sent in my team blind." The anger swirled in the room, and while Matthews tried to remain implacable, Wilcox's fury was incandescent. "The thing is, my team *needed to know* there was that possibility. It would've changed our tactics."

"We didn't have confirmed intel, only chatter. There wasn't any confirmation."

"Bullshit. The fact that they're after Dr. Martell, a known specialist in the field of antidotes was enough to extrapolate a likely outcome."

Chester agreed, and his own anger rose at Avery for having gotten him involved in the scheme to take over the research campus. He thought he'd known his cousin, and he would never have expected Avery to pull some anti-government crap before. Granted, they weren't best buddies, but Chester hadn't seen this coming.

"Given his familial connection with Max Louden, AKA Avery Gentry, was a concern, there was a possibility that he'd contact Louden and expose our operation."

Chester snorted. "Avery and I aren't close, Agent Matthews. The cousin I knew was friendly enough, didn't spout anarchist or anti-government sentiment, and I'd never expect him to lead a terrorist group. The moment the shooting started, I wasn't inclined to call him for the 411." He scowled and shook his head. "I haven't seen Avery in the last four years, and we aren't connected online. His involvement in the Eagle Militia is news to me." Chester traced a few lines cut into the surface of the table with his fingers. "But one thing I do know about him. Once he gets an idea into his head, he never stops until it's completed. He doesn't leave anything unfinished. So, if his goal is to find me, you can bet he won't stop until he does."

"Do you think he's aware that you've made it off campus, Dr. Martell?" Lt. Colonel Burke spoke up from the screen.

Chester shrugged. "If he isn't yet, he will be soon. His men fired on us as we crossed the grass to the fence line, but I don't know if he's searched the entire campus for me. He knows some people escaped."

"What do you think he'll do when he finds out you're gone?"

Chester shook his head. "I don't know. Do you have any idea of what he was planning to do with the biological weapon?"

Everyone looked at SAIC Matthews.

The FBI agent grimaced. "There were unconfirmed hints that he planned to use it on a large population center."

Chester snorted. "Then why is he here in Montana? If he was trying to hurt a large group of people, he'd be better off in Rapid City or Seattle."

"That could be his plan once he secured you, Dr. Martell." Matthews nodded.

"But that doesn't make any sense. Why take over the entire research campus just to get to me? He could've kidnapped me at any point outside of the campus. Why go to all this trouble?"

"Because all your equipment and supplies are here." The white woman beside Wilcox spoke up for the first time. "Whatever he needed you for would've been easier to make here rather than taking you anywhere else."

"But what about their escape plan? They had to know if they attacked the research facility, the FBI and others would be alerted. Once they got me to do whatever it is they needed, how would they get away?"

"I can think of a few ways," Wilcox remarked under her breath.

"Care to share, Captain?" Matthews scowled.

"How about *you* share, Special Agent Matthews? You're the one with the intel on this whole clusterfuck. Or I could make an educated guess, and you can tell me how right I am."

"Go ahead." Sarcasm oozed from Matthews's voice as he gestured smugly.

"Right, then. I'd say the Eagle Militia would hold the research campus for as long as they needed while Dr. Martell made their antidote to whatever biological weapon they have. Then to get out, they'd do what we did, albeit with a distraction, like a full campus explosion using C4 placed at strategic locations. The FBI and emergency services would be so busy dealing with the resulting fires and injuries, the Eagle Militia and their weapon could slip away unnoticed in the confusion. Then you'd find out which city they chose a few days later when the new threat comes in. How'm I doin' so far?"

Matthews had lost his smug look. "Did you see C4 while on campus, Captain?"

She shook her head. "No, but it's what I would do with this kind of incursion. But now that you've heard my take, I suggest you look at ways to make sure they don't get out even if they do blow up the buildings as a distraction."

"Would they blow up the buildings while all the researchers are still inside?" Chester couldn't help the horror in his voice.

Wilcox leveled her hard look on him. "You saw what he did in that room, Dr. Martell."

"What? What is she talking about, Doctor? What room?" Matthews sat up. "Did you see the weapon?"

Chester shook his head and swallowed hard. "No, but I saw Avery shoot someone in the head when they couldn't give him what he wanted."

An ominous silence filled the room as everyone digested that. Chester hadn't thought Avery would be willing to kill to coerce him to help the cause, but that was a naive belief.

Fuck, he drove trucks into the main building and had his men shoot the guards to get what he wanted.

He had a biological weapon of mass destruction, according to the FBI. Avery had already turned the corner on killing people.

"I think it's safe to say you don't know Louden very well." Wilcox crossed her arms over her chest.

"I don't know Louden at all, especially because of what he's done." Chester scowled. "But what little I do know about him is he'll keep coming after me to get what he wants."

Matthews nodded. "The FBI can put you in protective custody."

"You mean yank me out of my life and hide me away?" Chester crossed his arms over his chest. "Max Louden and his trigger-happy hillbillies are terrorists, Special Agent Matthews. You need to take them down and arrest them. I'm the victim here. You shouldn't punish me for their indiscretions."

"I'm sorry, Dr. Martell. That's the only option you have."

"Not the only option." Wilcox narrowed her eyes as she tapped her chin.

"What are you thinking, Captain?" Lt. Colonel Burke tilted her head.

"Ma'am, I agree with Dr. Martell. I'm not convinced the threat against him has abated. Yeah, we got him out of the research campus, but they won't stop coming until they get him. He needs to be protected until the threat is diffused. But not necessarily by the FBI."

"The FBI is more than capable of protecting Dr. Martell, Captain."

"With all due respect, Special Agent Matthews, I don't think the FBI is the best choice to protect Martell." Wilcox shook her head. "You hired us to go in and recover him, but didn't share intel. There were moles inside the research campus. How sure are you there isn't one in your investigative team as well?"

"Now, wait a damn minute—"

Wilcox held up a hand.

"I'm not accusing you of leaking info, I'm just saying that they came prepared and they'll keep coming for Dr. Martell. If the FBI takes him, they'll know right where to look because I'll bet dollars to doughnuts they know your tactics. The Sirens have a better place—a safehouse off grid where he can stay until you apprehend the Eagle Militia." She didn't finish her sentence, but *if you bother to apprehend them* hung in the air unsaid.

Matthews had the grace to grimace. Ever since Ammon Bundy and his home-grown terrorists occupied the Malheur National Wildlife Refuge in 2016, the FBI was unwilling to shoot or take down white militias despite their danger to the surrounding public. Chester remembered that siege and how frustrated he was that the powers-that-be had done nothing because the terrorists were white guys. Given the expressions in the people around the table, everyone remembered how that turned out.

"He's in FBI custody. He's not going anywhere." Matthews shook his head.

"And how safe do you think that will be if Louden decides to come after him again?" Wilcox raised a derisive eyebrow. "He already had two insiders waiting to help him carry this out. What's to say he doesn't have an idea of where you'd take Martell already? Louden isn't stupid or winging this. He's got plans on plans and he likely has a backup should the FBI get ahold of his doctor before he does."

"Are you suggesting my investigation is compromised, Captain?"

"I wouldn't go that far, because you hired my team and they didn't see us coming. But Max Louden probably has teams of hackers to break into your servers."

Matthews scowled. "That'll never happen. We're the FBI. We don't get hacked."

Wilcox shot a look at the woman beside her and they shared a smirk. "Whatever you say, Special Agent."

"That's enough!" Lt. Colonel barked from the screen. "Captain Wilcox is correct that the FBI doesn't have a great track record taking down domestic terrorists since the Mesquite fiasco of 2014. But we trust that the FBI can keep their servers safe so no information will be leaked. That said, because the FBI didn't disclose the intel regarding the biological WMD to the team you hired to bring Dr. Martell out, he will remain in our custody at an undisclosed location until you dismantle the threat of the Eagle Militia."

"That's not how this works. The FBI is in charge."

Burke shook her head. "That's not true. You didn't do the work, you just hired my crew as cannon fodder to do the heavy lifting. Until you do your jobs and take down these domestic terrorists, we'll continue to do our job to protect Dr. Martell. Are we clear, Agent Matthews?"

"Don't I have a say in what's going to happen to me?" Everyone's gaze switched to Chester as he waved. "The guy they're trying to hunt down here. I'm pretty sure I can choose to do what I want to, even against advice. Right?"

Frowns darkened Matthews's and Wilcox's faces.

"I'm afraid the time for you to choose is long gone, Dr. Martell." Matthews shook his head.

"Why? Am I under arrest?"

"No, but you are a person of interest in this investigation."

"I always liked that TV show, but this isn't Hollywood, and it's not make-believe. I'm not the problem here. You want to protect people? Start with taking down the Eagle Militia. If I'm not under arrest, I'll be making my own decisions about where I go and with whom."

Chester was done being pliable and amiable. His cousin probably assumed he'd be the same once Avery found him, and now the FBI thought he'd be too scared to do anything except listen to them.

But Captain Wilcox and her team were offering him a place to disappear, and he agreed with her about who'd done all the heavy lifting. It was time to make some decisions about what happened next and he was done being passive.

He wanted more time with Captain Wilcox, even if it was just as his bodyguard. She was the first woman in years to spark his attention and she did it all without the traditional feminine forms of distraction. Wilcox was genuinely who she was—woman, soldier, capable fighter, and knight-in-shining-armor all rolled into one. He rarely admitted that he'd liked fairytales as a kid, but he'd always wanted to be the rescued rather than the rescuer.

"What are you saying, Dr. Martell?" Wilcox tilted her head, her expression back to stoic.

"I'm saying, I'd rather be with Captain Wilcox and the Sirens, Inc. at their safehouse than in the direct custody of the FBI." He switched his gaze to Matthews and noted the scowl. "It's not like I'm going to disappear. You'll be able to keep tabs on me, and yet, the Eagle Militia and all their buddies, those you know about and those you don't, won't be able to find me before you take them down."

"That's not how this works, Dr. Martell."

"Well, that's how this is going to work or you can figure out that biological weapon on your own. I'm going with the Sirens."

Chapter Ten

Hermione chuckled to herself as she pulled the SUV off the main highway onto a well-maintained dirt road. A rustic-looking gate spanned the break in the trees and slowly swung open with a press of a button. Though it appeared to be made of wood beams, the gate was actually hollow steel posts painted like wood. Mini-cameras were positioned to give a view of the vehicle entering, the highway outside, and the rear-plate of the visitor. The only indication that there was anything beyond the gate was the street address numbers hanging on the crossbar.

"Something funny, Captain?" Dunwoody stretched and cracked her neck.

"Oh, I was just thinking of Dr. Martell's remarks to SAIC Matthews and the expression on Matthews' face." She snorted. "He hadn't expected Martell to lay down the law. He thought it was his job."

Dunwoody snorted. "Yeah, I didn't expect that, either. Martell seemed like a go-with-the-flow kind of guy. But yesterday, he made the decision for all of us. I swore the lieutenant colonel was going to smirk, but that woman's nothing if not professional. I noticed you didn't smirk either."

"Not on the outside." Hermione winked before checking the rearview mirror.

The gate closed behind them without problems, and she switched her gaze to Martell's slumped form. He'd fallen asleep somewhere around ten minutes outside of Broken Pass and hadn't moved since. He didn't even snore. He'd pillowed his head in his arm and dropped off. She approved. Not everyone mastered the ability to fall asleep anywhere outside of the military.

"You're wearing a dopey smile, Wizard."

Hermione blinked. "What? No, I'm not."

"Yeah, you are. Are you sweet on Dr. Martell?" Dunwoody smirked.

"Shh, keep your voice down, he's sleeping." Hermione jerked her attention back to the drive. "No, I'm not sweet on him. You've been reading too many romance novels."

"You may have a point," Dunwoody conceded. "But that doesn't mean I don't recognize when you like someone. Remember that brief hookup you had in Finland? You wore that dopey grin for days after."

"Seriously? A dopey grin? Ain't no such thing touched my face. Ever." But the truth of Dunwoody's words resonated in her memory.

Her brief hookup with one of Finland's army soldiers had scratched her itch for sex and made her feel being feminine might not be a bad thing from time to time. Her lover had been accomplished in bed and quite good at appreciating her womanhood, and then they'd both moved on, unattached and happier.

"Yeah, uh-huh, right. Keep tellin' yourself that, Wizard." Dunwoody snorted and shook her head.

Hermione would've said more but they broke through the trees to approach the safehouse. The original designer had made a horseshoe drive that ran under a portico for dry arrivals in inclement weather. Her idea of a cabin in the woods was a one room shack and an outhouse twenty yards away. Her parents' idea of a cabin had been a ten-bedroom, eight-bathroom, rustic chic mansion with full gym, sauna, hot tub, shooting range, six car garage with a workshop overhead, and sixty acres of hiking trails through the mountainous woods.

When her parents had abandoned their "rustic mountain cabin" they'd given it to her for whatever use she wanted. They probably expected her to have elaborate parties like they were used to hosting. Instead, as one of the founding members of Sirens, Inc, she'd offered it as their headquarters and training facility. Her parents thought it was a cute soldiers' club. She'd never corrected their assumptions.

She parked the SUV and turned around to wake the doctor.

"Hey doc, we're here." She waited for him to open his eyes and look around. "Grab your gear and head inside while I park the vehicle."

He took a deep breath in and stretched, tightening his t-shirt against his chest. She'd never expected a scientist to be in good physical shape, but Chester Martell had spent some time working out. She'd like to see him without a shirt, but she shoved those thoughts away as she waited for him to fully wake up.

"Whoa. This is the safehouse? Damn, it looks like a mansion."

Dunwoody snorted with humor before slipping out to the portico. Hermione rolled her eyes.

"Yeah, it's a rustic chic mansion donated to the Sirens by a wealthy benefactor." She didn't mention that it was she who was the wealthy benefactor. "We use it as our base of operations as well as our training facility."

"Doesn't seem like much of a safehouse if it's where you all train." He opened the door to get out.

"It's not on any map, and it's not where we meet prospective clients or give trainings. That's somewhere else. Just head in the front door and I'll meet you there."

He nodded and slid out of the car before grabbing his bag and striding for the door. Hermione didn't watch his ass as he walked away, so she didn't notice how his jeans fit or the breadth of his shoulders. Not at all.

Sighing, she moved the SUV into the six-car garage and parked beside one of the team's two jeeps. She shut the vehicle down and climbed out, berating herself. *He's a victim who needs protecting. He's not a potential lover.* And even if he could be, he hadn't shown any indication of interest in her.

Which means I need to keep my libido in check and use my toys when I'm alone.

She grabbed her own gear and locked the SUV before heading through the house door to the garage. She clicked the button on the garage door mechanism and waited for it to close entirely before stepping into the kitchen.

Corporal Roxanne "Tinker" Bailey stood at the island eating ice cream straight out of the carton as she read something on a tablet. Hermione waved and pointed at the pint.

"Don't let Chef Esme catch you doing that."

Roxanne rolled her eyes. "This is my personal stash. She can't say a thing beyond, 'hey that looks good.'"

Hermione laughed and looked over Roxanne's shoulder to see what she was reading. She expected Facebook or some other social media network, but she found schematics for a water filtration system. Hermione snorted and shot Bailey a smile.

"Doing some light reading?"

"Don't laugh. I trust corporations as far as I can spit out a dead sewer rat. Clean water is going to become a commodity—hell, it already is—and we have the money and foresight now to make this a reality." Roxanne pointed at the tablet. "You'll thank me when the bottled water corporations start charging for tap water."

Hermione snorted but nodded. "Talk to Gomez and have her order the parts. If it works well, we'll build a few of them to keep us in clean water without corporate help."

Roxanne smirked. "That's my goal."

"Well, then, carry on." Hermione gave her a one-finger salute before continuing through the archway to the main entry.

Dr. Martell stood with his head tilted back, looking at the massive wood beams that crossed the vaulted ceiling and the support columns holding it up. She took a few moments to look at him before he was aware of her. His broad shoulders made his waist and hips look narrower than they were, but his legs and ass filled out his jeans with delightful tautness. He'd grown some scruff on his chin and cheeks during their day and now looked deliciously rough when he'd been a hot nerd before. But he still had to push his glasses back up his nose to take in all the details of her donated mansion.

She'd be happy to push those glasses completely off his face while she kissed the hell out of him.

What's wrong with me?

She hadn't been this attracted to a man in years, more interested in being the best Army Ranger she could be. Men were either brothers-in-arms or opponents to take out. No one had tripped her trigger in a long time. But just a few hours with Dr. Chester Martell, and she was ready to play a whole different kind of doctor.

She cleared her throat and nodded when Martell turned around.

"Are you ready to visit your quarters?"

"Uh, yeah. I mean, yes, ma'am." He nodded and picked up his duffel bag. "Lead on."

She took him up the stairs above the kitchen. "You'll be in the west wing of the house overlooking the front drive. While it's not the sexiest view, it'll give us all the necessary heads-up should any-one come up the driveway. There's an exit on the end of the wing down into the garage by a secret door and servants' stairs. That'll be our escape route if we need to leave in a hurry. Understand?"

"Secret door and servants' stairs. Yes, ma'am." Chester nodded as she led him down the hallway.

"Good." She stopped in front of the second-to-the-last door on the left. "This is your room." She stood back to let him enter first.

Originally, all the rooms had luxurious furnishings as befitted the wealthy and their decadence. But since taking over the mansion, the Sirens had swapped out the luxurious for the modern and efficient. This room held a full-sized bed with a striped duvet in copper, brass, and black, a modern glass writing desk and chair, a tall six-drawer bureau, and a couple of bookshelves already stocked with everything from electrical engineering texts to trashy spy and detective novels—Dunwoody had taken all the romance to her quarters. Two tall, narrow windows opened on either side of the bed to look out on the drive.

"Wow, this is amazing." He walked in and set his bag on the bed beside a stack of rust-colored towels.

"The bathroom is through that door and shared with the room next door." She pointed to the right. "The closet is there opposite the bathroom."

Chester nodded. "And where will you be staying? You know, if I need to reach you?"

She pointed to the bathroom door. "Straight through there. We share the bathroom. I'm your suitemate."

She meant it like "roommate", but it somehow came out like "sweet mate" and an awkward silence followed her words. She wasn't prone to blushing, but the heat rose to her face and she glanced away as she cleared her throat.

"If we're ever breached, drop what you're doing and go straight through the bath to my quarters. I'll get you out from there."

He shot her a nervous look. "Have you ever been breached here?"

She smirked. "Not so far, but we're prepared if it ever happens. I'll let you get settled and meet you downstairs to give you the tour and the ground rules."

"Yeah, okay. Hey, Captain?"

She turned around at the door. "Yeah?"

"Thanks for doing this. I'm glad I'm here." He gave her his crooked, grateful smile.

And she was a goner, for sure. She nodded and ducked out, afraid if she stayed longer, she'd wrap him in her arms just to make sure he was safe.

Yeah, you need to stay away from him.

Except it was basically her job to be his bodyguard. She saw a lot of cool showers and private time with her sex toys in the future.

Shaking her head, she ducked into her quarters and checked that everything she needed was in place and all her gear was stowed. She could really use a shower after the long drive, but the time for relaxing was a few hours ahead and she had shit to do.

At least I don't smell like I've been in the bush for days.

She regretted the word she'd chosen immediately as it filled her mind with other things Chester could do with her and her 'bush.' Swearing a blue streak, she shoved the thoughts away and stomped downstairs.

Chester breathed a sigh of relief after Wilcox left. Not because he didn't want to be near her, but because he wanted to be near her too much, and that wasn't why he was here. He groaned and scrubbed his face with his hands, setting his bag on the floor near the closet. He avoided the bed because that made him think of horizontal activities and again, not why he or Wilcox were here.

Stop thinking with your dick, Martell.

Yeah, when it came to Captain Wilcox, easier thought than done.

While Chester had dated since he was seventeen, he still felt like an insecure teenager when it came to women, all big glasses, gangly limbs, and pimples with the grace of an orangutan. Granted, he'd grown into his body, and now had decent muscles on his frame, but he still had the glasses and the gracelessness.

"And the social acumen of a turnip."

He took a deep breath and set his belongings in the closet, before using the bathroom. He washed his hands and stared at himself in the mirror. He wasn't much to look at other than being fit and trim, and his beard was growing in despite having shaved that morning.

It's barely begun but I'm gonna look like a mountain man by bedtime.

He sighed and returned to the room to dig out his shaving kit. He made quick work of his rampaging whiskers and patted his cheeks. At least he'd appear presentable when he took a tour of the mansion. Captain Wilcox said there were facilities like a pool, library, and gym in the house available for use. A good thing because he might have to swim off his attraction.

He tucked his things back into the bag and returned to his room, trying to think of anything he needed to be doing. Should he be reading? Or researching his notes? He stowed his shaving kit on the bureau and surveyed the room.

Considering I was nearly taken hostage by a crazed militia, maybe I'll just relax for a few.

He headed for the door and found an old-fashioned key in the lock. It seemed rather low tech for a house of this stature, but on the other hand, a hacker would be of no use to getting into private rooms.

He locked his door and headed back toward the stairs, enjoying the sumptuous functionality of the huge house. He almost felt like a debutante making her entrance as he descended the stairs into the main entryway. Everything felt so grand.

He met Captain Wilcox at the bottom of the stairs and she gave him a nod.

"Ready for the Rules & Regs talk?"

He shrugged. "Maybe. If it includes the locations of all the cool facilities you mentioned when we first arrived, I'm all for it."

She laughed, and it zinged through him like a burst of adrenaline.

"Yes, I'll show you the pool, hot tub, and sauna that can be used after you bust your ass on the obstacle course through the woods."

He gave her a weak smile. "Oh, good, that too."

She laughed again and started the tour, giving him all the inside stories on how and why each amenity was built. He followed along, enjoying the cadence of her voice and the knowledge of the house.

"How do you know so much about this place?"

"Well..." Wilcox paused as they headed across the grounds from the obstacle course. "This was my parents' vacation cabin until a few years ago, and when they decided they were too old for roughing it, they gave it to me. I donated it to the Sirens for a training facility and barracks."

Chester coughed. "This is your parents' idea of *roughing it*?"

She grimaced and rubbed the back of her neck. "Yeah."

He reined in his incredulity and nodded. "All righty then. I think you've really done wonders for the place—really modernized it." He grinned as she snorted. "All kidding aside, you've made it a great training facility. Top notch. Nicer than all the gyms I've been to."

She smirked. "It better be. We made sure to model it after most of the military's training facilities, especially those for the Special Operations crews."

Oh good, so it's the easy course.

What was it the SEALs were reputed to say—the only easy day was yesterday? Yeah, except he wasn't a Navy SEAL or even in the military at all. He wasn't sure he could even attempt the course. Hell, he wasn't sure he could manage to even get up the courage to ask Captain Wilcox out on a date. How did those guys get up the courage to do it? He shot a look at Wilcox beside him and resisted the urge to just blurt out what he was thinking.

He'd never been very suave with the ladies, but his looks and efforts to keep his body in shape had made them willing to at least hang out with him. With Wilcox, he didn't know how she'd take it if he asked her out. Or hell, just to have dinner alone with him in the fancy dining room of their operations mansion.

And really, I shouldn't want to ask her out. Relationships based on tense situations rarely work out.

All of that was true, but it didn't stop him from wanting to make a move.

He was still wrestling with his courage as they headed back toward the house past the running track and the incongruous tennis courts. Wilcox seemed content with the silence and didn't push. Chester debated whether or not to take a chance that she'd welcome his interest. He liked her and how she'd made sure everyone got out of Broken Pass as safely as possible. He didn't know her well, but he really wanted to get to know her better.

The question is, does she want to know me better?

If he didn't ask, the answer would always be no. But it was hard to force the words past his lips.

"Okay. Do you have any questions before we go in for dinner?"

They hadn't reached the patio yet, but they were close.

It's now or never.

He cleared his throat and stopped walking. "Yeah, just one." He shifted in front of her and gathered his courage to meet her gaze. "May I kiss you?"

Wilcox blinked. "Kiss me?"

"Uh, yes, ma'am. I...you know what? Never mind. Forget I asked."

He turned to continue up toward the house, but she caught his arm and pulled him back to face her.

"I don't want to forget you asked. And the answer's yes."

Chapter Eleven

H ermione hadn't expected Chester to be interested in her at all. She'd thought her attraction was one-sided until his question. She'd been so surprised, she repeated his question like an idiot. Her response had been enough to make him retreat, but she'd been given the all-clear to act on her attraction and she wasn't ignoring it.

"I don't want to forget you asked, and the answer's yes."

She pulled him close, cupped his face in her hands, and kissed him. His arms wrapped around her waist, and he held her tight as she tilted her head to fit their mouths together. His lips were soft but firm, and he opened them to let her tongue in. She tasted toothpaste and a flavor uniquely Chester as her breasts brushed his surprisingly hard chest.

He wasn't shy about the kiss and gave as good as he got, his tongue sliding against hers as pleasure swamped her mind. This was the kind of kiss she'd missed getting for the last few years. Hell, she hadn't had any of these kinds of kisses in her marriage. She'd had some flings to scratch the itch of need, but no one had kissed her with such intention and effort.

They broke apart and stared at each other for a few moments before Chester smiled as a blush flooded his face.

"Yeah, that was a helluva kiss." He ducked his head and glanced around. "And you know, if you're okay with it, I'd like to do it again."

Hermione laughed. "Yeah, I'm always up for kisses like that. But right now, we should head in for chow, and to find out if there's any new intel."

"Yes, right. Okay."

He nodded and his smile was kinda goofy as he turned to head up the patio. But she grabbed his arm again. He raised his eyebrows in question as he glanced back.

"Don't think we're done here, doc. I'm gonna want to continue this experiment as soon as we can."

His smile widened. "Yes, ma'am."

She followed him up into the house, heat and another weird emotion filling her chest. What was it? It was different, not bad, per se, but not quite anticipation or excitement. It was softer than that. She frowned as she tried to put a name to it, but nothing came to mind.

What the hell? I'm not a teenager. Why don't I know what this is?

Her frown must have been significant because Dunwoody raised her eyebrows as soon as they stepped into the kitchen to dish up their plates. Hermione let Martell go first as she puzzled over her weird emotional reaction.

"You okay there, Captain?"

"Yeah, I'm good, why?" Hermione watched Martell head into the mess hall with his food.

Lisa shrugged. "You had this look on your face that said something didn't quite add up, but you didn't have all the intel."

Hermione laughed. "That's pretty damn accurate, actually."

"So, what is it? Something with this mission?" They carried their plates into the dining area they'd turned into a mess hall with trestle tables and benches.

It definitely has something to do with this mission. Or rather, *someone.* Not that she'd tell Dunwoody that.

"I'm trying to figure out why the Eagle Militia would've been going after Dr. Martell. He works with anti-venom. What the hell would they need him for?"

They sat down at one of the tables across from Chester and she tried not to show anything other than polite friendliness. Even if she did want to kiss him again. He smiled at her and she couldn't stop the heat from rising in her face.

Think about something else quick.

"I don't know." Lisa didn't appear to notice Hermione's blush. "What's anti-venom used for?"

"Snake bites, mostly." Chester gestured with his fork. "My intent is to make anti-venom for every poisonous critter out there in enough quantity so it won't be so expensive or difficult to get a hold of. I'd like to make it a common and standard item in First Aid kits."

"Wow, you mean like anti-venom for things like pit vipers and rattlesnakes?" Marine Corporal ret. Ann Ayeshe raised her eyebrows as she pushed her black braid over her shoulder.

"Yes, ma'am. I don't see any reason these anti-venoms shouldn't be included in region-specific kits." Chester nodded. "They're helpful in mitigating the effects of the poison and should be easily obtained."

"Damn, Australians would need an entire kit just of anti-venom. They have more poisonous creatures than the rest of the world." Marine Private First-Class Portia Giovinazzo laughed. Her honey and caramel brown eyes crinkled at the edges. "That was rough bush, for sure. We definitely could've used anti-venom by the buttload out there."

Lisa nodded. "But that still doesn't explain why the Eagle Militia wanted you, Dr. Martell. Why would they need an anti-venom specialist? We don't have that many toxic animals here in Montana."

"Yeah, but they're only here in Montana to get Dr. Martell. Who knows where they planned to take him?" Hermione took a sip of her water.

"*If* they planned on taking me anywhere." Chester waved his fork back and forth. "They took over the Broken Pass Research Center, knowing that's where I'd be and I'd have my equipment there. Maybe their goal was to get me to make something."

"Which brings us back to why would they need anti-venom?" Lisa set her fork down and sat back. "There's no way the Eagle Militia was going to go out there, round up a bunch of snakes and spiders, and strafe a community like the WKRP Turkey Drop. So, what did they need Martell for?"

No one seemed to have an answer to that so they moved on to other subjects, like the newest Marvel movie coming out and the latest Netflix series. Dunwoody remarked she was champing at the bit for the new historical romance show's season, and Porter asked if she meant season, or *Season* like in a Regency romance.

"I'm impressed you know the difference, Porter," Dunwoody remarked primly.

"Hey, I used to read Regency romance, but I got bored with all the stories of the women pretty much doing the same thing—going to parties, trying not to get caught alone with a man in a room, and waving fans." Beverly rolled her eyes. "And glory be, their stilted conversation where it took pages to get to the point! Give me a good romantic suspense any day."

The table erupted with either support for Regency romance or reasons why the other subgenres were better. Hermione shared an amused look with Chester over the vehement arguments either way and shook her head. She'd never been much of a romance reader since her own marriage had imploded.

When she'd gotten counseling for it, and that was minimal, she'd found other women in her group had turned to romance novels because they offered an escape where everything worked out, the bad guys got their comeuppance, and the heroine got the man of her dreams. And sometimes the hero beat the living shit out of the cheating lover, or abusive ex, or hell, shot the bad guy point blank.

But that rarely happens in real life.

Which was why most of the women had been reading them. It was a fantasy to escape to. Hermione hadn't been into them then, and she wouldn't pick them up now, but she understood why Dunwoody and others read them. Who wouldn't want to get the guy after going through hell?

Her gaze involuntarily shifted over to Chester, and something clicked inside her chest. She'd like to get *that* guy. If the kiss outside had been anything to go on, he'd be worth taking for a spin. He seemed just as interested in her. The problem was, she was supposed to be protecting him, not fucking him, even if he was the first man in over two years she'd been interested in.

My timing sucks.

The thought depressed her enough to slide out of the bench and take her plate back to the industrial kitchen where Bailey was setting up the dish cleaning stations. Hermione dropped her plate and fork into the first one full of warm soapy water, grabbed the scrub brush, and cleaned her plate. She yanked it out and plunged it into the next bin with rinse water, before depositing it in the drainer.

"Damn, woman, slow the hell down. What's got your goat?"

"Nothing. Let me know if you hear anything from the FBI or Broken Pass Research Center. I wanna know why the hell the Eagle Militia needed Dr. Martell." She stalked out of the kitchen and headed back to the dining room, looking for Chester, but he wasn't there.

Fuck.

She did an about-face and reentered the kitchen to get some coffee or tea, and damn near ran Chester over. They collided and she pivoted, ending up holding him bent over backwards in what looked like a waltz pose.

Which means it's the perfect pose to kiss someone.

And he definitely knew how to kiss. Their eyes met and held for a small eternity, and she forgot to breathe. Chester's hazel eyes were more brown than green, but flecks of silver glinted in the green against tiny veins of blue. He smelled like pine, fresh air, and warm man, and she wanted to reacquaint herself with his taste.

But they were in the middle of the kitchen and her colleagues were staring.

"Don't worry, doc. I got you."

"Uh, yeah, thanks."

She slowly stood, setting him on his feet and stepping back. He braced his feet wide and straightened his shirt, refusing to look at her.

"Wow, nice move there, Wizard. I haven't seen moves like that since Dunwoody streamed the Hallmark Channel." Bailey grinned as she leaned against the kitchen island. "Too bad you didn't kiss him, though. I mean, I always love it when the characters get into a waltz pose and kiss. It's romantic as hell."

Hermione rolled her eyes in hopes it would keep her blush at bay. Chester, on the other hand, grinned while he blushed, and it was adorable.

"It was an accident, but I couldn't let him fall." She shrugged one shoulder self-consciously.

"Uh-huh, sure." Bailey winked. "Say no more. I got it." She grinned and turned back to the dishes, giving Hermione a chance to escape.

Which was stupid because she'd gone back into the kitchen for tea or coffee. She stopped, closed her eyes as she tipped her head back, and groaned.

Do I really need tea or coffee at this time of day?

The answer in the military was always yes, but she wondered if it would be worth the razzing her teammates would give her. She had no idea how long she stood outside the kitchen door, but before she could finally make the decision, the door opened and Chester came out with two steaming mugs in his hands.

"Uh, hi, I brought you some black tea. Bailey said you usually have something hot to drink before lights out and figured that's why you nearly ran me over." He grimaced. "Her words not mine." He held out one mug to her.

"Yeah, despite being a hardened Special Operator, Bailey has a romantic streak two klicks wide." Hermione took the mug. "Thanks for this. I'm headed up to my quarters. Do you want to join me? Might as well get tongues wagging since they will be after that waltz pose anyway."

He laughed. "Sure. Besides, I remember you saying you were always up for kisses and I'm hoping to get another one."

"Hell yeah, doc. I like the way you think." She gestured for him to precede her up the stairs, and she watched his ass as well as the shadows.

Yeah, this house and estate were pretty damn secure. But while she didn't expect enemies to pop out of the shadows like Cato Fong from the Pink Panther movies, she'd survived her SpecOps career by being vigilant even in "safe" places. She still had her Ka-Bar and she could use the mug to subdue someone if need-be.

"Looks all clear, doc. Hold my mug while I clear your room."

He blinked. "You need to clear the room here?"

"Need to? Probably not, but I also don't take any chances. Stay here."

She ducked into the room and switched on the lights before clearing the closet, the bathroom, water closet, and her own quarters. She came back into his room and found him standing just inside the door, craning his neck to catch sight of her.

"You're supposed to stay out in the hall, doc." She grimaced and took her mug back. "It's all clear if you care to know."

"Yes, thank you. Please come in." He rubbed the back of his neck as she closed the door. "You can take the chair. I'll sit on the bed."

"Okay, doc." She settled into the armchair near the bookshelves.

"You can call me Chester. Since we've kissed, I think you've earned the familiarity of my first name." He paused and bit his lip. "Don't you think?"

She chuckled. "Yeah, we're pretty familiar now."

"Familiar enough for first names?"

She tilted her head as she considered his question. "Yeah, I guess so. My first name's Hermione."

"Like the character from that magical book series?"

She shook her head. "No, from my great aunt Hermione, my grandmother's sister on my father's side. Only she pronounced it "Hermian" instead of the British way. It helped the family tell us apart while she was still alive."

"Did you look a lot alike?" Chester sipped his tea.

Hermione grinned. "Nope. She was five foot nothing, and I'm five nine. She had white hair and glasses, and her voice shook. But the spelling made people blink. It was great for weeding out telemarketers, though."

He laughed. "I bet. So, how did you get the nickname Wizard?"

"Because of my first name and the movie series based on those kids' books." She rolled her eyes. "My BUD/S classmates thought they were so clever with the nickname. But it stuck because I could remember all the things I read, even if I'd only glanced at it. I became the resident know-it-all."

"You have an eidetic memory? Wow, I'm impressed."

"If that's all it takes to impress you, Chester, we'll get along fine." She smirked. "Tell me about you. You got any family?"

"Other than my cousin with terrorist tendencies?" He rolled his eyes. "I have two sisters who are both geniuses. Clara is a choreographer in LA with an internationally acclaimed dance company, and Vivian is an astrophysicist working at JPL on the Mars Rover program."

"Oh, so you were the slow kids at school, I see."

He barked a laugh. "Yup. The Nerd Herd."

Hermione joined in. "Wow, you had your own group name?"

"We earned it. I mean, one kid in drama and the other two were geeky scientists? We should've had t-shirts made." He nodded with a smile. "I might still do that for the winter holidays. It would be good to get the Nerd Herd back together."

"Do you see your family very often?" She couldn't help the wistful tone in her voice. She didn't have much family left.

If you don't count the other Sirens.

He shook his head. "Only at major holidays. Clara is so busy with her dance company she's not home often, and Vivian loves to work. It's hard to convince her to break away. Or harder than I'd have thought."

"You'd be happy with everyone back home, I take it."

He nodded. "Yeah. I mean, we're all so busy, but I love seeing them. They're amazing women." He shot her a smile. "What about you? Do you have family?"

She shook her head. "Not in the way you mean. The Sirens are really my family now."

"Were you ever married?"

She shrugged. "Yeah. It didn't work out."

"Why not?" Chester had the grace to blush. "I mean, if it's not too painful to talk about."

She sighed and rubbed her thighs. "It is and it isn't. The memories aren't very good. He was a mean bastard, and not just when he was drunk. So, I joined the Army and he couldn't do anything to me then." It wasn't that simple, but the details weren't important anymore.

"I'm sorry you had to go through that."

She nodded. "Thanks. It took me a while to realize that I'm not sorry."

He raised his eyebrows. "You're not?"

Hermione shook her head with a smile. "Nah, he taught me a lot, including how to stand up to him, how to find solutions when there appeared to be none, and made me a helluva lot stronger. He taught me warning signs, and what I didn't want. I don't exactly venerate him, but I'm grateful for the harsh lessons I learned from him." She let a smirk curl her lips. "It became very easy to spot abusers, even those who were sweet talkin' authority to get away with hurting their spouses."

"What gave them away?"

She shrugged. "The smooth ones are all dismissive and friendly, like they're trying too hard to find the bros who are the same. But they carry the meanness in their eyes. My ex wasn't as smooth, but he had a whole network of bros to vouch for his character. It didn't work nearly as well when I joined the Army while he was at work. Once I signed on the dotted line, he couldn't do anything about me leaving."

"I'd argue that he wouldn't have been able to stop you from leaving regardless, even if the US Military didn't have your signature."

She shot him a smile, though the shame still ate at her a little. "I wasn't always strong enough to say no to him. It was my first real act of rebellion to enlist. And I told no one. I even left for Boot Camp while he was at work. He came home to an empty house, my discarded cellphone, and deleted social media accounts.

I had my mail forwarded to my parents' house and set up a separate bank account for my pay. I basically ghosted him until I could get divorce papers drawn up." She shook her head. "He actually filed a missing person's report with the local PD, which ended when they contacted my parents. By then, I'd told them where I was, and it made him look like a stupid fool. Boy, was he pissed. Mostly because I'd taken all the choices from him—he had no say."

"How long did you serve in the Army?" Chester nodded.

"Twelve years. The first two were as a regular Army grunt, but I showed aptitude and took the officer's training. I was a butter bar lieutenant in five years and asked to join the Green Berets by seven. I made captain by the final year."

He frowned. "That's fast, isn't it?"

She shrugged. "Yup."

"Why did you retire from the Army if you'd made captain?"

"I'd gotten what I needed from the Army, and I didn't need more of their brand of it." Hermione sat up straighter. "My ex was out of the picture, I had my own friends and bank account, and I was ready to live my own life for me. I just didn't count on how hard it would be to get a job that paid me what I was worth."

"Sirens, Inc. wasn't around when you got out?"

She shook her head. "Nope, and you'd be surprised how much of the old boys' club pertains to former military in the civilian sector. Despite my skills being the same as the former military men, the men wouldn't hire me for anything other than being their personal secretary for the office. It was infuriating. So, when Lieutenant Commander Burke said she wanted to start her own paramilitary group that did exactly what the men did but with women, I jumped in with both feet."

"What does your group do?" Chester raised his eyebrows. "I've watched movies and TV shows about paramilitary groups, but I don't really know what they're for."

"We do hostage recovery, extractions, infiltrations, rescues, and sometimes we work with the FBI for domestic situations like this one." She grinned. "Might as well put all this training to good use."

"Wow, yeah." He nodded, but his expression said he was overwhelmed.

Disappointment stung her chest. Maybe she was too much for him. Glory knew she had been too much for a lot of men. Most of those in her past didn't matter, but Chester's opinion of her did. She sighed inwardly as he cast around for something to say and she rose, grabbing her mug.

"Well, I better let you get some rest. It's been a helluva day. Don't forget to lock the door after I leave." She headed for the door to the hall instead of the bathroom. "I'll see you in the morning."

"Hermione, wait." He scrambled to his feet as she turned at the open door. "You're going?"

"Yeah, it was a long day, and I could use some rack time. I'm sure you're tired."

"I—well, yeah. Are you sure?"

"Yeah. Get some rest, doc." She nodded as she stepped out into the hall. "Good night." She closed the door and stuffed the disappointment behind her eyes as she went to find something a little stronger than tea.

The beer in the fridge worked just fine, and she took her sorry ass out onto the front porch to nurse her whiny heart. She settled into one of the Adirondack chairs and popped the cap off the beer with her knife. Hermione rested her head against the wall and let the sounds beyond the porch of the cabin soothe her. She snorted. Cabin was a bit of a stretch for the rustic chic mansion that housed the Sirens.

Sittin' here with a beer on the veranda ain't bad, though.

Dunwoody stepped onto the porch and stretched before she turned and caught sight of Hermione.

"Captain? What are you doing out here? I thought you'd be in talking with Dr. Martell." She waggled her eyebrows as she came over and sat down in the chair beside Hermione.

"Yeah, I was. We got to talking about our pasts and, well, here I am with my beer." She raised the bottle and toasted the night filled with the sounds of crickets.

Dunwoody lost her smile. "He couldn't handle you having an ex?"

Hermione shook her head. "No, it wasn't the ex that set him off. More that he didn't know how to handle someone like me who does what I do." She sipped her beer. Maybe she wasn't cut out for a relationship in the civilian world.

Except I live in the civilian world and rescue them. I'm not military anymore.

But she wasn't strictly civilian either. And most civilians had no clue what it was like with military partners.

Hell, I can't remember what it was like with a civilian partner.

Well, she could, but most of it wasn't worth remembering.

"He couldn't handle what we do?" Dunwoody frowned. "You just rescued his ass. He *saw* what you do first-hand. How do you know he can't handle it? Did he say that?"

"It wasn't so much what he said, it was more what he didn't say. And his expression." She sighed and dropped her hand to her lap.

"I don't know how to make these kinds of relationships work. I mean, the last real relationship I had was with my ex-husband, and it went to shit fast."

Dunwoody sipped her beer and nodded. "Maybe you need to break up with him."

"How can I break up with a guy I'm not even with officially?"

"Come on. You've spent almost eighteen hours with him, and you just tucked him in for the night. You at least have potential." Dunwoody smirked. "Plus, I caught that kiss on the back lawn tonight. Dr. Martell was pretty into you from what I could see."

Hermione closed her eyes and groaned. "I take it pretty much the entire team saw it?"

"Oh yeah. Corporal Ayashe caught the whole thing and hit record on the cameras. It's on instant-replay now that she made sure the rest of us saw it." Dunwoody laughed. "You're famous."

Hermione snorted. "A momentary aberration. His reaction tonight makes me think that's all it'll ever be."

"Oh, come on." Dunwoody rolled her eyes. "How would you know if you don't talk to him about it?"

"There hasn't been time. We've only known each other for eighteen hours, remember?"

"And you've only had one conversation. You can't base your future interactions on such little intel." Dunwoody nodded sagely. "Give him some time. And get some sleep. You look like hell."

"Thanks." Hermione drained her bottle. "I guess you're right and he just needs a little time to get used to who I am. Glory knows I'm not going to change for a man. If my ex couldn't get me to do it, the doc won't."

"And if he needs you to, then he's not worth it, no matter how good he kisses." Dunwoody winked.

"You're not gonna let that go, are you?"

"Nope. Better than any romance novel I've read. Plus, I *know* the heroine." She grinned. "Perfect."

Hermione laughed as she rose and shook her head. *Romance, right.* But the insurgency of hope made a small incursion on her walled off heart as she staggered to her room and fell into bed.

"Fuck!"

Chester wanted to throw his mug against the floor, but it wasn't his house or his mug. The last thing he needed to do was piss Hermione off more than he already had.

She was right. He was tired and that made him say stupid things without thinking, but he hadn't meant to chase her out of his room. He just hadn't considered what she did for a living.

Which is stupid because of how I met her.

She'd saved his ass and those of his colleagues from a domestic terrorist group, and he hadn't had a problem with that.

So, what is my problem?

He frowned as the mug in his hands cooled like his hope at getting to know Hermione better. His problem was he'd never considered that women could be badass like men. Oh sure, everyone knew about SEAL Team 6, the operators who took down bin Laden, but the idea that women could do the same thing, had the same training, was too much for his sexist brain.

He grimaced and dropped his head. *I'm such a misogynistic asshole.*

The question was, could he outgrow the ideas he'd accepted for all his life? Could he get over Hermione's job? Hell, he'd witnessed her at work and had never felt so safe as with her. But would his old, long-held, unspoken beliefs override his personal observations?

He swigged the last of his tea and set the mug aside before heading to the bathroom to get ready for bed. He hoped Hermione had gone into her own room, but the space beyond the other bathroom door remained dark and quiet. He brushed his teeth and used the toilet before turning off the light and closing his door. He checked the bedroom lock to make sure it was engaged as she'd asked before setting his phone to charge and crawling into the bed alone.

I'm such a dumbass.

The question was, could he unlearn his dumbassery?

Chapter Twelve

C hester's usual five a.m. alarm went off and he reached over to shut off his phone. Except it wasn't on the bedside table where he always left it in his bedroom. Slapping the empty surface, he finally opened his eyes and looked around.

This isn't my room...

It took him a couple of minutes listening to his annoyingly cheerful alarm before he remembered he was in the Sirens' home base after escaping from terrorists. He'd put his phone on the charger on the bureau across the room. He groaned. He had aches and pains from all the running and hiding they'd done, and he didn't want to get up. But the damn alarm would go off every five minutes for the next fifteen.

He dragged himself out of bed and shuffled across the room to dismiss the alarm before stumbling back to bed.

When he woke up again, light was shining brightly in the crack between the blackout curtains and his body didn't hurt nearly as much. He still dragged his ass out of bed to use the bathroom before he moved to the bureau to look at his phone.

Holy shit! It's already ten o'clock?

He threw the drapes open and squinted against the late morning light. Sunshine bathed the estate and grounds in the brilliant colors of summertime. It was the perfect kind of day to spend outdoors with someone he liked.

Too bad I'm too much of a sexist asshole to get my wish.

He took a deep breath. He needed to go for a run. Maybe that would help him clear his head and find a solution to his sexism. He snorted. There was no way to quickly rid himself of old and erroneous beliefs, but running might at least exhaust his mind enough to get some insight.

He dressed himself in a t-shirt and running shorts before he put on his sneakers and shoved his phone and earphones into his pocket. He stepped out of his room and glanced around, not really wanting to talk to anyone. It was too late to hope they were still abed, so he locked his door and trotted down the hallway to the stairs.

He doubted he was as quiet as the women who'd rescued his ass from the Broken Pass Research Center, but he did his best to keep his footfalls silent. He made it to the ground floor without seeing anyone and breathed a sigh of relief.

Chester stepped out the door to the trails he'd seen the day before and did stretches to make sure his body wouldn't cramp up as soon as he started running. He groaned as he bent over, stretching his back and legs. Everything felt tight and unused, despite only a day having passed since his last run.

Maybe it's not my running muscles that are tight.

Yeah, he didn't even want to think about those.

Taking a deep breath, he set off at an easy pace, letting his body warm up to the idea of running distance. He'd once entertained the idea that he'd do marathons, but his ideal distance turned out to be about twelve miles max and anything over that was torture.

So, he ran for the pleasure of pushing his body to move steadily and strongly, but not fast or hard.

Chester appreciated the tour Hermione had given him the day before as he let his strides carry him into the forest. Someone had cleared trails for hiking or biking, but they were wide enough for endurance running. He let his mind shut off to everything but the sounds of nature and the exertion, and eventually the runner's high took over, letting him settle into a rhythm.

He'd been running for a little over a half an hour when he realized he was no longer alone. It wasn't anything obvious, but the world had grown a little quieter around him. He shot a look over either shoulder, but he didn't see anyone else. Unease prickled the back of his neck as he slowed and jogged in place near a boulder outcrop. The trail continued on between the rocks in a little dip, but something about it made him pause.

Good place for an ambush.

Hermione's voice echoed in his head, and he did an about-face, taking off the way he'd come. His pace was faster than when he started, but he no longer had the relaxed energy of his trip out there. He needed to get back to the house, back where he was safe from unknown threats, and had a team to protect him.

Hermione might be disappointed in him, but she'd still protect him. Of that, he had no doubt.

But she can't protect you if she doesn't know where you are, jackass.

Yeah, that was a bad miscalculation on his part. He'd just blithely ran out the door and into the woods without telling anyone. What if Avery had figured out where he'd gone and sent people after him? He hadn't informed his protection detail where he was as if his life hadn't changed. What was he thinking?

The crack of a branch and footsteps sounded off to his left, and his gut cramped.

Shit, there's someone out there!

The fear spiked his adrenaline, and he increased his pace again. He refrained from sprinting—he was too far from the house—but he no longer jogged.

Focus on the goal and you'll make it.

The voice in his head sounded remarkably like Hermione's though she'd never said those words to him. But he took them to heart and raced down the trail, listening and watching for anyone nearby.

At last, the rugged chic mansion appeared through the trees, and he dug deep into his reserves. He put on a burst of speed that carried him all the way to the back porch where he grasped the sliding glass door and opened it just wide enough to slip inside. He slid it closed and spun, sure he'd see his stalker skidding to a stop just outside.

Instead, he found Hermione trotting up the steps, her cheeks rosy from exertion. She grinned and waved before she reached for the door handle and pulled it open.

"Wow, doc, you're faster than I expected. I almost couldn't keep up with you there at the end."

He gaped at her a moment. "That was you following me?"

"Yeah. Shadowing you to keep you safe just in case. But damn, when you wanna haul ass, you kick on the afterburners." She put her hands on her hips and walked into the main foyer, the vaulted ceiling echoing with their breaths.

"Yeah, fear and adrenaline will do that." He shot her a dry look as he bent over and stretched his hams. "You could've let me know you were there and run with me."

"What's the fun in that? The view wouldn't have been as good." She winked and did her own stretches.

He snorted but watched her body as he twisted and reached. She was so astoundingly beautiful with her lithe limbs and elegant athletic curves. Plus, she was skilled, capable, and intelligent. So, why did he have a problem with her doing things that military Special Operators could do?

Because I could lose her before I've had a chance to keep her safe.

Whoa. He straightened and gaped at her. Where the hell had that thought come from? He'd known her a handful of days—and by handful he meant less than two—and he was already thinking about protecting her?

Yeah, like I have those skills. She doesn't need protection.

Hermione straightened and narrowed her eyes. "What?"

"I..." He scrambled to think of anything intelligent to say. "Uh...I definitely need some coffee."

She nodded slowly. "I'm sure. But what were you thinking just before? Are you feeling okay? Or did you come up with something about your cousin and the Eagle Militia?"

The Eagle Militia? Oh, right, they were a concern. "I gotta apologize."

"Huh?" She tilted her head.

"For last night." Where was all this coming from? He'd never been this communicative.

She opened her mouth to say something then thought better of it and held up her hand. "While I do want to hear more of why you're sorry for last night, I think this requires coffee to make sense, and maybe a space on the deck."

"Uh, yeah. Okay. Right." He nodded dumbly and followed her into the kitchen where a huge coffee tank reminiscent of a Russian samovar stood on one of the marble counters.

"Cream or sugar?" She filled a couple of mugs and headed for the fridge.

"Just cream please."

"Me too. Cream makes everything better." Hermione nodded with satisfaction as she doctored their cups then waved at the door to the deck. "After you, doc."

Chester led the way out to the deck and took a deep breath of the warm, fragrant air as she settled against the railing beside him and handed him the mug. It was muggy, with the scent of water, and he figured they'd have a thunderstorm later that afternoon. They both sipped their coffee at the same time, neither particularly interested in breaching the silence. But it was his apology and he had to back it up with an explanation. He just wasn't sure how to word it.

"Before I say something really stupid, I want you to hear me out and not jump to conclusions." That sounded reasonable, right?

"All right." She nodded. "Go ahead."

"Last night, you listed all the things your company does—scary things that we only hear about after the fact. It's unnerving to think you do this all the time. You go into dangerous situations that could get you killed repeatedly, and you do it willingly." He grimaced and rubbed the mug with his thumbs. "It's nuts and crazy. I can't imagine doing it at all, much less willingly."

He took a deep breath. "That said, I know there are people who do this, especially active military people. Granted, the ones I've heard about are men, which is probably due to the sexist media. SEAL Team 6, the Army Rangers, and whatnot, so I think of those men doing this, not women."

"There are women in the Rangers, just sayin'." Hermione's expression had closed down, but he held up a hand to forestall her protest.

"I know. It's sexist and misogynistic. You don't have to tell me. I'm aware of how stupid I sound. Hence the apology." He turned and met her cold gaze. "I'm sorry I reacted badly last night. I had to work through some of my hangups and unchallenged beliefs. Even though I've lived through the events with you yesterday, I still had ill-conceived notions in my head."

He dropped his head and gazed at the ground beyond the deck. "But I'm a scientist and testing hypotheses is my job. And you passed the test without even asking. I've seen what you can do—there's ample and direct evidence of your skills and abilities. Now, humans can ignore evidence for their own long-held conclusions, but I've learned to overcome those, so again, I'm sorry I was still too stupid last night to recognize that you're one of the people who do this work. It scares me, and yet I admire you for it. You're inspiring. Scary, but inspiring."

She grunted with what sounded like amusement as a half-smile curled her lips. "Thanks, I think."

He sighed. "I'm not saying this very well. I, uh, really like you, Hermione, and I'd like to get to know you better without people shooting at us. I know we haven't known each other long, so it might seem like a weird request. But the only time I have is now so I'm takin' a stab at it."

She nodded slowly before sipping her coffee. "You know I'm not going to change what I do for a living, right? I'm still going to rescue people who need it. Hunt down terrorists if asked. And save the world one person at a time. I'm not gonna stay at home, have babies, cook meals, clean the house, and knit. Although, I can knit, and I made a really nice sweater once."

"What?" He blinked.

"Yeah. Loved that thing. It was thick and warm and not scratchy." She smiled as she turned her head to meet his gaze. "It was perfect for me at the time when I was forty pounds heavier and a little bit bigger through the rib cage."

"I can't imagine that."

"What? Being forty pounds heavier or knitting?"

He blinked. "Both, actually, but I really shouldn't be surprised at the knitting. I've seen how you handle weapons. I suspect you're just as capable with anything you choose to do."

"Does it bother you that I'm so capable with weapons?"

He shook his head. "No. It's a skill used for a specific need in our world that we can't get away from, and I'm grateful you have it. I certainly don't."

She sipped her coffee again. "But last night…?

"Yeah, last night." He sighed and leaned on the railing, supporting his mug between his hands. "I was younger and less experienced. I've grown up since then."

Her eyes widened and she blinked a couple of times before she threw her head back and laughed. He grinned and enjoyed the sound of her laughter. It warmed his heart and made him want to say more things that set her off. But he enjoyed the sound until she ended with chuckles.

"Okay, then, doc. Since you've grown up in that time, maybe we can start with getting to know each other like ordinary people."

He snorted. "I don't think that's possible. You have skills straight out of an adventure movie, and I'm a hard-core nerd who likes poisonous creepy crawlies. 'Ordinary' isn't even in the neighborhood of who we are."

"Heh, you're probably right. But we can still do ordinary things like dates and stuff. Right?"

He dropped his brows. "How?"

She waved at the grounds ahead of her. "We could go on a day hike and take a picnic. Or we could have a dinner date with a movie."

He raised one eyebrow. "How can we go out to dinner and movie without being seen?"

"We won't go out. We'll make dinner here and watch a movie in the theatre downstairs. I think we have pretty much all the streaming services pumped into this place." She shrugged one shoulder. "Despite my colleagues giving me the hairy eyeball about this being a 'rustic cabin,' they sure did appreciate being able to Netflix & Chill whenever they wanted."

He coughed a laugh. "Yeah, I can see that. I haven't seen a movie in forever. I'm always too busy either working or reading. Plus, I don't have a regular movie buddy."

"Okay then. How 'bout I be your movie buddy while you stay here? I'm gonna go take a shower and get the latest sitrep on the tangos. But I'll meet you back in the kitchen for lunch around thirteen hundred, yeah?" She held out her hand for his empty coffee cup.

"Yeah, that sounds good." He nodded and released the mug.

"Right, I'll see you then."

Hermione ducked back into the house, and Chester settled back against the railing. He was going on a date. A real date with a sexy, strong, capable woman. An unfamiliar feeling settled in his chest. Was it excitement? Nervousness? Fear? All of the above? He tried to pinpoint the emotions pinging around in his mind.

He let it swirl inside without trying to direct it. Some of it felt like he was back in high school again, the nerd with a big crush and no game. But Hermione had already agreed to it so he didn't have to do anything more, at least in terms of convincing her.

Right, but now's the hard part.

He scrubbed his face with his hands and took a deep breath.

Damn, I need a frickin' shower.

Except, Hermione was probably already in their shared bathroom showering. His hands froze on the lower half of his face as his mind filled with an image of her standing naked under the hot water, clear rivulets sliding down her athletic curves. Would she have scars from her work in the service? Would she have ink? He didn't know the answers, but he closed his eyes and imagined her body.

Her breasts were small, a perfect handful for his palms, and he could almost feel the taut nipples against his skin. His cock saluted the thought, and he shifted his weight to make sure his running shorts gave him some extra space. He wanted to reach down and massage the stiffness, but he was too exposed on the back deck. Any one of Hermione's colleagues could see him and enjoy the show. Glory knew what kind of cameras had been installed.

I should really go back up to my room.

He straightened and headed in the door of the house. No one seemed to be around, for which he was very grateful, and he hurried up the stairs to his room. He slipped inside and shut the door tight with a sigh of relief. He leaned against it and tried to calm his racing heart. What was wrong with him? Why was the prospect of going out with Hermione electrifying him so much?

Because she's incredibly sexy and she likes me, too.

Jeez, he was such a nerd. A pretty woman looked at him and suddenly he was as twitchy as water on hot metal.

She did more than look. She agreed to go on a date with me.

He really needed a shower, and he yanked himself off the door to head toward the bathroom. He'd reached the door when he heard the water running and stopped, remembering that Hermione had said she needed a shower. He groaned and leaned his head against the door.

The images of her wet and washing filled his mind again, and his dick hardened even more.

Okay, jackass, at least find a towel and rub one out before you see her.

Chester retreated to the bed with one of the hand towels he'd been given. He stripped off his sweaty running gear and peeled back the sheets before settling, naked, on the bed. Then he closed his eyes and listened to the sounds of the shower behind the bathroom door.

Hermione's body coalesced in his mind's eye, streaming with water as she dipped her head under the spray. He grasped his aching cock and stroked it with his fist, imagining her turning to face him and smiling with her green hazel eyes sparkling with heat. She smiled at him and ran her hand down her body until her fingers tangled in her wet pubic hair on her mound.

Chester moaned and stroked his shaft. He wanted his own hand to be on her mound. He'd peel apart her lips and let his fingers strum her clit until she grew wet. She purred in his imagination and threw her head back as he rubbed her slick folds. The sound made his dick harden more, and he groaned in concert with her.

"Oh, glory, yes, Chester. Your hand feels so good on my pussy." Hermoine's voice was breathy for the first time, and he loved it.

He moved his hand with languid motions, coaxing her arousal to greater heights. He crowded her against the walls of the shower and let her soft breasts press against his chest. She moaned under his hand as he slid one of his fingers into her hot, tight sheath. She clamped down on his finger and arched her hips to get closer to his hand.

"Oh yeah, that feels so fuckin' good. Fuck me with your fingers."

She rocked her hips in time with his thrusts and her moans increased with the speed of his motions. Water streamed down her body, warming her skin and his hand as he stroked her.

"Do you like that, Hermione? Do you like my hand in your pussy?"

"Yes." She whimpered as she rocked her hips harder. "Glory, yes. Fuck me faster."

He did as she asked, increasing the frequency of his strokes until she bucked against his hand. She gasped and clamped down on his fingers just before throwing her head back and groaning with ecstasy. He kept rubbing her through her orgasm, enjoying the sweet flush that stained her skin all the way to her toes.

Eventually, she stilled and opened her eyes as her chest rose and fell with her breath. The green in her eyes glowed with lust and need, and she pushed him against the cold tile before dropping to her knees in front of him.

"What are you doing?" He had his cock in his hand and massaged it slowly, keeping the arousal mostly in check.

"I'm repaying the favor. I'm gonna suck on that cock of yours to show you my appreciation." She reached out and stroked his balls as she gazed up his body.

"Oh, you don't have to—"

His breath stalled in his chest as she wrapped her lips around the tip of his dick and licked the slit. The warmth of her mouth raced from his groin all the way up to his chest, and he moaned with the pleasure of it. He couldn't remember anything feeling quite this good and he realized he hadn't had sex with another person in way too long.

"Damn, Hermione, your mouth is so frickin' sexy."

She pulled back and raised a sharp, elegant eyebrow as one hand closed around his shaft. "Frickin'? Really?"

"It's not polite to swear in front of a woman you're trying to court."

She snorted and shot him a burning look, full of mischief and arousal. "I've been in the SpecOps community for years, Chester, and the women there have far more dirty mouths than anything you could come up with."

He grinned as he met her gaze. "I don't need their mouths. I need yours. On my fuckin' cock. Now."

Her arousal flared in her eyes, and she matched his grin.

"Yes, sir."

She opened her lips and leaned forward, taking the entire head into her hot mouth. He hissed as the pleasure hit his nerves and filled his entire awareness. Damn, her lips were tight and her mouth scorching. He groaned and tried to keep his thrusts steady, but the heat of her mouth was too much for him.

"Holy shit, Hermione. Your mouth feels so fuckin' awesome on my dick."

She grinned and hummed around his shaft, her tongue painting intricate designs on his sensitive flesh. He arched his back and rocked his hips as he grasped her head between his hands. Glory, her hair was soft and slick in his palms as she suckled on his shaft.

He wanted to take his time enjoying everything about her, but his orgasm built too fast for him to hold back for very long. Her mouth squeezed down on him just as his balls tightened and his release shot out his shaft. He moaned long and hard as he came into his fist, the image of Hermione swallowing down his cum shattering against reality.

At last, he came down from his erotic high and lay on the bed with his spent cock in his hand. Euphoria settled around him like a soft tropical breeze, warm, comforting, and satisfying. Damn, that had been a good fantasy. He reached over and grasped the hand towel to clean up, amused that he'd damn near hit his chin with his cum.

I was kinda excited about Hermione sucking my cock.

His chuckle echoed in the silent room, and he rose to head to the bathroom. Except, he didn't know if Hermione had finished her shower. Should he check and open the door? He glanced down at himself, naked and sweaty. Yeah, maybe he should throw on some shorts before he ventured into shared spaces.

He headed for the bureau as he listened for sounds from the bathroom. Silence met his ears.

Oh, shit. Did she hear me jacking off?

He bit his lip and shot a look toward the closed bathroom door. Jeez, he hoped she hadn't heard him or it would make their dinner date weird. Chester rubbed the back of his neck and listened through the door.

Nothing.

He cracked it open and peered around the edge inside. The mirror still had condensation on it, but the room was empty. He grabbed his towel and slipped inside to get his shower before anyone noticed.

Chapter Thirteen

Hermione's face heated and she grinned as she finished drying her hair with the towel and hung it over the chair in her room. But the sight of Chester on his back with his hand wrapped around his cock as he masturbated was one she wouldn't soon forget. Glory, he was sexy and far better built than she'd first surmised.

When she'd initially heard him moan, she'd cracked the door to his room open to see if he was okay.

And holy shit, he was more than just okay.

He was gorgeous with hair the same color as on his head running across his pecs and arrowing down to his groin. His chest and belly had sculpted muscle, more so than she expected in a scientist who spent his day in a lab, and his biceps and forearm bunched as he stroked his hard shaft. She stood there a few heartbeats too long before she remembered to retreat and shut the door.

I should've known not to open the door.

She grabbed her brush and swiped at her hair to comb out the tangles on the long side, thinking about the flush on his skin and the moans he emitted. Her heart raced and her nipples pebbled against her shirt in arousal. She put down the brush and sat in her chair, trying to ignore her aching core.

Damn, he'd been so beautiful. She had no idea what he'd been thinking of, but whatever it was, it had turned her on just to watch for a moment. Her pussy clenched with a need she'd forgotten feeling, and she had to shift her weight until the tension passed.

She so wanted him to take care of that for her. Hell, she'd even be happy with in-person mutual masturbation. They could watch each other pleasure themselves. It would be good, clean, kinky fun.

It would be more fun to sixty-nine, though.

Yeah, that would be more fun, but she wasn't sure he'd accept her suggestion. And she didn't really want to tell him she'd enjoyed the show.

She took a deep breath to calm down and headed for the closet. She needed to get dressed and find out the latest news on the Broken Pass Research Center situation. Had the FBI finally shut the domestic terrorists down or were they still pussy-footing around?

She grimaced. She'd rather keep thinking about Dr. Chester rubbing his own cock. She threw on some clothes—a t-shirt that read "I'm my own hero" and a pair of lightweight cargo pants before she shoved her feet into her Teva sandals and headed down to the situation room they'd set up for all sorts of surveillance and communications.

Petty Officer Ret. Susan King sat at her bank of monitors and clicked on her mouse as the images changed depending on what she was looking at. Half the time, Hermione felt like she'd entered the *Matrix* movies with the gobbledygook that passed on the screens, but she didn't say anything. The woman was a wizard in both the tech worlds and the latest online roleplaying game.

At the moment, King nodded her head to the music she heard through huge orange and white gamer's headphones. She looked a little like an X-wing pilot jamming out to space tunes. Her braids had been pulled back into a ponytail and they waved along with the beat.

Hermione waved and met her friend's gaze in the little, strategically placed mirror in between two monitors. King's fingers swept over the keyboard and she stopped bouncing.

"What's up, Wizard? Kiss anymore hot scientists?"

Hermione snorted. She should've known King was watching.

"Not today, no. But the day's young." She nodded as she stepped up beside the chair. "What's the word on the Broken Pass Research Center? Have the Feds cleared out the terrorists yet? Or are they just letting those idiots have the run of the place?"

"Well, you know how they treat good ole white boys." King's mouth flattened. "No shots fired and they're listenin' to demands. Just the usual stuff."

Hermione scowled. "I'll never understand why they don't just send in a team and shoot the bastards. They're terrorists. Those assholes won't learn unless there are consequences—bad consequences."

"Yeah, I know, Wizard. Preachin' to the choir." King nodded. "No word on their demands, if they're even smart enough to have some, but no one else has tried to get onto the campus to shut 'em down. And they haven't used snipers."

"That's only for two reasons."

"Oh, which are those?"

"Homeboys are white, and there are still hostages on site. But if you ask them, they'll claim it's the hostages keeping them from shooting white terrorists."

King scowled. "You know it'd be totally different if the terrorists were brown, Black, or women."

"Yup. They'd be dead already."

"Well, when I'm Queen of the Universe, that shit's gonna be the first to change."

Hermione grinned. "You should run with that as your campaign slogan. I'd vote for you."

"Ain't no voting necessary. It's a calling." King flashed a bright smile. "I'll have lapel pins made."

"Sounds good. Any other news to report?" Hermione headed for the door.

"Nope. All quiet on all fronts so far." King twisted around to meet her gaze. "You gonna go spend more time with the cute scientist?"

She tried not to think of the image of Chester on the bed with his dick in his hand and failed miserably. She cleared her throat in an effort to clear her mind.

"Yeah, actually. I have a lunch date with him. Lunch and a movie."

"Ooh, girl, well done. And still plenty of time for evening hot stuff, right?" King wiggled in her chair and winked.

"Yeah, don't do that. You're weirding me out with that shit. And just to clarify, there are no cameras in the rooms, right?"

King grinned. "May-be."

"Note-to-self: Pick up a frequency jammer ASAP." Hermione rolled her eyes and left the room to King's laughter.

Chester spent the morning after his shower catching up on emails—mostly colleagues in other parts of the country worried about him—and reading some recent scientific journals he'd put off. But he had a hard time concentrating with the images from his shower fantasy intruding on him.

I gotta get this under control before I see Hermione at lunch.

Because she had no idea what he'd been doing or thinking, and he didn't need to blush the moment he saw her. He could just see how that conversation went:

"Why are you blushing, Chester?"

"Well, see, I was fantasizing about you sucking my dick and…"

Yeah, probably not what a woman of Hermione's character wanted to hear. Especially after he'd apologized for being sexist and misogynistic. Adding creepy to the mix didn't seem to be the right path toward spending more time with her.

He sighed and shook his head before going back to his emails. He'd received a strident email from his sister Vivian and decided he'd use the burner phone the Sirens had supplied to call his family.

"Vivian Martell." His sister's voice came over the line, and some of his unease slid away.

"Hey, Vivi, it's Chester."

"Chester! Oh my glory, are you all right? Are you hurt? Where are you? I saw the Eagle Militia people took over your research campus, and I was so worried you'd gotten hurt." Vivi blasted her concerns through the phone with the same softness of a high-pressure water hose.

"Yeah, I'm okay and I'm safe, and no, I didn't get hurt." Shit, he'd forgotten to check on how Tessa was doing. He made a mental note to ask Hermione later. "It was a scary thing, though. Do you know much about the Eagle Militia?"

"Only that they're anti-government whack-a-dos who think they're 'free people' while unironically waving an American flag and demanding the same rights they get under the Constitution—which they don't recognize." He could hear her roll her eyes. "Why?"

He didn't know how much he could share without endangering himself or the Sirens.

"Yup, that's them. I didn't talk to them when they took over the campus, but they weren't in the mood to do anything but shout and shoot people."

"Oh, my glory. That's frightening. What are the authorities doing about it? Are you still there?"

"No, I'm safe, but I have no idea what they're doing. I just hope everyone is okay."

"Haven't you been watching the news? These asshats are ranting about overpopulation and disease and the wrath of God or some such BS. I don't know if they've shot anyone, but they still have hostages. But you're okay?"

"Yeah, I'm fine. I want you to pass it on to the rest of the family that I'm okay, and..." He bit his lip. "Has anyone seen or heard from our cousin Avery Gentry lately?"

There was a pause on the other end of the phone. "I don't know. *I* haven't heard from him, why?"

"Because I could've sworn I saw him among the Eagle Militia members who stormed the campus. It was only a quick glimpse, but I'm pretty sure he was one of the gun-toting crazies in the building."

There. That wasn't too revealing, but he'd said enough that his family could start to track Avery down and make sure they understood not to defend him when the shit hit the fan for him.

"Are you serious? Have you talked to Aunt Janette? Does she know about this?"

He shook his head even if Vivi couldn't see him. "No, I haven't talked to them since the reunion last year. I didn't talk to Avery then, either, so I have no idea if she knows about his activities. But some of those people were killing the hostages inside. I saw them, so don't think he wouldn't do anything like that. He's gone completely insane."

"Chester..." She sounded cautious. "Did you see Avery kill someone?"

Dammit, his sister wasn't stupid, and he'd revealed too much. He shot a look around his empty room, hoping there weren't any listening devices.

"Yes, I did."

She gasped and it took her a while to get her breath back. "Sweet glory."

"You can't tell anyone yet, Vivi."

"What are you talking about? I have to tell the family."

"No, listen to me. You can't say anything yet. Not until the FBI and powers-that-be make a move. You could be endangering me and everyone at the research campus." He grimaced. "I probably shouldn't have told you, to be honest, but I need someone in the family to know other than me. Pay attention to the news reports. Check out who the face of the Eagle Militia is. You'll see all you need to know."

"What I've already seen will give me nightmares." Vivi sounded angry. "And you're sure you saw Avery?"

"Yes. Please keep this to yourself until either I message you or the FBI makes an announcement. I don't want to fuck up their case against the Eagle Militia."

"Okay, I promise. I'll just tell everyone you're safe. Because you *are* safe, right, Chester?"

"Yes, I'm safe. If you talk to Mom and Dad, let them know I'm okay and I love them. Clara, too. And I love you, too, just in case you were worried." He bit his lip, hoping she knew he meant it. He loved his sisters even if they were even more amazing than him.

"Oh, I was *so* worried." The snark was back in her voice before it grew serious again. "Take care of yourself. We wouldn't have the Nerd Herd without you, and we have to keep up our membership."

"I will. I have a whole team of people looking out for me now. Take care, Vivi, and I'll talk to you later."

"Okay, Chester. Love you."

They ended the call, and he smiled at the phone in his hand. That had gone better than he hoped, and he knew Vivi wouldn't say anything to anyone until he gave her the go-ahead. At least the family would know he was fine.

He checked the time on his computer. Almost lunchtime. His heart jumped into overdrive at the idea of seeing Hermione for a lunch date. Should he dress up?

Oh yeah, like I brought date clothing with me when I packed for being at a safe house.

But he had a few nicer shirts, plus a classy pair of navy cargo shorts that would make a decent impression. Okay, not the most elegant of date clothing, but they weren't threadbare or stained so he'd just have to take what he could get.

He dressed and shaved to make sure he looked presentable, brushed his teeth, and combed his hair, making sure he didn't smell like sex or sweat. He didn't have any cologne, but women liked clean and soap-scent, right?

Damn, he was nervous. More nervous than he'd been when he took Mallory Prescott to the junior prom, and he'd been dressed to the nines that night. But he couldn't dance. He'd fixed that problem and tons of others, like being able to talk to a woman in complete sentences, but Hermione was beyond his expectations and experience. She was so amazing, and he wanted to make a good impression.

You mean, you want her to like you.

Well, yeah, that too.

He checked the clock and straightened his clothes before he stepped out of his room, locking the door behind him. He took a deep breath and headed toward the stairs. He didn't have a chance to get some flowers, but he couldn't just run out and pick some up. Maybe he could make some popcorn or something.

He made it to the kitchen just as the clock clicked over to 1300 and stepped inside. Hermione stood at one of the counters, chopping vegetables while her blonde colleague named Dunwoody stirred a large pot of spaghetti sauce. The kitchen smelled like an Italian restaurant with its savory spices, and Chester's mouth watered.

"That smells good. Can I help with anything?"

The ladies turned and both smiled. Dunwoody nodded.

"Yeah, the pasta's done. You can dish it up for everyone." She waved at the pile of plates on the counter beside the sink.

Everyone?

So much for an intimate date. Though he shouldn't have been surprised. Making food for just two people when a whole team lived in the house didn't make much sense.

"Right. How many are eating right now?" He grabbed a clawed pasta spoon and served up the first plate.

"Six, but we'll leave you and Wizard alone for your date."

Hermione shot Dunwoody a dry look as the other woman winked and turned off the stove.

"Sauce is done. Should be perfect like my grandmama used to make it." Dunwoody held out her hand. "Plate, please."

Chester handed her a plate full of pasta and she smothered it with the delicious-smelling sauce. She handed it back, and they repeated the process five more times while Hermione served everyone salad and dropped a roll on the side. While she grabbed two bottles of water, napkins, and silverware, Chester carried their two full plates and followed her out to the dining room. A single table had been pushed off to the side, and someone had lit a candle in a vintage red restaurant candle holder.

Chester laughed as he sat down. "That's perfect."

"You like it?" Hermione took the chair across from him. "I found it in the back of the China room. I think my folks bought them back when they were the latest thing in Italian restaurants. Mom just had to have the IT thing."

He nodded. "Clara is a little like that when it comes to dance and performance fashion. I usually just nodded and smiled. But the candle and holder definitely set a certain ambiance."

"Cheap date night?"

He laughed. "Or all-you-can-eat date night. Not that I had many dates. But I had a lot of all-you-can-eat dinners."

She tilted her head. "You didn't have many dates?"

He shook his head. "Nope. Nerd Herd, remember? I might have known how to talk to women back then, thanks to my mother and sisters, but women were still more turned on by the jocks than by the guys who liked snakes and spiders."

"Yeah, about that." She shot him a confused smile. "Why *did* you get into studying venom?"

"Spiderman."

Hermione blinked. "What?"

"Spiderman got me into studying venoms. I wanted to know if I could actually get superpowers from being bitten by a radioactive spider." He grinned as she barked a laugh. "Much to my disappointment, venoms don't work that way, but that's what started me off."

"That's kinda cool. The boys around me when I was growing up basically used the comic books to learn to read and then pretend they were superheroes." She snorted. "Only two of them went into the military, and none into SpecOps so those were just fantasies rather than aspirations."

"But you became the real deal. I'd definitely call you a superhero." He paused and frowned. "Or is that 'supershero'?"

"Nah, it's all good. I'm not really a fan of spangly jumpsuits and capes. They get caught on all sorts of things, and you can never go pee when you want to." She grinned.

He laughed again, and they took some time to eat. But the conversation flowed from there into personal things. He asked about her knitting and if she still did it, and she asked him what he did beyond running for exercise. They shared their favorite books and movies, if they preferred Netflix to Prime, cats to dogs, and Mac to PC.

Chester found himself more and more entranced by Hermione's wit and depth as he learned more about her. He loved the way her eyes sparkled when she talked about joining the Sirens and the work they did, even if the work still freaked him out a little. But she made it sound easy and fun, despite the seriousness of it.

That's because it's easy and fun for her.

Kind of like when he discovered a new property about a neurotoxin in a jellyfish or snake.

Yeah, neither one of us is normal.

They finished their lunch, and he'd never been so satisfied with either food or company.

"All right, what do you want to watch?" Hermione grabbed their plates and took them back to the kitchen as he followed with the silverware and cups.

"Let's watch an action adventure where the good guys thwart the bad guys and save the world all in under two hours." He shot her a grin as they put their things in the dishwasher.

She laughed. "That sounds perfect."

She led him deeper into the house to a room with no windows and a set of solid double doors.

"This is the theatre. There's a DVD player, a streaming connection, and I think there's even an old VHS player in the cabinet."

"Seriously? What, are you hoping you'll find a random Blockbuster around here somewhere?" He raised his eyebrows as they stepped into the room. "Wow. This is great."

Six rows of chairs marched toward the large screen against the far wall. While it didn't have curtains like the old theatres he remembered, it did have the tilted floor so those at the back of the room sat higher than those at the front. And the chairs themselves were comfortable without being wide enough to house an elephant.

"Yeah, my folks went all out with this room, but they're the ones with the VHS player." She smirked as she grabbed the remotes from off the table at the back. "Pick a seat and a media source."

Despite the nostalgia associated with the VHS player and tapes, he picked a streaming service and they settled in the third row of seats. The remotes also had a dimmer switch so the lights would dim enough to clearly see the screen.

"What do you want to watch?"

"I dunno. Maybe a series that isn't too serious?"

"Serious?" Hermione raised an eyebrow. "What does that mean?"

"You know, where it's about murder or police work or stuff like that." Chester grimaced. "I'm living it at the moment, and I'd rather just turn my brain off than worry about more of it."

Hermione laughed. "I never thought of it that way, but it makes sense. So, what would you rather watch?"

"How about one of those creative reality shows? You know, like the guys who all try to make knives and swords for a prize of ten grand?"

She raised an eyebrow as she switched on the system. "You don't want to watch guys using weapons, you'd rather watch guys making them?"

He grinned. "Yeah."

"Well, okay, then." She nodded and clicked over to the streaming network. "Making Weapons 101 it is."

They watched a show about blacksmithing, and he watched Hermione. She started off watching with amused patience, but soon her expression intensified, and she would cheer or gasp when surprising events happened. All Chester could think of was how beautiful she looked and how much he wished they could do this every day.

Which is ridiculous because she saves the world on the regular.

But it didn't stop him from wishing.

Chapter Fourteen

Hermione had never enjoyed watching Making Weapons 101 as much as she did with Chester. He seemed as fascinated with the construction of each blade as he was with the use of it, and he'd share her surprise and concern when the contestants' weapons didn't work. Overall, it was just plain fun to hang out with him on their movie date.

They'd watched about three hours of show when Chester turned the TV off and sat back with a grin.

"That was amazing. Can you imagine trying to make something useful and functional in like five hours?"

Hermione gave him a half-smile. "I can, but I've never had to do shit like that in the field. However, I have used what's around me to get a mission accomplished."

"Really?" He blinked. "Can you tell me about it? I mean, if it's not top secret or anything."

She shrugged. "Yeah, so me and my team were in this tropical locale and we'd been called in to retrieve an asset without raising the suspicions of the local government. The thing was, this was a tropical island paradise kind of deal. The whole place was full of guests for this big wedding going on. We had to blend in."

"Did you go in as staff, like catering people?"

She shook her head. "Nope. We had to look like college kids on spring break—bikinis, sarongs, flip-flops, and sunglasses. The only good thing about the sarongs was the ability to hide knives."

"Surely they kept you cool." Chester grinned.

She snorted. "No one stayed cool. It was a tropical island in the summer. But at least we weren't humping sixty-pound packs and body armor in the tropical jungle. Although I missed my pack for the gear I could carry. I had to make do with a duffel bag.

"The asset was a teenager who'd graduated from MIT at the age of fifteen. Smart cookie was putting it mildly, but she was there for her father's wedding to wife number three. She was under eighteen so she couldn't just refuse to go, but she was working the surly teenager gig pretty hard." Hermione grinned. "I liked her first thing."

Chester laughed. "Your kind of girl?"

"Hell yeah. If she was old enough, I would've recruited her to be part of the team. She made me feel mentally slow." She let her smile mellow a little. "We thought this would be easy. Cozy up to her guards—yeah, her daddy had her under guard—get them to think we were just some beach bunnies, take the girl shopping, and be outta there.

"But the guards were annoyingly sharp, even the horny ones, and we had to play the long game of being simpering party girls for most of the week-long celebrations. At least I got to work on my tan." She rolled her eyes.

"How did you get the asset out?"

Hermione smirked, satisfaction rolling through her. "Good old-fashioned misogyny."

"Huh?" Chester blinked.

"Do you know why my team is so damn effective?"

He frowned a bit. "Because you're special operators."

She shook her head. "Because men never see women as threats. Their misogyny is their own downfall. They expect other men to be a threat, but not women in bikinis who wear makeup and have bangin' bodies. They never saw us coming when we made our move."

"It's a good thing we have popcorn. This is getting good." Chester sat back and shoved some kernels in his mouth through his grin.

She laughed at his antics, warming to her story. "There were four of us, which we'd hoped meant two per guard, but we'd run out of time to get the asset off-island using a RHIB, rigid-hulled inflatable boat, on the far side of the island before a typhoon took out all transport." Hermione put her feet up on the chair in front of her and snagged some popcorn. "We arrived at the guards' shift change so there were four of them. We'd expected to take them down and get the asset out easily. With two extra guards, all four of us had to take one down. Each one of them had to have nearly a hundred pounds and a couple inches on us. Plus, they got to wear real shirts rather than sparkly tank tops, and were armed with personal weapons."

"How did you get past them? I mean, wouldn't it seem weird to them that four sexy, grown women were coming to see a teenager?"

She shook her head. "We'd been doing it all week, so they just thought we were friends she met at college and invited to the wedding. I was more weirded out that there were four grown men guarding a teenager, to keep her from leaving on her own. The guys let us in the resort suite and we had to each take one down at the same time or someone would get a shot off and alert the whole place.

"Fortunately, they were distracted by my colleagues' boobs in their sparkly shirts that were fucking tied on with dental floss. I hated the stupid things, but they had the desired effect, and we had all four laid out on the floor in a matter of minutes. Then we moved the asset, but we had to still look like a group of giggling socialites. It was excruciating."

"How did the teenager take being abducted from the island?"

"Heh, she helped us disable the cameras in the hotel with her *phone*, and kept us appraised of the weaknesses in her guards. That kid was a force to be reckoned with." Hermione shook her head with a grin. "The only place where it got hinky was an opportunistic guard who noticed us heading for the golf carts meant only for the staff to transport guests to the hot springs near the jetty. That's when we had to get creative."

"Creative? I'd say you were already fairly creative."

Hermione shrugged, but his words warmed her heart. "We had the other guards' weapons, but again, a gunshot would attract too much attention. So, we had to take this guy down as quietly as possible. While the asset turned off the security cameras, Dunwoody and I took the guy down, but we didn't have any rope or zip ties to secure him. All we had were those stupid spaghetti-strapped glitter shirts. So, we stripped the guard, tied him with the straps from our shirts with his hands to his ankles, and left him in his skivvies in the bushes. I took his t-shirt and Dunwoody just stayed in her bra until we reached the RHIB with the rest of our team."

"And you got away?"

"Yup. It took daddy a good five hours to realize she was gone—it was his wedding, after all and he couldn't be bothered with his offspring—and by then, she'd exposed her father as the war profiteer funding domestic terrorists threatening to take out Oregon's governor because they were non-binary."

"Whoa. Seriously?" Chester shook his head. "That's a stupid reason. Where's the girl you rescued now?"

"Honestly, I don't know. She entered WITSEC and disappeared. But she's brilliant. I wouldn't be surprised if she works for the NSA at this point."

Chester snorted. "You could just tell them by whispering into your phone or TV that you'd like to talk to her."

Hermione grinned. "Can't. We sweep for bugs and signals daily to make sure not even the NSA comes to visit."

He laughed. "Wow, you have all your bases covered."

"Yeah, well, though we might not be guarding national secrets, we take our security very seriously. Especially when it comes to our snacks."

He blinked. "Snacks?"

"Oh yeah." Hermione nodded sagely. "Never get in the way of King and her Cheesy Corn Puffs. It's like a religious experience for her, and if they're gone, the world might as well pack it in."

Chester's grin widened. "You gotta be kidding me."

She folded her hands together and bowed her head with a serene expression. "This is the way."

"The world ends because of a dearth of Cheesy Corn Puffs?"

"Well, maybe not ends, but it definitely gets hard to be around King if we're out. The Quartermaster makes sure we have them on hand all the time."

"Good to know. But I have a question. What is one thing *you* can't go without? The sillier the better. What's that one thing?"

She sat back in her chair and dropped her hands to her lap. What was the silliest thing she loved to eat? It took her a few moments, but when she did, she rubbed the back of her neck as her cheeks flushed.

"It's really silly."

He nodded. "Excellent. What is it?"

"Organic chocolate gems."

He grinned. "Chocolate gems?"

"Yeah, they're like M&Ms but without corn syrup in the candy shells. Perfect little balls of happiness and you can eat as many or as few as you like." She shrugged though the blush still heated her cheeks.

Why the hell am I blushing? There's nothing wrong with loving chocolate.

He reached out to grasp her hand. "I promise to tell no one this intelligence to keep your secret safe." Then he brought her knuckles to his lips.

Her eyes widened, but she didn't jerk her hand free from his grip. She liked the old-fashioned feel of his lips on her hand. He froze a moment as if remembering she could take him out through her training, but she squeezed his hand and smiled before pulling her hand free and leaning toward him.

She grasped his head to tilt it before fitting her mouth over his.

He tasted like their lunch and popcorn, and she couldn't get enough of him. She wanted the feeling of his tongue against hers, because Chester wasn't a wilting flower by any means. He moaned a little as his hand snaked around the back of her head. Usually, she was the one in control, but the way he gave into the kiss and took initiative made her feel strangely feminine.

When they pulled apart, she blinked at him. "Wow."

"I concur." He nodded. "Please, ma'am, may I have another?"

She laughed. "Yeah, but maybe not here where the rest of the team can see us. Just in case we want to go further than making out."

"Great plan."

He kept her hand in his as they rose and left the theatre room before dropping off their popcorn bins in the kitchen. They headed back toward the bedroom wing as casually as they could, though she doubted they fooled anyone. She caught the looks her sister soldiers shot her as she passed them in the halls. There were a lot of sly smiles and elbows to each other's sides. She refrained from rolling her eyes at the juvenile responses, but she couldn't quite quell her grin.

Aw hell yeah, she was gettin' some.

"Hey, you still with me?" Chester's voice pulled her out of her thoughts and she reminded herself to keep her situational awareness.

"Yeah, why?"

"I asked if you were good with this after all the ribbing we caught." They'd made it up to the bedrooms and stopped in front of his door. "I wanted to make sure we were still on the same page about this."

"Are you planning to kiss me more?" She raised an eyebrow.

"Yeah, hell, yeah. Every place you'll let me." He nodded, his expression guarded but hopeful.

"Then I'm all for it. Let's get to it, doc."

His smile turned shy, and his cheeks flushed with heat. "Right." He pushed the door open and led them inside, before he kicked it closed and pulled her close. "I've been waiting to do this forever. Ever since I watched you work in the underground labs."

He slanted his lips over hers and her heart thundered with the pleasure surging through her. She loved when a man took charge, showing her what he wanted without treating her like some delicate flower that couldn't take his loving.

When they came up for air, she met his gaze with a grin.

"I like the way you kiss."

"You do? That's good. Maybe we can do some more, but naked." He winked.

"I'll think about it." She tilted her head and placed her index finger on her chin. "Yup, thought about it, and I'm all good with it."

He laughed and tugged her over to the bed. "Good. Let me get undressed and then I'll be right with you."

But she shook her head and stopped his hands at his belt. "Let me. Please?"

"You want to undress me?"

"Yeah... is that okay?"

"Fuck yeah. That's sexy as hell." His cheeks flamed again, but his eyes glittered with arousal.

She leaned forward and brushed his lips with hers before she went to work on the buttons of his shirt, sliding them through the holes. She opened his shirt slowly, revealing the physique she'd seen laid out on the bed earlier. She loved the way the hair outlined his pecs and his abdominal muscles. She kissed the space between them as she continued to open his shirt.

He gasped and shivered as her lips brushed the skin. She grinned as she stood back and pushed the shirt off his shoulders. He watched her with rapt attention as she walked around him and pulled the shirt from his arms, kissing the muscles of his back. She tossed the shirt behind her and slid her hands around his sides to pull him gently against her body.

"You smell good, doc. Did you bring cologne?"

He shook his head. "Nope, it's all just soap and shampoo."

"I like the way it smells on your skin." She shifted around him, following the hand that slid across his nipples and down to the waistband of his shorts. "Let me see what else I like the smell of."

She stopped in front of him and opened the button on his shorts before pushing down the zipper. The hard ridge of his cock pressed against the cotton of his underwear, and she couldn't resist sliding her hand inside his fly to caress it.

"Oh fuck." Chester groaned and rocked his hips to press the length against her palm.

"Yeah, we'll get there, doc." She grinned up at him as she tugged his shorts off his hips. "But first, I'd like to suck on your cock. Do you want me to do it while you stand or sit?" She went to work on his underwear and pushed the briefs down after carefully stretching the waistband around his erect penis.

He hissed as she cupped his balls in her hand and laid a gentle kiss on the underside of the shaft.

"Fuck. Sit. Definitely sit or my damn knees might give out."

She laughed and rose, leading him over to the bed. "Okay, you sit there and look handsome and sexy."

"That's it? You don't want me to do anything?" He settled on the bed with his thighs splayed enough to give her access to his cock and balls.

"Not yet. You'll have your turn."

She stepped back and unbuttoned her own jeans before shimmying out of them and her underwear. Simple cotton briefs without ornamentation. She was a no-frills kind of girl. But it felt good to wiggle her hips for him as she undressed. She kicked the clothes to the side before she knelt on the floor between his legs and grasped his shaft.

"Ready, doc?"

"Yes, ma'am." He licked his lips and nodded. "But aren't you going to take off your shirt?"

"Not quite yet. I want to tempt you a little bit more. You good with that?"

"Oh glory, yeah. I'm good with that." His cheeks blazed with heat, and he swallowed hard.

"Alrighty then. Give me some good dick, doc."

Hermione leaned forward and took the tip of his cock in her mouth. The tangy taste of his precum hit her tongue and made her groan along with him.

Holy shit, he tastes so damn good.

She'd never really liked giving head before. Most of the time the men she'd been with didn't want to eat her out so what was the point of making an effort for them? Besides, fucking was less intimate and easier when they were just scratching an itch.

But Chester was different. She didn't want to just fuck him. She wanted to pleasure him until he was moaning and crying out her name. Hell yeah, she wanted him to want her as much as she wanted him.

And she wanted him bad.

She brushed her teeth over the edge of his cockhead then soothed the sharp scrape with her tongue. His cock flexed in her mouth, and a little dollop of precum dropped on her tongue. She smothered a giggle of pleasure—who the hell giggled while sucking cock?—and tightened her lips around his girth.

"Oh, fuck yeah. Your mouth feels so fuckin' good on my cock, Hermione."

She loved his voice full of arousal, and she would make good on his pleasure. She set up a constant rhythm of sucking on his tip before sliding her mouth down the base as the tip hit the back of her throat. When she pulled back, she squeezed with her palm on the shaft.

"Oh shit, that's so damn good. Suck me hard."

His fists tightened in the bedclothes, and his hips rocked in the rhythm she set with her mouth. She held back her grin as she worked him over with her tongue, teeth, and fist. He moaned and threw his head back as he arched his back. She could tell he was enjoying himself but he wasn't quite there yet. She reached up to caress his balls with her free hand, and Chester cried out with surprise. His cock hardened to silken stone in her mouth, and his cum jetted to the back of her throat as he rocked his hips hard and flopped onto the bed.

She swallowed down his cum as great satisfaction filled her chest. She'd brought the handsome scientist pleasure enough to leave him somewhat boneless on the coverlet. She sucked and licked him until his dick was clean, then she released him and stood.

"Damn, doc, you look good pleasured and relaxed." Hermione grinned.

He gave her a tired laugh. "Yeah, well, I'd like to see you the same way." He sat up and motioned to the bed beside him. "Crawl on up here and let me take a look at that pussy you've been teasing me with this whole time."

She raised her eyebrows. "This pussy? I haven't been teasing you with it."

"Oh, hell yeah, you have." He grinned as he slid his naked ass off the bed. "I could smell your arousal as you sucked on my cock and it just made my mouth water. You smell so damn good." He rose and pointed at the bed. "So lay down and let me taste what I've been smelling the whole time."

She shrugged as if his words didn't turn her on like a fuckin' light switch. She crawled onto the bed, showing him her ass, and he reached out to caress one cheek.

"Damn, even your ass is sexy. There's nothing like a fit, taut, athletic woman to make me hard." He followed and waited for her to turn on her back before he leaned over her, his hardening shaft between her legs. "My cock really wants inside you, Hermione, but I want to taste you first. Look at you, too. Let's take off your shirt."

She sat up and pulled the shirt over her head then tossed it to the side. He smiled at her lack of bra and leaned forward to take a nipple into his mouth. They groaned at the same time, and her pussy clenched at the hot sensation of his tongue on her tit.

"Yeah, I'm gonna have to come back to those." He pulled back and slid down her body to fit his shoulders between her thighs. "Right now, I need to do an inspection of your equipment, ma'am. Is everything in order?"

"The last medical checkup I had said yes, but I'm not averse to a second opinion."

"Excellent. Let me put your legs over my shoulders so I get a good view." He helped her lift each thigh and draped them down his back. "Ah yes, I can see it much better now." He grinned up at her.

She laughed until he pressed his lips to her nether lips and slid his tongue between them. Her laugh ended as the searing heat cut off her breath. She gasped and moaned as he settled in to press kisses to her vulva. Each brush of his scruff against the hairs on her pussy lips sent tickles of sensation straight to her head.

"Oh fuck, that's good." She lay back and closed her eyes.

Chester was a master at eating pussy. He took his time, his touches light and teasing as he slid his tongue between her labia. She fell into the pleasure as he used his thumbs to peel her lips apart and pushed the tip into her sheath.

A high-pitched whimper left her lips, surprising her, but she forgot it immediately as Chester sucked on her clit. The threat of her orgasm entered her awareness, and she tightened her hands into the covers on the bed to keep it at bay. She wanted to hold out, to make the pleasure last, but he was very good at what he was doing.

He hummed against her vulva, licking every surface he could reach, and she was helpless against the pleasure building to a crescendo. She grabbed his head and rocked her hips against his mouth, trying to hold on. But he inserted one finger, scrubbing her G-spot with determined strokes, and she was lost. Her orgasm got away from her, crashing through her before she could hold it back. She cried out and rocked against his thrusting fingers and slick tongue as she flew into a thick blanket of pleasure. He kept up with her, licking and humming throughout her release, until she came down to the bed with a satisfied thump.

Chester gently laid her legs on the bed before crawling up beside her to gather her into his arms.

"You are the sexiest woman. Absolutely fucking stunning when you come." He rubbed his hard cock against her hip. "And when you come down from that orgasm, I plan on giving you another one."

She would've made a snarky comment, but she couldn't find the breath or the energy to do anything other than laugh amid the glorious pleasure still coursing through her. It had been so long since she'd been pleasured to the point of floating relaxation, and she wasn't ready to leave.

If this is what he does with his mouth, what can he do with his cock?

The thought made her summon the energy to move and roll over on top of him. She straddled his hips and notched her pussy lips against his hard length. His eyes blazed with renewed arousal and he rubbed his shaft on her clit, making her moan as the sensations shot through her.

"I want another orgasm, and I want to give you one, too." She wiggled her hips until she saw stars. "Fuck, your shaft is so damn good."

"Aw yeah, I can hardly wait to get inside you." Then his eyes opened wide and he froze. "Fuck, condoms!"

He rolled, flipping her onto her back with a whoop, and shot off the bed toward the bathroom before she could say anything.

Damn, he's strong.

She hadn't expected that kind of athleticism from someone who spent a lot of time looking down microscopes and writing notes. She watched his taut ass disappear into the bathroom and hoped he was successful in finding condoms. She normally had some in her kit when she went into the field to keep the muzzle of her rifle dry, but they didn't usually make it into her quarters.

"Got them!" Chester's voice came from the bathroom just before he appeared, brandishing a strip of condoms triumphantly.

Hermione laughed in amusement and relief. It would've been hell if they couldn't finish what they'd started. And she wanted some serious dick before the day was over.

He tore one of the condoms from the strip and set the rest on the bedside table before crawling back onto the bed.

"Here, let me. I've wanted to get my hands on your dick for a while now." She took the condom and tore it open.

His eyebrows went up as he lay on his back beside her. "You have? You just had your hands on my dick earlier."

"Yeah, but I want more." She grinned as she smoothed the latex down his shaft. "Damn, doc. You fill this thing completely, don't you? I'm gonna have a damn good time riding you."

"I love how plainly you speak. It's sexy as hell." He answered her grin with his own and grasped her hips when she swung her leg over him. "Come on and ride me. I love the idea of filling your pussy completely with my cock."

She nodded and positioned his shaft at her entrance then lowered herself onto it. He was big and she appreciated the stretch of her inner vaginal muscles around his girth. She moaned a little as he sank deeper and deeper into her body. When she was fully seated on his hard shaft, she closed her eyes to savor the fullness of him inside her.

"Fuck, Hermione, you're so tight." He gritted his teeth and the muscles in his neck stood out hard against his skin.

"I hope you like it because I love the feeling of you tight in my pussy." She rolled her hips a little and the friction on her clit made her see stars. "Oh glory, yeah. You feel so damn good, doc."

She pulled off then slid back down onto him with a continuous slide, and they both moaned. Hot pleasure swelled from her pussy up her spine to remind her what she'd been missing for months. True, she had toys to take the edge off, and they worked great, but there was something wonderful about a hot cock attached to a handsome man to make her truly satisfied. She loved the rock and roll of riding a man and watching pleasure suffuse his features as she took hers.

"I'm gonna fuck you hard enough to say my name." Hermione rocked her hips, impaling herself on his cock hard, making him groan. "You're gonna say my name, you sexy scientist, and I'm gonna fall into bliss the moment you do."

"Two can play that game, my hot warrior woman. And the name is Chester." He grinned fiercely as his hands clamped down on her hips, dragging his shaft almost all the way out before slamming back inside. "Come and take what you want as hard as you want it."

That was all the encouragement she needed. She rose over him, bracing her hands against the bed on either side of his head, and let go. She slammed her pussy down over his cock hard and fast, building the friction on her clit against his shaft. She kept her gaze locked on his as she pounded onto him.

"Oh glory, Hermione, fuck me hard. Yeah, fuck yeah."

His evident pleasure made her orgasm come out of nowhere. One moment she was building the arousal up to a crescendo and the next she was screaming out Chester's name as she fell over the precipice of pleasure. He matched her shout, her name ringing out as his hips jerked and his cock stiffened in her sheath.

They fell together into a heap of tangled limbs and sweaty bodies, satisfaction beating through her with every pump of her heart. This was what she missed the most about only using toys. The bone-tired satisfaction of bringing pleasure to herself and another. She slowly gathered her wits and pulled off his half-hard cock before removing the condom and taking it to the bathroom.

She dropped the condom in the trash and grabbed a washcloth to run under hot water. She brought it back to the bed and cleaned him off gently and lovingly.

"What are you doing?" He blinked up at her.

"Cleaning you up." She finished and got up again. "I'll be back."

"But that's my job. I should be cleaning you." He rolled to his feet and followed her into the bathroom, crowding his naked body behind hers against the counter. "Give me that."

He took the washcloth and ran it under hot water as his gaze met hers in the mirror. She loved the way his gaze traveled over her body. It electrified her and made her nipples tighten to little peaks.

"Cold?" He stepped closer and ran the warm washcloth over her pussy lips. "I promise to warm you up as much as you'd like. Anytime you like."

"This is good. I like being warm."

She met his eyes as he fondled her with his sure touches, cleaning away the remnants of their sexual exertions. He tossed the cloth in the sink before wrapping his arms around her and pressing his hard chest against her equally hard body.

"Thank you." He leaned his forehead against hers. "That was the best afternoon I've had in months."

His words warmed her more than she expected. It was great sex, for certain, but she hadn't expected more. Most of her trysts had been quick and enjoyable, meant to scratch an itch. But this connection to Chester felt different—deeper, stronger, and fuller.

Which scares the hell out of me.

It was true. Yet, she didn't want to turn away from it despite the fear. Chester wasn't anything like her ex, and she wasn't the same naive girl she'd been when she'd first gotten married. She knew who she was and what she wanted.

"Yeah, me too. If we have time, let's do it again."

He grinned. "Deal."

Chapter Fifteen

The next few days had Chester in heaven. Hermione was not only interesting as a woman, but she was a helluva lover with great stamina. While they didn't have sex all over the mansion, they did have sex in many different positions and styles at various hours of the day or night. Chester should have been exhausted, but he found himself invigorated by the challenge of wondering when and where they could try again.

He'd kissed a few women over his adult life—hell, his first kiss was with Jenny Bridgeport at the Sadie Hawkins dance in junior high—but nothing in his previous experience compared to kissing Hermione Wilcox. And he wanted to keep on kissing her after all this business with his stupid cousin and his homegrown terrorist organization had ended.

Despite being the object of their mission, Chester hadn't heard how anything was going. He knew he should be concerned about it, but the idyll of hiding in a luxurious mountain mansion with several highly intelligent and beautiful woman around him kept him happily distracted.

Until Hermione and the team was called in to talk to the FBI.

Apparently, they had some new intel on the weapon Avery planned to deploy and they needed Chester's expertise to explain it.

Hermione made it clear exposing Chester to the outside world was a no-go—he was supposed to remain in hiding until the FBI took care of things at the research campus. Too many cameras—either cellphones, security cameras, or press—made it too easy for the terrorists to realize where he was, and she couldn't take the chance they had someone on the outside reporting back to the terrorists.

But the FBI insisted.

They loaded into the dark SUV, Giovinazzo driving while Hermione sat in the passenger seat up front. Dunwoody and Subramani sat in the back bracketing him as they pulled out of the gated drive. Hermione didn't even look back at him, and he swallowed hard. Things had just gone from relaxed and fun to intense and serious, the real world intruding on the idyll he'd been enjoying.

Guess it was just a fling. The thought soured his gut.

When they arrived at the temporary FBI headquarters in Broken Pass, Hermione had reverted back into the hard SpecOps soldier she'd been at the beginning. Gone was the soft, easy woman who watched movies and made love with him. In her place was a deadly, sharp-eyed operative who wouldn't hesitate to kill. Chester swallowed hard and tried to shove the disappointment aside.

He entered the building surrounded by fearsome warriors, and the show of force surprised and impressed the FBI, if their expressions were anything to go by. They walked him straight through the building to a conference room with no windows to the outside. Three agents sat at the table working on computers and tablets while two others stood behind them, watching the screens. One looked up.

"Dr. Martell, thank you for coming so quickly." Agent Matthews gave him a sharp nod and shook his hand.

Chester nodded. "What can I do for you, Agent Matthews?"

"We managed to get search warrants for Louden and Terrorist #2's email. In them we found correspondence with someone who calls themselves The Dart." Agent Matthews turned one of the laptops to show a screen full of equations and hand-drawn molecules. "Apparently, they were willing to sell Louden the plans on how to construct this particular toxic agent and how to make it airborne. Can you tell us what they're making?"

Chester studied the screen for a while. From what he could tell, the molecule was a powerful neurotoxin, but it wasn't one he'd seen before. He frowned, tracing the lines between the compounds with his fingers. Parts of it were familiar, but others were completely unusual.

After studying it for a good ten minutes, he asked for paper and a pencil. Once they appeared, he started writing down what he could see, breaking things apart and separating them into their building blocks. He wrote down two pages of equations before he sat back and looked up at the screens. Excitement and grudging admiration for The Dart filled Chester.

"I'll be damned." He shook his head. "This is brilliantly devious. It's a compound with aspects of Gaboon Viper, King Brown Snake, and Diamondback Rattlesnake venom."

Agent Matthews raised his eyebrows. "How do you know that?"

Chester shot him a dry look. "A PhD and twenty years of experience?"

No one snickered, but all four Sirens smirked.

Rein in the sarcasm. You can't blame him for ruining your time with Hermione.

Actually, he could. If the FBI had taken Avery and his goons out, Chester wouldn't have to focus on terrorists.

He sighed. "Because you have properties here that will replicate the inhibitors in the venom of each snake. See this one?" He pointed to one part of the molecule. "It's from the Gaboon Viper, and it shuts down the nervous system just like ketamine—you're there, but you can't move. And this one?" Another portion of the molecule. "This is the part where the body forgets to breathe, and you suffocate. This is a potent mix that will target pretty much every human and quite a few mammalian species if it's released. And a lot of people will die because this kind of thing acts fast."

"How fast?"

He glanced at his notes. "Within minutes of contact with it. But I'm not sure how they're going to deploy it. Water-borne? Aerosol? I'm thinking they're going to go for max coverage, so they'd make an airborne toxin." He tapped his chin. "I can make an antidote that will combat all three, and help block against the worst of the symptoms, like an inoculation. But ideally, you'd want to stop this weapon before it's deployed. I can make sure there's an antidote for when it is. There's just one problem."

"What's that, Dr. Martell?"

"All my equipment and my notes are in there." He pointed at the map of the research campus. "I have to get back in there to do this."

"No, that's impossible."

He spread his hands. "It's all we've got. The research center doesn't let us take our supplies or equipment home. It's proprietary. But getting in is not impossible. We got out. It's just a matter of distracting Avery and his yahoos, and getting the samples." He pointed at the equations of the chemical weapon. "I know what they did to make it. I can reverse engineer an antidote and you can inoculate anyone who comes in contact with it. I just need my equipment and my notes to make it. Once we have it, you can mass produce doses at another lab."

"Oh, is that all? We just get you back in there and distract the tangos, and that's it?" Hermione threw her arms out. "Are you fucking kidding me? That's insane, doc!"

"No more insane than letting this bastard release that neuro-toxin over one of our cities and watching everyone die." Chester tightened his hands into fists. "I heard Avery say he wanted me to develop an antidote for him and his gang. So, I'll do it, but I'll do it on a massive scale, and I'll give it to all of you first. So even if he releases his horrible weapon, you'll have a way to survive. The problem is I need my equipment and enough time to get it done."

"No, there's no way you're going back in there, Dr. Martell. You can just make it at another lab." Agent Matthews shook his head. "We can get you anywhere you need to go."

"You're not hearing me, Agent Matthews."

"Then explain it to me like I'm five, because there's no way we can let you go back into the Broken Pass Research Center, Doctor."

Chester took a deep breath. "Everything you want and need—everything *I* need—is right there."

"Being held by home-grown terrorists." Hermione crossed her arms over her chest. "Getting you out without getting killed was hard enough. You now want us to take you back in there, endangering your life and those of my team? That's insane." She pointed at the screens showing the Eagle Militia wandering around the grounds. "They won't hesitate to kill us, doc. The only way to get back in there is to shoot our way in."

"The way I see it, we have two problems." Dunwoody's drawl settled into the tense silence. "The first is we need an antidote to this here bioweapon and we need it now. Dr. Martell can do what we need, but he's gotta get into the lab to do it. The second problem is there's a whole bunch of terrorists occupyin' the research facility Dr. Martell needs. But mostly you just need the notes you have on the various venoms, right?"

Chester shrugged but nodded. "Yeah, mostly the proprietary notes."

"Are they digitized and held somewhere like on a cloud server?"

He shook his head. "No, they're on my personal laptop that I left in the lab when we had to evacuate."

"Don't you have a backup?" Dunwoody tsked and shook her head. "You always should make a backup, doc. And a backup of your backup."

He scowled, trying not to shuffle his feet like a toddler taken to task. "I did make a backup. Several. But they're on an external hard drive, disconnected from any network... Kept in the lab for proprietary reasons."

"So, no matter what, someone's gonna have to go in there and bring at least the laptop or the hard drive out." Dunwoody shot Chester an exasperated look. "I'm gonna teach you about cloud servers, doc. This kind of retro crap ain't good in the long run."

"No one's going in, and that's final." Agent Matthews shook his head.

"Then you're dooming everyone who comes in contact with that weapon to death because you aren't willing to do anything."

Chester raised his chin as his temper flared. "Hell, what are you doing about taking these guys down and arresting the lot of them?"

"We're doing what needs to be done—"

"You aren't doing shit!" Chester pointed at the monitors. "People died in there, agent. Died, shot to death by terrorists. I don't give a shit if they're white boys from farm country. They're killing people, and you're letting them. You haven't taken a strike force in to do anything about them. Are there still hostages in there? Have you just left them there?" He swung his gaze around to the agents in the HQ, some of which wouldn't meet his gaze. "Holy shit, you have! You've left them to Max Louden and his band of delinquent thugs."

"It's complicated, Dr. Martell—"

"It's not, Agent Matthews." Chester swung around to face him. "It's really not. Either send in a covert team to take those assholes out—we don't negotiate with terrorists, right?—or at least send me in there to make an antidote to this weapon of mass murder with a team of professional sneaks. Seriously, it's not complex at all."

"The whole point of engaging the Sirens was to get you out of harm's way, Doctor." Agent Matthews sounded like he chewed on gravel. "They got you out. That was accomplished, and you survived. There's no way we can send you back into the place where we liberated you."

"You liberated me and a few others, but not everyone." Chester scowled. "And you didn't 'liberate' the very knowledge you need to save anyone if they release that damn weapon. So now you get to make a decision. Send me back in there with a small team to get my research so you can save more than just me, and maybe take out a few of them along the way. Or don't, and let a lot of people—probably more than just this town—die."

Agent Matthews scrubbed his hands over his face and clenched his jaw. "I can't send you back in there, Dr. Martell. That would defeat the purpose of sending the Sirens in the first time." He leaned on the table in front of him. "What if we sent in a team to recover the laptop and the hard drive? Would that be enough?"

He wanted to nod and say yeah, but he remembered Tessa telling him to save his work and lock it all in the biometric safe in the lab. He shook his head, grimacing.

"No. The laptop and drive are locked in the biometric safe at the back of our lab. You need my eyeball and my fingerprint along with my combination to get into it." He held up his hands. "I can give you my fingerprints, but I'm not handing over my eyeballs."

Agent Matthews didn't smile, but Hermione snorted and Dunwoody smirked.

"Well, as it turns out, you won't need to give us an eyeball—at least not physically." Dunwoody rested her hip against the table. "There's this nifty-cool app now that can take a detailed pic of your iris. We can use that to let the camera scan it and bob's your uncle."

Chester blinked. "Really?"

"Yup. So, then we'll have your fingerprints, your eyeball, and the combination for the keypad, and we can pull the hard drive and the laptop." Dunwoody nodded before fiddling with something on her phone. "I can get an image of it right now." She shrugged. "Going back in is gonna suck, but it's doable. Especially if we get the go-ahead to use lethal force to get in."

"I can't authorize that."

"But everything I need to make the antidote is right there—the equipment, the samples, the data, and the computers. If the Sirens can get me in there without the terrorists noticing, it's a done deal, and everyone can be inoculated." Chester spread his hands. "All we have to do is get in and do the work."

"Behind a wall of terrorists!" Agent Matthews threw his hands out. "We just got you out of there. We can't let you fall back into their hands. That was the whole point of getting you out."

"But if they release that WMD, it'll kill a lot of people, including you, me, and the town of Broken Pass."

"And if they get their hands on you, not only will we not have the protection of an antidote, but they could release it and kill everyone anyway. No." Agent Matthews shook his head. "No, you're not going back in there, Dr. Martell." He swung to point at Hermione. "And I can't authorize lethal force."

"Well, someone's gonna have to because that's the only solution that ensures the least amount of bloodshed, Agent Matthews, no matter who goes in. Either we're getting the tech out or we're taking the doc in." Hermione straightened and pointed at the maps on the table in front of them. "Either way, we won't be able to go in the way we left because they most likely have that hole in their defenses plugged. But you've been watching these assholes for almost a week now. Give my team the data on their movements. They're gonna run out of food here soon, so they'll turn on each other when they get too hungry with no change in the situation. That'll work to our advantage."

She looked down at the map again for a few moments. "Once we analyze their movements, we'll need you to set up a diversion to get all their attention to the front gates. Try the negotiation tactic to get them talking and focused on you. That'll allow me and my team to either escort the doctor into the building or get tech items and get our asses back out alive."

"You're crazy. There's no way this will work."

"You got a better idea, Agent Matthews, I'm all ears. Dunwoody's right. It can be done if we're given the permission to kill anyone in our way." Hermione fixed him with a hard look. "Just pretend they're bank robbers stealin' rich people's money and that should be justification enough to use lethal force."

Agent Matthews scowled. "That's not funny."

"I wasn't making a joke."

"I have a question." Chester frowned as he looked down at the map. "Thinking logically, in your assessment, how much time do we have before the terrorists actually release the WMD they've built?"

"What do you mean? They're not inoculated against the poison they're holding." Agent Matthews shook his head.

"They're going to get desperate for something to happen. In your assessment, when they reach that point, will they set it off anyway, killing all the hostages left in the labs and the people in the surrounding region? Or will they try to get it out of the lab and take it to a larger population center?" Chester waved at the map. "Here's the real question you have to consider. How long will they wait? Because it's going to take time to go into the research center, retrieve the computer and hard drive, get back out, then find a lab with all the materials needed to craft an antidote to this thing. Not many labs around the country have all the venoms needed, nor the equipment to do it. This is one of the few. Plus, I know this lab and all the items in it. I know what I'm doing and I can do it fast."

"But the terrorists have control, doc." Hermione scowled. "We got you out so they wouldn't have you, too."

"I know, and I appreciate that, believe me. But we have a time limit here. Too many people will die if I don't craft the antidote—which I can easily do, in my own lab."

Chester had to wonder at his own sanity. He was arguing to *go back into* the lab while Avery prowled like a loose lion?

"I hate to say it, but it's the best and fastest solution to your problem. If you inoculate everyone but them, even if they set off the device, only they will die. Hell, you can go in, guns blazing, and take them down on your own terms because they'll be defanged."

"I'm all in favor of guns blazing," Dunwoody remarked.

"Me, too." Hermione nodded.

She met Agent Matthews's angry gaze with a flat one, and Chester swallowed hard. This wasn't the soft, funny woman he'd spent the last few days with. This was the battle-hardened soldier who knew the risks and the price of her actions.

"I can't authorize that."

"Then who can?" Hermione asked as Dunwoody moved over to the console of their surveillance monitors. "I thought you were Special Agent in Charge. Doesn't that make you the guy who makes all the decisions? Come on, Matthews. We're gonna do this no matter what. Don't hamstring us when we're here to save your ass in more ways than one."

Chester watched the thoughts chase themselves across Matthews's face as he tried to find a way to tell them they couldn't do what needed to be done. Chester normally wouldn't encourage the use of lethal force. But after he saw Avery put a gun to a scientist's head and pull the trigger when they couldn't answer his question, Chester had no problem removing the Eagle Militia from the equation.

"Fine."

Chester swung his gaze around to Agent Matthews. "Really?"

"This is what you wanted, Doctor. You're going back into the lab to get your laptop and the hard drive with the Sirens. You'll synthesize the anti-venom in the lab, inoculate the team, and get the hell out of there." Matthews pointed at Hermione. "You can use lethal force, but only as a last resort. If you have to kill anyone, do it quietly and out of sight of the press. The last thing I need is a bunch of reporters going ape-shit over the deaths of cousin Bobby and his band of merry thugs."

Dunwoody snorted. "Dibs on Cousin Bobby when we go in." She sat down beside the surveillance techs. "Patch me in and give me the last four days of their movements."

"All right, Captain Wilcox, what do you have in mind to get back in there?" Agent Matthews ran his hands through his hair.

"We're gonna need the surveillance feeds, but while Dunwoody works on that, tell me what they've been doing since we left with the doctor."

While Agent Matthews and Hermione went over the movements of the Eagle Militia, Chester found himself pushed out of the conversation until he seemed to be an afterthought left at the back of the room. Normally, he wouldn't mind, preferring to work on his own quietly and without fuss. But this was different. Not only would he be going in with the team to work behind enemy lines, but Hermione would be leading the mission in the line of fire. He didn't like the idea of her in harm's way. So much could go wrong and they'd had a helluva time just getting out.

It was your stupid idea, jackass, and she's trained for this while you're not.

There really wasn't a better solution, and they didn't have a lot of time. His notes, data, and equipment would decrease the time it took to build an antidote to Avery's death machine. Who knew how desperate Avery would become when they couldn't find Chester? He could set the biologic weapon off, his thugs be damned, and no one would be safe.

It took well over two hours for the FBI and the Sirens to come up with a plan to get in and out without the Eagle Militia noticing their return. Chester sat out of the way with Giovinazzo and Subramani flanking him as guards, as if the FBI and their people weren't to be trusted to keep him safe.

I wouldn't put it past Hermione to feel that way about Agent Matthews.

His gaze unerringly found her as she stood beside Dunwoody and went over the maps and video surveillance from the FBI for the thousandth time. His stomach growled in hunger, and he grimaced as Subramani smirked but her gaze kept moving around the room, keeping watch. No one else seemed to be in any hurry to head back to the house, so Chester sighed and settled in for a long wait.

The planning session took far more time than Hermione expected, but she never did anything half-assed, especially when it meant the lives of herself and her team. She and Dunwoody ran over it again and again, coming up with alternatives if their primary routes were compromised by too many goons. She planned to kill as few of the terrorists as possible to appease Agent Matthews, but plans only worked as far as the first engagement. After that, it changed on the fly.

They had the best plan they could work out, with the FBI causing a distraction at the front of the campus by demanding to talk to Louden or one of his lieutenants in person. If that failed to get the Eagle Militia's attention, Ayeshe and Gomez would blow up an old junker at the edge of the campus as an extra diversion while Lin Su took overwatch and kept the terrorists away from the infiltration team. Either of those events should give Hermione, Dunwoody, Subramani and Giovinazzo time to get Chester into the tunnels of Building Two via Building Three, lock down the lab so he could get to work, and get back out again without being detected.

"I got one last question before we head out, Wizard." Dunwoody stowed her tablet in its case before she fixed Hermione with her steady look.

"Yeah, what's that?"

"What happens if we come across the WMD while we're traversing the tunnels? Are we just gonna leave it there, or are we gonna disable the damn thing?"

Her immediate answer was to shoot anyone nearby, secure the weapon, and take it with them, essentially disarming the Eagle Militia's threat. But she didn't know how unstable the thing was or how big. They couldn't afford to waste time collecting, securing, and humping it out.

"If we come across the WMD, we'll photograph it and send it back to FBI HQ so they can figure out what to do with it. We can't afford to take the time to fool with it. That could kill too many people, including us. Can't risk it." She shook her head and met Agent Matthews's gaze. "You better have someone on standby who knows something about bombs and WMDs. We'll send back what images we get, but we're not going to touch it."

He nodded. "We'll have someone available from the bomb squad."

"Good. Then I think we're done here." She gathered up her notes she'd made to study on her own later and nodded to Dunwoody. "We'll go over this until we know it without looking and be back here at 23:30 hours with our gear. Copy?"

"Got it. Are you sure this is going to work?" Agent Matthews hadn't liked their plan but he wasn't going, so his opinions were just that.

"Yup. Giovinazzo and Subramani, let's move out." She turned and headed straight for Chester where he leaned against the wall between her women, his eyes closed. "Come on, doc. Time to regroup, get some chow, and some rest. We'll be going into the lab tonight."

He opened his eyes and stood, but some of his vitality had diminished since that morning. She frowned but refrained from asking him what was wrong. It wasn't the time or place in the FBI HQ surrounded by agents and staff. So, she kept her mouth shut and they moved as a unit back out to the SUV.

They didn't speak as they loaded up and headed out. Hermione kept her gaze moving, searching for anyone watching them too closely, but nothing was out of place. She wanted to talk to Chester and reassure him that they had a good plan, but again, it didn't feel right to talk about anything in the car. The only sounds were those of the engine, the tires against the road, and Subramani's voice when King called from the mansion.

"Yeah, we're on our way back." Subramani paused as she listened to King's voice. "Yeah, new plan. We'll fill you in when we get there. Sounds like it's going to take a six-person team, but we'll discuss logistics when we arrive. ETA twenty mikes."

Hermione glanced over her shoulder at Subramani. "We all good?"

"Yes, ma'am. The team will be waiting for us."

"Good." She turned her head more to look at Chester, but his attention remained out the window past Dunwoody. Unease and sorrow beat against Hermione, but she shoved them away and turned to face forward. "Good."

No one said anything else and the rest of the drive was made in silence. She wished she could prove to Chester how going in with her team wasn't the best choice. The Sirens were well trained and capable, but now they had to keep him safe. At least the lab had limited entrances, though it still had a shit ton of windows.

We're just going to have to lock down the whole building once we get there.

She nodded to herself. That might work. Block the entrances of Building Two except the one they needed, creating a bottleneck they could easily defend. It would make escape harder if the tangos noticed them, but they could be sure no one came at them from their flank.

And if it all went according to plan, they'd get in, get the antidote, and get out without detection, lickity split.

As long as Murphy stays the fuck away.

Yeah, she knew it wasn't likely. The plan always lasted until the first shot was fired. If they were lucky, no shots would be fired at them, and no one would notice they were there. King could set the cameras for Buildings Two and Three on a loop so no one would notice, and they could let Chester have as much time as he needed. All she had to do was keep him alive long enough.

Yeah, and keep us all from getting shot. No biggie.

They arrived at the mansion, and everyone unloaded. Hermione got out of the vehicle and waited for Chester so she could escort him inside. He shot her a look of surprise, but he didn't smile or say anything else. She felt his silence like a physical blow, but she shoved the unease away until she could talk to him privately. She still needed to organize the mission that would take place that night.

"Will I see you at lunch, Hermione?"

She blinked as she came back to the present. They stood in front of Chester's door as he unlocked it, and he stepped across the threshold before turning to look at her.

"Uh, no, I don't think so. I need to plan our insertion mission with the team."

"Ah." He nodded. "How about dinner, then? You're going to have to eat some time."

She grimaced. "I can't promise anything like our last dinner, but we'll definitely talk by then. The mission's happening tonight so you need to be ready. We have a lot of planning to do before we go in. But I promise we're going to talk to you about it. This isn't gonna be easy, doc."

He straightened, and his expression shuttered into a polite mask. "Yes, I know. I have no illusions that it's anything less than insane. I just can't think of a better way."

She sighed. "The hell of it is, I can't either. I hate taking a civilian back into that mess, but if we're gonna do it, we have to plan the hell out of it. Copy?"

He nodded. "I'll be ready."

"Good." She clapped him on the shoulder. "I'll send Gomez to you with the necessary gear for you to wear. She's our Quartermaster and can get anything that you need. You'll listen to her and wear everything she offers because this is non-negotiable. Safety is everything."

"I understand." Chester nodded again. "Good. In that case, I'll be expecting Gomez. Good luck, Captain."

He stepped backward and closed the door. Hermione stood there a few moments, wondering why he'd shut more than just the portal to his room. Had she imagined his complete withdrawal?

Probably. He's probably just worried about the mission, like I should be. But the thought sounded hollow in her head and she wondered if she'd hit FUBAR between them without even trying.

Chapter Sixteen

The plan was in place. Hermione checked her gear for the fifth time as she rode in the surveillance van with Dunwoody, Subramani, Giovinazzo, Moriarty, Porter, Lin Su, and Chester. Hermione went over the plan again in her head. Moriarty would stay in the van and monitor both the communications and the cameras, keeping track of the tangos as well as the team. She'd also make sure the cameras in Buildings Two and Three were in a loop so no one noticed anything about them. Porter would remain on standby to help with any injuries and provide cover fire when they made their return escape.

Dunwoody, Subramani, Giovinazzo and Hermione would infiltrate Building Three with Dr. Martell from the north end, and subdue any tangos on the way while Moriarty ran surveillance interruption. They'd enter the building on the surface and while Hermione took Martell down to the tunnels and into the lab in Building Two, the others would secure all the doors until they were ready to leave. They'd all converge on the lab to secure it while Chester did his thing.

Easy peasy. She snorted too quietly for the others to hear in the moving van. *The only easy day was yesterday.*

Agent Matthews promised to cause a disturbance at the front of the compound to make sure all eyes were pointed toward him, but Hermione didn't trust him to hold up his end of the deal. He was all about by the book and so far, his book hadn't gotten very good results. She'd instructed Ayeshe and Gomez with help from Lin Su to make sure the terrorists were focused on them no matter what the FBI did. They'd rely on their skills to go undetected and let the rest take care of itself. And if all else failed, Lin Su would clear the way if any tangos didn't take Matthews's bait.

"Comms check." Moriarty's voice came over the earwig in Hermione's left ear.

"Siren One, check."

"Siren Two, check." Dunwoody gave a thumbs-up as she steered the van closer to the perimeter fence of the research facility.

"Siren Three, check." Subramani's grin flashed briefly in the dark van.

"Siren Four, check." Porter met Hermione's gaze and nodded.

"Siren Six, check." Lin Su didn't bother to open her eyes as she spared her night vision and her inner calm.

"Siren Nine, check." Giovinazzo tied her hair up in a tight braid and pinned it to the back of her head.

Hermione waited for Chester to sound off, but he sat tensely at her side with his head down.

"Doc?"

"What?" He jerked his head up. "Oh, right. Uh, check, yeah, I hear you. Yes."

"All clear, Captain. Reading everyone five-by-five." Moriarty gave a thumbs-up from her console along with a smirk.

"ETA to perimeter fence two mikes." Dunwoody turned them onto the frontage road, and they bounced over the uneven ruts.

"Lock and load, ladies." Hermione strapped on her helmet with her NVGs and focused her mind on the mission ahead. "Doc, stay in between Subramani and me. Giovinazzo will cover our sixes."

"Yes, ma'am." He swallowed hard and nodded.

By the time the van stopped, they were ready, and silently slid out of the vehicle into the starry dark. Even Chester did a decent job of moving without noise. No moon meant they'd have a better chance of getting into the building undetected, but after their escape a few days earlier, surveillance showed members of the Eagle Militia making more regular patrols around the buildings.

Matthews gave us permission to use lethal force. The Sirens would take advantage of it.

Once they were all out of the van, Lin Su immediately disappeared into the darkness. She'd already made a sniper's nest in the nearest Ponderosa and would radio in when she'd reached overwatch.

"Sirens One, Two, Three, and Nine with boots on the ground. Package secure." Hermione shot a look at Chester. "You ready, doc?"

He swallowed and nodded. "Yes, ma'am."

Hermione tried not to let his acknowledgment please her. "Good. Sirens One, Two, Three, and Nine moving out with the package." She led the way to the break in the fence.

"Readin' you loud and clear, Wizard." Moriarty's voice settled into her Georgia twang. "Be advised. Two tangos to your eleven o'clock on a smoke break. Looks like they're bored as hell."

"Siren Six in position. I see them. Want me to take them out, Wizard?" Lin Su's voice held an undercurrent of suppressed excitement.

"Hold. Let's see if they move on, Pin." Lin Su's nickname in Delta had been "Pinpoint" because her shots had been that accurate. "Moriarty, any other tangos in the vicinity?"

"Negative, Wizard. Just those two."

"Standby, Pinpoint. If they stay longer than five minutes, take them down."

"Roger that." Lin Su's voice had cooled into deadly calm.

Everyone waited in tense silence. Part of her hoped the men would be smart enough to move back into their patrols and save them a bullet. But another part wanted them out of the way permanently.

Good riddance to bad garbage.

The seconds ticked by, and Hermione settled deeper into mission-mode, watching the terrorists smoke away. She wanted to move and head straight for them, but she'd given them five minutes. She was a woman of her word.

At four minutes and thirty-nine seconds, the men crushed out their butts and headed in opposite directions around the building. Hermione let out her breath and gestured to the others when the men disappeared.

"Let's move. Doc, stay between us."

He nodded and they started off across the darkened lawn. No one spoke and they moved fast, though Chester didn't have a stealth mode despite his fitness. She suspected his anxiety made silence damn near impossible. She didn't blame him.

They neared the building's side door, and Dunwoody moved ahead to pick the locks. The others stood with their backs to the door, keeping watch in case the tangos decided to make their rounds faster than expected.

"We're in." Dunwoody inched the door open and peered inside.

"Nothing on the Building Three cameras, Circuits. You should be clear." Moriarty gave them the go-ahead.

"Roger that. Let's move, Sirens." Hermione held the door open as the women filed through, keeping Chester between them. "Door closing. Loop cameras, Moriarty."

"Way ahead of you, Wizard."

Hermione closed the door behind them and scanned the hallway. No one but her Sirens and Chester filled the space, and only the nightlights cast small spots of light along the way. She held up her hand to stop everyone and they paused, listening to the sounds of the building. No voices or foot scuffs came to their ears, and Hermione eased them back into motion.

"Subramani, Giovinazzo, fan out. Dunwoody, take point. I've got your sixes."

She just hoped Murphy would keep his damn Law to himself.

They all moved as a unit, creeping down the hallway as they headed for the central staircase to the lower level. Chester felt like a clumsy deer amongst bobcats, his footfalls making more noise than the four predators around him. It gave him a greater appreciation of just how deadly these women were.

Glory help anyone who gets in their way.

They stopped in front of the doors at the bottom of the stairs and Dunwoody signed for silence before she cracked a door open. Chester held his breath as he waited for her to give the all-clear. The seconds ticked by, and sweat ran down his back as his heart thundered in his chest. The Sirens didn't move or breathe as far as he could tell, their focus on Dunwoody.

"All clear, Wizard. No movement."

"Copy that. Move out to the tunnel entrance to Building Two."

"Roger that."

Dunwoody and Subramani slid through the door and held it open as Wilcox followed Chester and Giovinazzo through. They made no sound as they crept, heel-toe, down the hallway. He tried to mimic their moves, but he just didn't have the coordination.

They reached the tunnel doors and paused, listening for footsteps. Nothing sounded, so Dunwoody pulled open the tunnel door. This tunnel had a mural of the plant cycle through time, with the development of flowers and ferns and trees. He'd forgotten about it because the last time they were in this tunnel, he was carrying Avondale.

When they reached the end, Dunwoody raised her hand in a fist before peeking through the doors to the underground of Building Two. After a couple of moments, she nodded.

"All clear, Captain."

"Roger that. The lab is third door on the right past the bathrooms. Move out."

They made it to his lab without incident, and he opened the door to find the room pretty much as he'd left it. Even the windows were still intact. He switched on the lights and headed for the safe as the Sirens closed the blinds and locked the doors.

"Giovinazzo, keep watch. Subramani and Dunwoody, help the doc in any way he needs. Keep your eyes and ears open, people. This can go south at any time."

Chester swallowed hard and focused on getting the safe open. He forced himself to shove the worries and threats to the back of his mind as he let the safe scan his hand and his eye. The thing beeped and unsealed, the lights flashing green. He let out the breath he hadn't realized he was holding and pulled open the door.

His laptop and the external hard drive with all his data sat where he'd left them, hidden only by Madigan's matching equipment. Taking a deep breath to settle his thoughts, he brought them out to the workstation and booted up the laptop. Once it had gone through its startup and he imputed his login credentials, he connected the external hard drive.

He sighed when everything worked correctly. Taking a deep breath, he extracted the notes he'd taken on the molecule from the Eagle Militia and spread it on the counter beside the computer.

"All right, this could take some time, but I should have a working prototype in about a half an hour." He settled into his chair and opened the anti-venom program.

The world faded around him as he focused on the formulae needed to construct an antidote that would cover the three types of venom in the weapon. Though he hadn't said anything to the FBI or the Sirens, the bioweapon made by the terrorists was both horrendous and elegant. If their goal was to kill and cause insurmountable havoc, they'd created the perfect instrument.

Excitement bubbled inside Chester for the first time in months. He had a puzzle to figure out. A deadly toxin to dismantle and mitigate. This was his arena, and he excelled in finding these sorts of solutions. He settled into his zone and worked the problem.

Time ceased to exist as he worked, using the program to make tweaks and theoretical tests to combat the elements of the deadly molecule. Despite his earlier promise, when he finally had something to physically test, it had been seventy-five minutes. He looked up to find the Sirens still vigilant at their posts, but tension rode their shoulders more than when they'd arrived.

"How's it going, doc?" Hermione's voice was barely above a whisper. "Got something?"

He blinked and nodded. "Yes. I think it will work." He held up three samples. "It *should* work, but without a sample of the weapon's concoction, I can only surmise. If nothing else, it will severely curtail the effects of the biotoxin from the email."

"You sure?" She moved closer to look over his shoulder.

He grimaced. "Ninety-eight percent. Without physically testing, I won't know for sure. But I know these toxins and I know how to mitigate them. This should work."

"Close enough for government work," Dunwoody remarked as she resettled her rifle in her hands. "If you're done, let's pack up your laptop and hard drive, and get the flock outta here. No point in pussyfootin' around. Need help storing the antidote?"

"Uh, no. Let me just save everything and shut down before I package up the samples." He hit save on every open window, but Dunwoody shook her head.

"Samples first, doc, then the computer. We don't want to miss anything."

He nodded and moved to collect the sealed vials. "Copy that."

"Just a heads-up, we have some tangos headed your way, Captain." Moriarty interrupted the silence.

Hermione lost any softness she might have had as she moved to the front of the lab to peek out the window. "Talk to me, Mo. What's going on?"

Chester quickly re-saved his work on his computer—backups of backups—and closed the laptop so no light shone in the lab. He held his breath. The darkness seemed to encroach on his mind as the radio in his ear filled with Moriarty's voice.

"Bunch of guys entered the main floor of Building Two. No indication as to why, Wizard."

"Fuck. Are they headed underground?" Hermione moved to the blinds and peeked out.

"Negative, Captain. They're fanning out and checking all the rooms upstairs."

"Roger that. We'll move to another building for exfil." Hermione morphed back into Captain Wilcox as she turned back to face the lab. A shiver ran down Chester's back.

"Time to go, doc. We're losing our window to get outta here without casualties. Pack your shit and let's go."

He wanted to protest. "I can't just—"

"You have to. We don't have time. Pack up the laptop and external. We'll take them with us." Wilcox held her rifle against her chest with the barrel pointed at the floor as she gestured to the others. "We're gonna have to leave from a different building to avoid detection. Do we have all the samples secured?"

"Yes, ma'am." Dunwoody shouldered her pack and grabbed her rifle. "Which way you wanna go, Wizard?"

"Mo, which is the clearest exfil, Building Three or Building One?" Wilcox's face turned to stone as Chester shoved the laptop and external hard drive into his bag.

"Depends on which problem you wanna deal with. Heading to Building Three means you're gonna be farther away from the vehicle and overwatch. We got spotted and had to move. We're now closer to Building Four. Heading to Building One puts you right in the thick of the bad guys' HQ."

"Got any better suggestions?" Hermione scowled as she checked her ammo.

"What about the Hub?" Dunwoody glanced out the window before aiming her gaze at the captain.

"The Hub?"

"Yeah, it's the underground atrium at the center of the campus—I think there's a fountain or some shit on ground level. In any case, tunnels from all buildings lead there and split off." Dunwoody shrugged. "We can choose whichever building we want from there, and our ride can move closest."

"Not a bad plan, Circuits. I vote the Hub." Mo's voice held approval.

"might get you closer to the vehicle, but you're gonna have to go past the staircase to the upper floor in Building Three to get there and the tangos will be using it any moment. Pick your poison, Captain."

"Shit." Wilcox chewed her lip for a few seconds before nodding. "We're heading to Building Four via the Hub and will exfil out the eastern entrance. Giovinazzo, you got any zip ties?"

The dark-haired woman with a Roman nose grinned. "You bet your ass, Wizard."

"Good. Let's go. Dunwoody, take point. Subramani, stick to the doc. Giovinazzo, go with Dunwoody and use those zip ties on the door handles to the upper floor. I'll cover your sixes. Let's move."

"Copy that. Come on, Dr. Martell." The woman with east Indian features and beguiling brown eyes gestured toward to door. "Do you still have your vest on?"

"Yes, uh, yes, ma'am." He nodded as he shoved the last of his samples into his courier bag inside a special pouch and straightened his shoulders. "But I have to pee." He grimaced and handed Subramani the bag. "Take this. All the doses are there. I'm going to run to the bathroom."

Wilcox let her breath out between clenched teeth. "Doctor..."

"I'm sorry, but no one knows we're here. I promise not to flush, plus we're going right past the bathrooms." He moved to the door and looked out. "I don't see anyone."

"Hold up. Moriarty, has anyone entered Building Two beyond the tangos upstairs?" Wilcox leaned against the door to keep him from opening it.

"Negative, Captain. No one has come in or out." Moriarty's drawl hit Chester's ears, soothing some of his tension.

"What about through the underground tunnels?"

"Well, shit, Wizard. Now why didn't I think of that?" Sarcasm filled the comms. "No one has been in or out since we took over the cameras."

"Copy that." Wilcox scowled and pointed at Chester. "Five minutes. Clock's ticking, doc. Get moving."

"Uh, yes. Right. Moving."

They filed into the hallway, listening for anyone else in the building as Wilcox turned off the lights and closed the lab door.

Chester peered into the darkened hallway with trepidation, but his bladder threatened to overflow and he hurried to the men's room door. To his surprise he found the lights on inside and paused. Had someone already used the room? He remembered they were on a timer to mitigate electricity use.

These shouldn't be on.

He froze as someone came out of one of the stalls, his heart sinking.

He recognized the man immediately. Brown hair cut short in a militaristic style, three-day scruff on his cheeks and chin, sharp blade of a nose over thin lips, and the same torn denim vest over a dirty long-sleeved t-shirt.

Avery...

Only his eyes were different. Gone was the friendly, slightly distracted look Chester remembered from family reunions. Instead, avid zealotry stared out over a slight smile.

Oh shit.

"Cousin Chester. At last. Just the man I've been looking for."

Chapter Seventeen

"What are you doing here?" Okay, not his most elegant of responses, but his heart raced and his brain damn near forgot coherent thought.

Avery gestured to the sinks. "Washing my hands. And you?"

"Uh, using the bathroom." Chester glanced back at the men's room door before he ducked into one of the stalls. "I'll be just a moment."

"Take your time. I'm so happy to see you. How've you been?"

Chester shuddered at the casual way Avery spoke, as if he hadn't orchestrated the takeover of an entire research campus and shot people without a thought. Chester swallowed hard and finished on the toilet, not flushing as promised. He zipped up his pants, buckled his belt, and straightened his shirt under the vest, before stepping back out into the main room.

"Don't forget to wash your hands. Germs, you know." Avery gestured to the sinks.

"Right." Chester nodded and moved to the counter to turn on the water.

"That's quite an outfit you got there. All black, complete with face paint. I didn't know you were into sneaking around at night like a soldier. I thought you avoided anything associated with the military."

Chester blinked. *Oh shit, I forgot about the face paint.*

"Uh, yeah, well. I didn't want to get shot on sight." Chester nodded at the gun in a holster on Avery's hip as he rinsed his hands. "Why are you carrying that, anyway? No one at this campus is armed."

"Oh, we both know that's not true." Avery shook his head. "The armed guards weren't going to let us in here without a fight. But they're no longer a problem." He shrugged, and his smile widened. "We could've avoided all the unpleasantness if they'd just told me where you were. Have you been here the whole time and we just missed you?"

Chester swallowed hard as he shut off the water. What the hell could he tell Avery? He'd never been good at lying, but the last thing he wanted was to put the Sirens in danger. He took a deep breath and shook his head as he grabbed a paper towel from the dispenser.

"No, I haven't been here." That was somewhat true. "The FBI asked me to come in here to make some sort of antidote." He tried to shrug nonchalantly. "So here I am."

"Well, thank you for volunteering. It makes my job so much easier. Toss those." Avery gestured to the towels. "How about we go to your lab? I wouldn't want to stand in the way of your work."

"Uh, wait. How does this make your job easier?"

Chester tried to stall, but Avery escorted him out the door into the hallway. What if Avery saw the Sirens? But to his relief, the hall was empty.

Where the hell did they go? He tried to breathe normally though sweat ran down his back as Avery pushed him over to his lab's door.

"Because now I don't have to search for you and kill anyone else to find you." Avery motioned to the door. "It took me long enough to find your lab. This is an opportunity not to be missed. In you go, *Doctor Venom*."

Chester shivered at the derision in his cousin's voice as they stepped into the dark and silent lab. He switched on the lights and looked around, expecting to see the four Sirens exposed, but the lab sat empty. Where had the women gone?

"You know that's a nickname someone else gave me, right?" Chester went over to his workstation and turned to keep Avery in his sights. "I don't go by that anywhere."

Avery shrugged. "It doesn't matter. It's who you are and the skills I need." He gestured to the table. "So, let's get started."

Chester thought hard. The laptop and hard drive were out of the lab in Dunwoody's pack. There wasn't any way to do the work again, though he remembered some of it. He had to stall.

Stall for what? No one's rescuing us.

But the Sirens were around somewhere and he had to hope they'd come for him and get him out.

It's my own damn fault I'm here. If I'd just held it until we got back to the vehicle.

"Chester? I said, *get to work!*" Avery barked the command, and Chester jumped.

"Hey, if you want me to do this, you can't yell at me. It might work for your Meal Team Six thugs in their blacktical gear, but it doesn't work on me." Chester scowled as he moved through the lab toward the safe. It was empty, but he had to make this look good.

"Look who's talking. Aren't you dressed in your own 'blacktical' gear?" Avery sneered. "Fine, I won't yell, Chessy, but you better get to work, or else."

"Or else what, Avery?" He punched the code into the safe. "Are you going to shoot me like you did the rest of the people in here?"

"If those people had just told me where you were to begin with, none of this would've happened." His voice held a mildly frustrated whine as if they'd simply inconvenienced him. "They should've just told me so we didn't have to go through all this unpleasantness." Though the way he smiled made Chester think he hadn't minded the killing.

Holy fuck, there's something really wrong with him.

Chester glanced up at him. "Avery, what are you *doing*? This is crazy."

"The name is Max!" He shouted the words as he stepped closer to Chester. "Max Louden and I'm on a mission to save the people from the government."

The government of the people, by the people, made up of people? But Chester kept his mouth shut. He didn't think logic would work on Avery.

"And now that you're here, you can make an antidote to my beautiful little monster."

Chester paused. "What monster?"

Avery grinned and swung a backpack off his shoulders to set it on the nearest table. He unzipped the bag and pulled out a large, silver cylinder with rounded ends that reminded Chester of a giant, metal gel cap vitamin.

"Isn't it pretty?"

Chester swallowed hard. "What is that?"

"This is my invention. Isn't it amazing?" He caressed the cylinder like a beloved toy. "This will ensure they listen to the people when we demand change to make everything right."

Right for whom?

"But what is that thing? How will it make anyone listen to anything?"

"By threat." Avery beamed. "If they don't adhere to our demands, we'll shoot this baby into Broken Pass to show I mean what I'm saying. Broken Pass is our test run. Once you make the antidote, of course."

"Antidote to what? Avery, you're not making sense." Chester tried to move away from the safe, and the cylinder, but Avery shook his head.

"Please try to keep up. This lovely thing is a shell containing a deadly neurotoxin created by my dear friend Mr. Schicksal." He stroked the canister. "It can be shot from a mobile weapon like a Howitzer so it's easily positioned and virtually unnoticed. In and out, and no one the wiser. It's perfect, elegant, and effective."

"For what?" How long would it take for the Sirens to come back?

"For convincing the government we're right. We shoot this thing into a population center like Chicago or New York, and kill thousands—maybe even millions if it's dense enough—and they'll have to listen."

"Wait, you want to kill others to prove how right you are? Is that what you're saying?"

Avery leveled him with a patronizing smile. "We tried getting their attention through normal channels—talking, voting, protesting. But the politicians are already in someone's pocket and distracted by nonsense—climate change, women's rights, gay marriage. Bah! This will make them listen."

"It's not that simple, Avery. Killing other people, those you perceive as your enemies, only proves them right in what they're saying about you."

"Oh?" Avery's eyes blazed with curiosity. "What are they saying about me, then?"

"They're calling you a terrorist. Someone willing to hurt others to get what he wants."

Avery shrugged. "Those who refuse to learn, listen, and change reap the consequences of their willful ignorance. History will describe me differently—as a patriot who overthrew oppression, and restored the voice of the people."

"Killing innocent people doesn't restore anyone's voice. You're harming those you claim to support." Chester shook his head. "This isn't logical. You can't kill innocents to prove you're fighting for them."

"Sheep!" Avery roared the word as he threw out his hands, knocking a beaker off the table so it shattered on the concrete floor. "They're fucking sheep who follow whatever their overlords tell them to do. They won't be missed or needed." His wild eyes softened as he took in Chester's tension. "But don't worry, Chessy. You're very important. I need you to construct an antidote to keep me and my militias safe from harm so we can do the work necessary to save our country."

Oh, sweet fucking glory. Avery had gone insane, and nothing Chester said would fix it.

"So, what do you need to do to make my antidote?" Avery blinked at him with a half-smile, like a curious kid at a science fair.

"Uh, well, I need to know what it's made of, specifically the formula of what went into the toxin."

Avery nodded and drew out a folded piece of paper. "Absolutely. Mr. Schicksal wrote it out clearly for when I found you." He held it out but lifted it out of reach before Chester could grasp it. "This must stay confidential. We can't have our enemies knowing the make-up of this little gem. Right?"

It's not a gem, it's a goddamned plague.

Chester gritted his teeth. "Right."

Avery held the paper a little longer, eyeing Chester with suspicion, but when Chester didn't move or flinch, he handed it over.

"Thank you." It occurred to him it was stupid to thank Avery for giving him the chemical formula for a toxic substance that could kill millions of people, but old habits died hard. He hoped the FBI had been close in their interpretation of the toxin.

He opened the paper and scanned the figures written there, relief cascading through him. He'd gotten the antidote right. Nothing had been changed or refined from the information the FBI had gathered.

Thank goodness I gave everything to Dunwoody. He straightened. *Oh, shit, I gave everything to Dunwoody.*

"Something wrong, Chessy?" Avery cocked his head.

Chester took a deep breath. "Nope. It's all good." He shoved the paper into his pocket as he approached the safe in the wall. "I just need to get out my laptop and hard drive. All my notes are there."

They weren't there. The safe was empty. He just hoped he could pull off authentic surprise so Avery didn't shoot him on the spot.

Hermione checked her watch and growled. "What the fuck is taking him so long?"

"I dunno, Wizard. Don't men pee faster than women?" Giovinazzo shrugged as she came back from securing the doors to the stairs. "Doors secure. The tangos upstairs aren't getting down here anytime soon."

"Copy that. Subramani, crack the door and see what's going on. Everyone else, prepare to move out."

Subramani nodded and headed for the door to the bathroom, but she stilled and held up her hand in a fist. Everyone froze.

"Voices, Wizard. I think the doc is talking to someone."

"What?" Hermione sidled closer as Subramani laid her hands against the door. "Are you sure?"

"Yeah. Give me a second. I'll try to get a visual."

She pressed her weight forward, letting the door crack open just enough to let the light spill out in a sliver. What they saw through the crack made Hermione's blood freeze.

"Don't forget to wash your hands. Germs, you know."

The man labeled as Max Louden gestured at the sinks, and Martell swallowed hard when he moved to the counter to wash his hands.

Fuck!

Subramani eased the door shut and backed away. "What do we do, Captain?"

Hermione scanned the hallway. There wasn't anywhere to hide except in the labs, but more than likely Louden would take Martell back to the venom lab. She pointed at the door across the hall.

"Dunwoody, get that door open, quick. We'll wait there to see what happens. Hurry."

"What's going on, Captain?" Mo's voice came through their earpieces.

"Louden has Dr. Martell."

"What the fuck? He didn't show up on any of the feeds!" Furious clicking sounds came over the comms. "I swear, no one else was in the building, Wizard."

"Copy that. Time to improvise. Standby."

Dunwoody got the lab door open and the Sirens ghosted inside, closing it behind them with a soft click. Hermione dropped the blinds on all the windows as the other Sirens settled into watch-mode. She cracked one of the blinds and waited.

No more than fifteen seconds later, the men's room door opened and Louden escorted Martell back to the venom lab. He carried a backpack that hung off one shoulder with something weighing it down and a pistol on his hip.

"Holy shit," Dunwoody breathed. "That was fuckin' close."

Hermione nodded as they watched the men open the venom lab's door and step inside. The lights came on through the blinds on the lab's windows, and she took her first breath since they hid.

"What are we going to do now, Captain?" Giovinazzo's face and voice were as stoic as ever. "We've got the laptop, the hard drive, and the antidote. When Martell opens that safe and it's empty of his things, Louden's gonna flip."

"Copy that. It just means we need to take him out of the equation." She checked over her weapons, making sure her Glock was loaded. It would make less noise than the rifles. "The FBI said we could use lethal force. I don't see a reason to keep Louden alive."

"Copy that, Captain." Dunwoody nodded as she checked her own weapons. "When do we move?"

Hermione checked the hallway. "Mo, what's going on upstairs?"

"Nothing so far, Captain. Them boys are just hangin' out like they're waitin' for somethin'. It's weird. They aren't even tryin' to go downstairs."

"Anyone else around? Pinpoint?"

"Negative, Captain. The guards are still patrolling, but aren't doing anything else. No one seems to know you're inside."

"Anyone patrolling near Building Four?"

"I don't have a great visual from overwatch. Humping to a new perch." Lin Su sounded breathless with effort.

"Roger that. Check in when overwatch established."

"Copy that."

Hermione bit her lip and nodded. "All right. Dunwoody, Giovinazzo, head for the door to the Hub beside the elevators and wait. Secure our exfil. Subramani, you're with me. We're going to get the doctor out of here."

"What about Louden, Captain?" Subramani met her gaze.

Hermione shrugged. "Take him out. Secure his cargo."

"Copy that."

"Right. Let's move."

They slid into the hallway, and Hermione and Subramani headed for the venom lab while Giovinazzo and Dunwoody moved toward the door to the tunnel at the far end of the building. Subramani grasped the door handle and met Hermione's gaze.

"What's the plan, Wizard?"

"I'll know when we get in there. Low and quiet."

"Roger that."

"Siren Six in new overwatch position, Captain."

"Copy that. Going in. Stand by."

Subramani lifted one finger, and Hermione nodded. A second finger went up as her other hand pushed down on the handle. When the third finger went up, she pushed the door open and dropped low. Hermione followed with her Glock in her hand. They entered the lab quick and quiet to find both men staring at the empty safe with varying expressions of dismay and anger.

"What the fuck are you saying, Chessy?"

"I'm saying someone stole my things!" Chester turned on Louden. "My laptop and notes are all gone. Are you sure your men didn't come in here and break into the safe to take them? How well do you know these people?"

Louden scowled. "None of my people have the skills to break into a safe—"

Chester's scoff cut him off. "That's bullshit, Avery, and you know it."

"Okay." Louden nodded. "Fine, no one with those skills are here in this building." He stopped and tilted his head. "How long were *you* in this building before you used the bathroom?" He pulled his pistol and aimed it at Chester.

Hermione gestured to Subramani to sneak closer around the other side of the central counter in the middle of the lab. If she got behind the men, they'd have a better chance of getting Chester out alive. She remained hidden behind the counter near the exit.

"What are you talking about, Avery?" Chester put his hands up as he shifted his back to the empty safe.

"The name is Max. How long have you been in this building tonight?" The barrel of the gun rose as Louden aimed at Chester's torso. Chester swallowed hard but lifted his chin.

"I came here to get my laptop and notes. That's why I'm here. Wait." He narrowed his eyes. "Are you suggesting I stole my own things? Seriously? Why would I do that?"

Hermione had to hand it to the doc—he sounded convincingly outraged. She couldn't see Subramani from this angle, but the clicks in her ear said her teammate had shifted closer to the tableau.

"To keep them away from me and my people."

Chester rolled his eyes and caught Hermione's just as she peeked out from her hiding place, stilling just a moment before he looked back at Louden. "That's ridiculous. You're the one who needs me to do this, right? And this is the only lab in the country that can build what you want. I came here looking for my things, but they're gone. Are you sure you can trust your people? Maybe someone went behind your back."

"No one would ever do that. They're loyal and believe in the cause as much as I do."

"Really? What about the people who were working here already, those supposedly on your side? You sure you can trust them?"

Damn, Chester's selling his surprise fuckin' well.

"Who, Dirk Olsen? He's not smart enough to know anything about the lab work."

Now we know that jackass is a mole.

"Maybe, but he's worked here a while and he knows most of the researchers. He could've gotten one of them to open the safe for him." Chester scowled, though Hermione could see he was sweating. "What about the researcher on your payroll? They're smart enough to get into the safe and take my things to sell my research on the open market."

Louden scoffed again, but his expression darkened as Chester's words cracked his certainty. "Dr. Miller doesn't have access to the labs in this building."

I knew that bitch was shady as fuck.

"But she has friends here. She could've convinced them to open the safe."

Louden growled. "You're just trying to hide your own theft of your tech."

"Where would I put it, Avery? Where?" Chester threw his arms out and spun in a circle. "I don't even have a backpack. It's not like I can stuff a laptop into my pants."

Hermione would've smirked if Louden's frustration hadn't boiled over and he grabbed the doc, shoving his pistol against his head.

"If you don't find the laptop, I'm going to kill you."

"If you kill me, you'll never get your antidote." Sweat poured down Chester's face, but his gaze held steady despite the gun pressed up against his head.

"I can find another venom specialist to do the job for me. If you can't do it now, you're useless to me." He chambered a round in the gun.

"Almost in position, Wizard," Subramani whispered.

"Copy that. Causing distraction. Signal me when in position." Hermione rose to full height and stepped into view, moving forward. "Hey, Louden, nice to finally meet you in person." Chester jumped, but Louden never moved.

For a moment, Hermione didn't think he'd turn, his gaze riveted on Chester, but he slowly rotated his head to look at her.

"This must be the rest of your team, Chessy. I knew you hadn't come here alone."

"I never said I was here alone. I said the FBI sent me in here to get my things." Chester was breathless, but he kept his hands out in a gesture of surrender.

Louden scowled and yanked Chester in front of him, using him as a human shield. "I should've remembered you have a fascination with the accuracy of words, cousin. How many others are here with you?"

"Right now, there's only Wilcox."

Technically true since he couldn't see Subramani.

"Let him go, Louden. Killing him won't get you what you want." Hermione kept her gaze and her weapon steady, her voice even. Her heartbeat settled down as she drew the terrorist's attention to her.

"How do you know that, Agent Wilcox? I assume you're FBI, sent in here to protect dear Dr. Venom, right?" Louden sneered. "Bang up job you're doing. They should've known better than to send in a woman." His lips curled in disdain at the last word.

Hermione debated the best way to keep distracting the tango until Subramani signaled.

"That supposed to piss me off, Louden? Your sexism and misogyny are well-documented." She shrugged, but her Glock never wavered. "I'd have to care what you think to make it affect me doing my job. A for effort, F for results. Let Martell go."

Louden's expression shifted through frustration to his maniacally amiable smile. "I think not. I think I'll be taking cousin Chessy with me and you're gonna let me leave or I'll kill him."

"Not gonna happen, Louden." Hermione didn't move. "The only way out of here is past me and I'm not moving. Let Martell go and I might negotiate."

Except, I don't negotiate with terrorists. I just shoot them.

Louden laughed and jerked Chester tighter against him. "No deal. What's the motto of the FBI? Oh yes, you don't negotiate with terrorists, and that's what you've branded me. But I'm a patriot and a sovereign citizen of this country, so you're gonna let me leave because I have rights."

So did all the people you shot and killed, jackass.

Clicks in her ear told her Subramani was in position.

"In position. Make him step back and I'll have a clear head shot."

Hermione let her breath out slowly and took a step forward. "Sure, I'll let you leave when you release Martell."

Louden took a corresponding step back and moved his head behind Chester's. "Cousin Chessy is coming with me. He's family after all."

A loud gunshot sounded in the room, and Louden's head exploded, painting the wall with blood and soft tissue. Chester shrieked and ducked as Louden's body crumbled behind him.

Hermione shoved her Glock into its holster and shot to Chester's side on the floor.

"Holy fuck! Holy fuck!"

"Are you okay, Martell?" Her heart thundered in her chest as she took in his blood-spattered appearance. "Any injuries?"

Subramani moved to the body to check for life. She raised her gaze to Hermione's and shook her head.

"No, no injuries. Fuck, that was close. I swore I was dead. Who killed him?" Chester started to turn, but Hermione thumped his shoulder.

"Hey, focus on me right now. Let's get you cleaned up and out of here. We don't know if his thugs heard the gunshot." She pulled him to his feet and dragged him closer to the door, hoping she could keep his mind away from the dead body. They stopped at the counter with a sink, and she found some paper towels. "Stand there and I'll get the blood off you."

"There's blood?" His face paled and he swayed a little.

"Hey, Martell, focus on me right now, okay? We still have to get out of here safely and I'd rather not have to carry you." She wet a towel and wiped off his shoulders to get the worst of the viscera, trying to keep her touches light but efficient. "How close were the FBI on the formula of the toxin? Did you make the right antidote?"

Some of the haze cleared from Chester's eyes. "Yes, uh, yes. The formula was right, and the antidote should work. It needs more testing, but it should work."

"Good. You're cleaned up. Let's get moving." She nodded to Subramani as the other woman slid past them.

"Wait, I need to grab his backpack. The weapon is in there."

"What?" Subramani paused. "What weapon?"

"The shell he was going to use to kill all the people in Broken Pass." He moved to find the backpack, but Hermione stopped him. "We have to bring it with us. We can't leave it here and maybe someone can reverse engineer it or something. The FBI needs to know what they're dealing with." He tried to move back toward the body.

"Okay. Subramani will get it and bring it out to you. Let's go out to the hallway, doc." Hermione forced him to head toward the door as she waved at Subramani. She had to get him away from the body or he might lose his composure and they were out of time. The other Siren nodded and grabbed the pack, stuffing the big silver shell back into its confines. "Let's go and meet up with Dunwoody and Giovinazzo."

He met her gaze, his face still chalky in pallor. "Is Avery dead?"

She nodded. "He won't be coming back from this shot."

Chester swallowed hard. "Okay. Let's go."

He stumbled away from her toward the door without looking back, and Hermione kept an eye on him as she waited for Subramani. She hoped he wouldn't freak out until they got well away from the research center. The other Siren came on her heels and turned off the lights in the lab as they exited to the hallway.

Dunwoody and Giovinazzo waited beside the elevators, weapons in hands and feet braced apart. Chester reached out for the pack in Subramani's hands.

"I'll carry it."

Subramani hesitated. "I don't think it's a good idea, Doctor. There's a possibility someone will be shooting at us. If that shell gets hit, you could die from exposure."

Chester scowled. "So could you."

"Yes, but I can't make more of the antidote if that comes to pass. I'll carry the shell."

"Right, let's move out. Giovinazzo, take point in the tunnel. Doc, I need you to stay between Dunwoody and Subramani. Move when we move, stay low when we say so, and we'll be out of here without a scratch. Copy?" Hermione hustled them to the doors to the tunnel.

"Copy, er roger. Uh, yes, ma'am." His expression showed shell shock and a kind of distraction that meant he was only going through the motions as he nodded. "What are you going to do?"

"Cover your sixes. Let's move."

Giovinazzo eased the door open, checked the tunnel, and moved through to take point. Hermione stepped up to hold the door, hoping Chester would make it, though he still looked wobbly.

"Move out, doc. I'll cover your six."

He shuddered and hurried through, his expression tightening as if he'd just realized everything that had happened. Hermione made sure the door closed them into the tunnel with a soft click, grateful that Moriarty had control of the cameras. The last thing she needed was a shoot-out while they were trapped.

"Mo, any movement from the tangos upstairs?" Hermione waited for Moriarty's response before the distance from the building cut off all communication.

"Negative, Wizard. Looks like they didn't hear the gunshot."

"Copy that. Going silent until we reach the Hub. Will try to re-establish comms there."

"Roger that."

Hermione took a deep breath as she nodded to Dunwoody.

"All right, we're on our own until we get to the Hub. Let's move."

Chapter Eighteen

C hester was swept along with the Siren tide as they almost ran down the tunnel to the Hub at the center of the research campus. He wished he could focus on the walls, but his mind kept going back to the utter terror of Avery pressing a gun to his head before abruptly letting go. And the sound of the body hitting the floor after Chester was sprayed with some warm liquid.

Blood. Hermione said it was blood.

A full body shudder worked its way up from his knees to his shoulders, and his stomach threatened to empty onto his boots. He swallowed against the bile working its way up his esophagus and kept his eyes on the end of the tunnel, which was weirdly dark.

Isn't death supposed to be all 'don't go into the light'?

All he had to do was make it to the Hub and he could focus on getting home safely, and maybe forget about the smell of blood and shit, and the sound of Avery's head breaking apart like a smashed melon.

Don't think about it. Fuck!

They made it to the end of the tunnel, and Chester tightened his hands into fists that hurt, just to give himself something to feel other than panic. Why had he thought coming back into the campus was a good idea? He wasn't built for this shit.

To save the world from a biological attack that would kill thousands. Right.

They stopped just before the exit, and Giovinazzo held her fist up to stop everyone. The other members of Wilcox's team did the same, their expressions stoic and watchful. He'd always thought women were especially expressive in their faces, but these women were harder and scarier when working than any of the military men he'd met.

"Everyone sit tight for a few. Dunwoody, clear the Hub underground."

"Copy that." The blonde Siren slipped into the dusky darkness and disappeared.

Chester studied the Hub. He'd never been there before, preferring to be outside. It was a large open space where sounds echoed, dark except for the solar lights in the tunnels leading away. He couldn't see much beyond Subramani's and Giovinazzo's shoulders, but he'd have to remind himself to come back and take a look.

When the place isn't overrun by terrorists.

Dunwoody was gone no more than a few minutes before she reappeared, but it felt like forever to Chester. "All clear, Wizard. No tangos in any of the tunnels."

"Roger that. You take point. Exfil out Building Four. Move out, team." Wilcox nodded sharply. "Mo, do you read?"

Silence met her question, and Chester swallowed hard.

"I repeat, Mo, do you read us?"

They waited a few more seconds before Hermione swore. "Sirens, be advised, comms are down all the way out to the Hub. Keep eyes and ears on for tangos. Move out to Building Four."

"Roger that."

Chester nodded and swallowed against the fear trying to crawl up his gut as they crossed the Hub and entered the tunnel to Building Four. He didn't have time to panic yet—he could do that later when back at the rustic mansion where he'd kissed Hermione.

If I'm going back there.

Given how the night trip had gone, he wasn't sure where he'd end up. Or if Hermione—Captain Wilcox—would want to be with him after she'd seen how he'd lost his shit. Was currently losing his shit while they tried to get out.

Military women don't want panicky men.

And he didn't know how she wasn't panicking.

Once they dismantled the domestic terrorist threat of the Eagle Militia, he'd go back to his ordinary life of research into anti-venom and solitary living. Which was probably for the best. He wasn't cut out for this kind of work, and he wasn't sure he'd be okay knowing Hermione did this every day, like a 9-to-5 job. How could she live with this kind of danger day in and day out? Could he be okay with knowing she put herself in danger, dealing with terrorists and biotoxins all the time?

He swallowed against more bile.

He didn't know if he could handle it. Maybe it was better if they just chalked their connection up to being a fling during stressful circumstances and let it go at that.

It's probably not the worst idea.

But even as he thought it, the words made his stomach tighten with disappointment and dread.

Or maybe the feeling is from us stepping into another tunnel where the terrorists can pick us off like fish in a barrel.

Time would tell.

They made it down the length of the tunnel to Building Four, then stopped at the door to the basement. Hermione checked in and re-established comms with Moriarty. The surveillance specialist confirmed the basement was all clear and the cameras had been looped. The Sirens all checked their weapons before Dunwoody opened the tunnel door to the building.

Deep breaths, Martell. We're gonna be fine. His inner thought sounded like a desperate lie.

They crossed the basement hallway to the central stairs in near silence. He'd never experienced so many heavily armored people moving so silently. It was eerie as hell, and he swallowed hard.

It's a damn good thing these people are on my side.

They'd reached the reception desk near the elevators before Giovinazzo raised her hand in a fist.

"Shit! Tangos incoming from upstairs. Your twelve o'clock!"

Moriarty's warning hit their ears just before the doors to the staircase opened. Panic surged in Chester's gut. There wasn't anywhere to hide before the bad guys started shooting, and bullets traveled in straight lines.

We're so dead.

Except Dunwoody closed in on the men coming through, their conversation on "the stupid G-men think they'll get Max to come out? Idiots." They never saw her. The first one dropped from a rifle butt to the temple, crumpling into a heap on the floor. The second man tried to yell and bring his weapon around, but she knocked his rifle aside and kicked his feet out from under him. He went down, and she finished him with a blow to the head. All in silence.

A chill ran up Chester's back. These were not women to mess with.

Dunwoody stepped over the bodies and eased the door they'd come through open a crack. Subramani and Wilcox zip-tied the terrorists' hands and feet with restraints purloined from the men's pockets.

Pretty damn useful they brought them for us.

"Let's go, doc."

Wilcox's voice in his ear made him jump, and he jerked his attention back to the situation at hand. She herded him into the stairwell, and the rest of the team surrounded him as they ascended to the ground floor. Dunwoody and Giovinazzo held their rifles at the ready as Wilcox moved to the next door.

"Mo, tell me what's going on in Building Four." She stood at the door with her Glock in her hand as she waited for a response.

"Copy. Be advised, two tangos present in the lobby near the info desk, two more roamin' the halls. The roamers are located in the west end of the building so they won't know about y'all hittin' their buddies for a bit, but don't tarry at all."

"Roger that." Wilcox turned her head to meet each person's gaze. "Okay, here's what we're going to do. Giovinazzo and I are going to take down the two tangos in the lobby. Dunwoody, Subramani, wait here with Martell until you receive the all-clear. Then we all move, fast and quiet, to the east end exit leading to the outer perimeter. Copy?"

"Copy that."

All the Sirens nodded, and Chester took a deep breath, shoving everything into the back of his mind to make sure he could survive until they made it out. Wilcox and Giovinazzo pushed open the doors and headed straight to the reception desk.

Avery's guys didn't see them until the Sirens were nearly to them, and they tried to fend the women off. But the first went down from a throat-punch and a knee to the nose, while the other one took a swing at Giovinazzo. The smaller woman ducked and hit the guy with a punch to the gut below his blacktical vest. The guy dropped, and she finished him off with a blow to his nose. He fell and remained still.

Holy shit, that was a lot easier than I expected.

"Let's go, doc. Move." Dunwoody shoved him through the door and followed.

Chester forced himself to focus on running through the hallways of Building Four without making too much noise. Dunwoody and Subramani took point, while Wilcox and Giovinazzo fell in behind them, covering their backs.

The hair on the back of his neck stood up, but he refused to look back. He needed to keep going. What was it that cartoon fish kept repeating?

Just keep swimming.

Yeah, they weren't swimming, but he was swept along with them as they jogged around the corner toward the hall leading to the exit. He made his feet move, but he ran as if in a dream, bent over and crouch-ran like the others just to fit in. He didn't want to present an easy target.

They made it to the solid steel door and slowed to a stop. Dunwoody gestured toward the outside and back at her eyes. Wilcox nodded before she tapped her mic.

"Pinpoint, are you still on overwatch?"

"Affirmative, Wizard. I now have line-of-sight on the exit door. No guards currently in your vicinity, but they make rounds every five mikes in teams of two around Building Five, which gives them line-of-sight to the east end of Four. Last pair just passed three mikes ago."

"Copy that." Wilcox held up a hand to Dunwoody. "Do we have enough time to make it to the fence line before the next pair comes into sight range?"

"Negative, Wizard. The next pair will be in range in the next thirty seconds. Standby."

No one said a word for a few moments. Chester listened for any voices in the building as they waited for the guards outside to clear away. He shot a look over his shoulder, but the hallway remained dark behind them.

"Thirty seconds and they'll be at the door, Wizard."

"Copy that, Pinpoint."

Dunwoody nodded, and everyone settled in to wait. Chester tried counting in his head, but his heart beat so loud, he couldn't keep the counts steady. Instead, he dropped his hand to his thigh and tapped his fingers in time with the seconds, not daring to look at anyone.

The seconds crawled by, and his anxiety increased with each breath. He tried to focus on his fingers, but the fear built as he waited for some news on anything. He was tired and keyed up, and he just wanted to go home.

"Wizard, this is Moriarty. You have tangos moving through Building Four to your location."

"Fuck." Wilcox shot a look down the hallway. "How much time do we have, Mo?"

"Estimated sixty seconds until they discover the bodies. Alarms on the outer doors disabled."

"Fuck. Pinpoint, give us some good news, woman. We need to haul ass."

"Copy that. The guards will be out of range in forty seconds. You'll have approximately ninety seconds to make it to the fence line before the next pair of guards come into range."

"Roger that. Give us the go command when time." Wilcox glanced down at her watch, the face glowing red. "It's gonna be close, ladies. Dunwoody, get us outside and cover our exfil, watching to the west. Subramani, it's your job to get the doc to the fence. Giovinazzo, keep an eye on the eastside guards. I'll make sure the door closes quietly and watch your sixes. Copy?"

"Copy that."

The Sirens got into position, and the tension hit a screaming pitch. Chester tightened his hand into a fist and swallowed against the urge to whimper. How the hell did the women put up with this kind of stress?

They could hear voices of the guards deeper in the building, and he hoped they hadn't found the bodies of their compatriots yet.

"Guards clear, Wizard. Your ninety second window starts now."

"Go, go, go!"

Dunwoody pushed the door open and took off about twenty yards ahead, before she turned and scanned the area to either side of the building. She gestured for them to come after her and Subramani shoved Chester in front of her.

"Run, doctor. Now."

They bolted away from the building, and Chester focused on the fence behind Dunwoody while Giovinazzo ran bent over as she kept an eye on the eastside guards. Chester didn't know if Wilcox closed the door quietly or not as he pounded toward the fence.

Moriarty stood on the other side, clipping the links in the fence to make a door. She finished the last one and peeled open the chain links just as he and Subramani made it to the fence.

"Welcome back. Get your ass on this side of the fence, doc." Moriarty held the links open so he could duck through. "Subramani, don't lollygag, honey. I understand you're carrying hazardous cargo."

Subramani hustled him into the trees and shoved him against a trunk while she crouched and took aim back toward the buildings. Chester braced his chest against the tree and peeked around to see how Giovinazzo and Wilcox were doing.

Oh, glory, Hermione. You gotta make it.

"Watch your six, Wizard. Two tangos to your five o'clock." Moriarty's voice sounded calm despite the western guards catching sight of the Sirens headed for the fence.

"I got them."

Pinpoint's voice held confidence as two shots rang out. Both the men running after Hermione and Giovinazzo stopped dead and dropped to the ground. Chester swallowed against bile as the two Sirens made it through the fence. Their vehicle pulled up, and Chester realized Subramani had taken over holding the fence open while Moriarty retrieved the SUV.

No one said a word as the vehicle's side doors opened. They simply flowed inside, and Subramani grasped Chester's arm to haul him along with them. Hermione jumped in and pulled him inside before reaching for Giovinazzo and Subramani. The vehicle started to move as the women jumped in, settling beside him. He glanced back at the buildings fading behind their tailgate to see two men at the door shooting at the SUV.

"Hold on, it's gonna get entertaining here for a moment." Moriarty yanked the wheel to the right and the vehicle shot into the trees, narrowly missing some of the trunks on either side. They bounced over rocks and debris, mowing down a couple of bushes as they outran the automatic rifles' distance.

When they broke through the trees, they skidded on the pavement and sped toward the FBI's mobile command post. Chester breathed a sigh of relief that they'd made it and no one got dead.

Except Avery.

Yeah, that was going to be hard to explain to Aunt Janette and Uncle Milton.

If I'm allowed to talk about it at all.

Who knew what the FBI would allow to get out. More than likely Chester would have to sign some sort of NDA having to do with national security or something equally frightening. He grimaced as they pulled up in front of the command center. He just wanted to go somewhere and sleep. He wasn't cut out for this kind of high-stress action. It had been a rough couple of weeks and he was ready for some normalcy.

They all got out, and the next few hours were spent going over the mission. The shell was turned over to the FBI along with the formula Avery had given Chester and all the samples of antidote he'd made.

Then he, Hermione, and Subramani had to explain what happened with the shooting of Max Louden AKA Avery Gentry, over and over, until his eyes started to close and he couldn't see straight.

"One more time, Dr. Martell. What happened when you encountered Max Louden in the bathroom?"

"You know what, Agent Matthews, I bet you could tell *me* what happened at this point better than I can tell you, so I'm done. You know the story backward and forward, up and down, left and right, and I'm done talking. I'm exhausted and hungry, and I just want to go to sleep. So." He slapped the table and stood. "I'm going to go. Mmkay? Right."

Chester slipped away from the table and headed for the door.

"Please, Dr. Martell, we need to know the story. One more time." Matthews gestured back to the chair at the end of the table.

"Nope, I'm done." Chester shook his head. "You know everything I do already." He pushed through the door to the hallway and headed toward the front doors.

"Dammit, Martell!" It gave him a small measure of amusement that Matthews didn't get his way, but his give-a-fuck was busted and he couldn't get it repaired until next Monday. "Where is he going? Get him back here!"

Chester made it out into the darkness before anyone knew to stop him, and he started walking. The nice thing about Broken Pass was its small size. He could walk home from work if he had time, and since it was nearing four in the morning, he had plenty of time. Hell, he'd jogged farther around town.

He made it to the main road before common sense kicked in and he sat down to breathe in the warm night air. The last thing he wanted to do was piss off the FBI, so he waited for them to catch up to him. It didn't take them long.

But instead of putting him back in an interrogation room, Dunwoody and Moriarty showed up and drove him back to the Cabin. He asked where Wilcox, Subramani, Giovinazzo, and Pinpoint were, but apparently, they had to stay behind to debrief about all the shootings. He shuddered at the thought and gratefully let himself into his room without fuss.

He wanted to just fall into bed, but he needed to remove the grease paint on his face and wash the sweat off his body. Dunwoody had handed him little packets of makeup removal wipes and told him to clean himself up before she left him. He did as she recommended, then showered, trying not to think about all that had happened that night.

He managed to keep the memories at bay until he crawled into bed. Then they crowded his brain in random order, fueling fear and elevated heart rates. How the hell did Hermione do the job all the time? What if she got killed on the next mission? Could he handle that?

Chester didn't know, and the worries chased his thoughts around for another hour before exhaustion sucked him into a dreamless sleep.

Chapter Nineteen

C hester sat on the bed in his room and took a deep breath.

So, it was over.

The Eagle Militia had been subdued, the FBI was tracking down the mysterious man Avery had been working with to make the WMD, and the Broken Pass Research Center was free to resume their usual work.

I don't feel like I can.

He'd done his part, made the antidote to the horrible toxin Avery would have unleashed, and even turned over his notes to the FBI so it could be replicated around the world. He hoped they would share the antidote with the world, but he had to wonder how 'sharing and caring' Agent Matthews would be, especially with a solution to a horrific toxin.

Chester took another deep breath and scrubbed his hands over his face. It would be time to leave the 'rustic' mansion soon. He'd slept for a good twelve hours once he fell into bed, and hadn't seen anyone since he'd woken up. Moriarty had called his phone to let him know he was free to go home and someone would give him a ride into town at 1330 hours. It took him a little bit to realize that was 1:30 p.m. in the afternoon.

So, now he was packed and ready to go, but feeling a little lost and bereft. It had been an intense adventure that he hadn't chosen to take, but now that it was over, he wasn't sure what he would do now. Could he just go back to his quiet life, studying venoms and toxins in an attempt to make antidotes? Could he walk into the lab as if the hostile takeover was just a minor blip in his life? Could he work in a lab that had blood and viscera spattered all over it when Subramani had ended Avery's life?

Chester knuckled his eyes, trying to scrub away the memories of Avery holding a gun to his head, then the sound of the gunshot and the spray of warm liquid. He groaned and shook his head to clear it. How the hell was he going to get over that memory?

He shot a look toward the bathroom that he shared with Hermione, but no lights shone under it and he hadn't heard any movement from her side. He wished he could see her and talk to her about what happened, but he'd heard she'd returned sometime during his marathon sleeping, and now she was the one resting.

As much as he wanted to talk to her, he couldn't wake her up after all they'd gone through. She needed her rest as much as he did, and now it was time for him to go home. Back to his ordinary life, with fewer friends, and a lot more distrust of the world.

A soft knock sounded on the door, and he rose, an irrational hope that Hermione had woken up and wanted to talk to him. But the bathroom remained dark and quiet, and the knock came again from the bedroom door. Sharp disappointment stabbed his chest.

His shoulders dropped as he moved to the bedroom door and opened it.

"Hi, Dr. Martell. I'm Captain O'Connell here to give you a ride home."

The woman on the other side of the door wasn't tall—maybe five and a half feet tall—with short, wavy auburn hair more red than brown and freckles across her nose and cheeks. Sharp, intelligent green eyes looked out over pixie-like features appearing almost fragile compared with the rest of her curvy body.

"Captain? Like Wilcox?" Chester retreated to pick up his packed duffel bag.

O'Connell tilted her head and scrunched her nose. "Not quite. Captain was my rank in the Coast Guard, and old habits die hard. Wilcox is the captain of our crew here in Montana. I'm the transportation manager. If it rolls, floats, or flies, I'm your girl." She flashed a wide grin.

Chester couldn't help but smile back. He shot one more look at the bathroom door before he followed her out of the room into the hallway.

"Coast Guard, huh? A long way from the ocean here in Broken Pass."

O'Connell grimaced. "Yeah, not my ideal, for sure. But I still get to fly helos, and sometimes I do the gnarliest white water rafting I can find, and that helps."

They chatted about some of the best rivers as they made their way down to the main floor of the house. Chester liked O'Connell's easy, straight-forward humor and friendly conversation. She had an intensity that was different from Hermione's, but they had similar qualities. Both women were no-nonsense warriors, but where Hermione was quiet, calculating, and thoughtful, O'Connell was brash, confident, and adventurous.

They loaded up in yet another SUV and headed into town, talking about the best hiking and white-water rafting places around

Broken Pass. He let O'Connell do most of the talking, content to listen to the cadence of her voice to keep himself from thinking about Hermione behind him and his empty apartment ahead of him.

Though the terrorist threat and the WMD had been resolved, Chester had no idea where he stood with Hermione now that the action, and her part in the rescue, was done. She had a whole life of being badass, going where she was needed, extracting 'packages,' and making sure the world was saved for another day. Did she fall for all the people she rescued? Did they fall for her like he had?

"All right, here we are, Dr. Martell. Safe and sound."

Chester came out of his thoughts with a start and realized they'd arrived at his apartment.

"Oh, right. Thank you very much, Captain O'Connell. I appreciate the ride." He unclipped his seatbelt and opened the SUV's door. "Please convey my thanks to everyone in your crew. I'm grateful for all their hard work."

"Of course. We're happy to help. You take care, now."

"Thanks."

He closed the door and waved as she drove off. Then he shouldered his bag, dug in his pocket for his keys, and headed into his apartment.

When he opened the door, the air smelled musty and unused, with a hint of rot. He wrinkled his nose when he realized he'd left some garbage in his place and it had festered in the heat of the days he'd been gone. He dropped his bag and immediately took out the trash before he vomited and made a worse mess. Then he opened all his windows to let the afternoon breeze air his place out.

He emptied his bag and threw his clothes in the washer, along with any other laundry he'd left, and tried to find some comfort in the familiar around him. But his mind kept going back to Hermione, and how she worked at a job that had the potential to kill her. He still hadn't made the decision if he could handle that long-term, but sitting around thinking about it wouldn't get him the answers. He needed to talk to Hermione.

He got up and searched his things for his phone, but remembered with dismay that it had been left and possibly destroyed at the research center, and he'd returned the burner phone the Sirens had given him. Worse, he hadn't memorized Hermione's number or her email, and didn't think the Sirens would just give out that information.

Chester sat down in his most comfortable chair, his head in his hands. Even if he got a new phone, he wouldn't be able to contact her. He leaned back in the chair and closed his eyes in dismay.

I never got to say goodbye.

Chapter Twenty

H ermione sat on the back porch overlooking the lawns surrounding the Cabin, listening to the summer rainstorm pound the grounds. A beer rested on the armrest of the wooden Adirondack chair, the glass sweating despite the rain. Her emotions matched the rain drenching the land and forest beyond the porch. It had been a helluva couple of weeks since the Sirens went in and killed Max Louden AKA Avery Gentry. She had mixed feelings about the mission and the aftermath.

But things weren't all bad. The FBI had managed to send in SWAT teams to take down and arrest all the remaining terrorists occupying the Broken Pass Research Center. Those who didn't come quietly were shot fighting back. They found Louden's body where the Sirens said it would be with the injuries described. Apparently, the other members of the Eagle Militia hadn't found him before SWAT came in, another reason they didn't have the cohesion to repel the incursion.

Hermione snorted. *It helped they were given permission to use lethal force like we were.*

Shooting terrorists made it a lot easier to retake the campus.

Interrogations of Meal Team Six had them singing like an opera choir, and six more shells intended for large population cities like

Los Angeles, Seattle, Portland, Chicago, New York, and Atlanta were found in the possession of one Herbert Meinke AKA Mr. Schicksal, a German word meaning "Fate". Along with an old WWII Howitzer gun towed behind his Suburban.

Meinke threatened to set one of the shells off to keep the FBI at bay, but they'd already mass-produced Dr. Martell's antidote and inoculated the raiding teams with it.

Essentially making Meinke's threat toothless.

Hermione smirked and sipped her beer as Dunwoody came out and sat in the chair beside hers.

"What are you smirking about?" The blonde woman set a cup of tea on her chair's arm and shot Hermione a smile.

"Just thinking of the declawing of the Eagle Militia thanks to Dr. Martell's antidote to their super toxin." She put her fingers up in air quotes. "Wasn't so super after that."

Lisa shook her head. "It would've wreaked havoc on the cities if Martell hadn't done his thing, though. He's a damn hero."

Hermione nodded. "Yes, he is. Saved the day and kept his cool. Did you see him working on that antidote? The man was F O C U S E D, *focused.* The rest of the world didn't exist while he worked. It was freaky."

"He's obviously very good at what he does." Lisa nodded. "Speaking of which, have you talked to him since we were de-briefed?"

Hermione grimaced and shook her head. "No. By the time I got back to the Cabin, he was completely zonked out, and when I woke up, he had gone home. I haven't seen or spoken to him since then."

Lisa turned to fix Hermione with a dry look. "You haven't called or texted, or hell, emailed him? At all?"

Hermione shook her head. "Nope."

"Why the hell not?" Lisa narrowed her eyes. "Were you just using him as a fuck buddy while he was here? Just get some hot dick, then 'wham, thud, thank you, stud' and you're out the door? Bitch, that's some fucked up shit, right there."

Hermione scowled. "What the fuck are you talking about?"

"Come on, Wizard. I saw how you two were together. He was really into you, and I thought you were really into him. I never took you for a love 'em and leave 'em kinda girl." Lisa tsked in disgust.

"What would you have me do? Communication devices work both ways. He hasn't called or texted me, either." Hermione shrugged uncomfortably. "Besides, I don't chase after men who aren't interested."

"How would you know? You haven't bothered to talk to him about it." She gasped and opened her eyes wide. "Oh, my glory! You're scared."

"What? No, I'm not scared. There just hasn't been time with the debrief and the paperwork and the clean-up."

"Bullshit. There's always time to talk. You've just been avoiding it. And we both know why that is." Dunwoody sipped her tea and stared out at the rain.

"Oh yeah? What?"

She rolled her eyes. "Fear of rejection. Plain and simple."

Hermione scowled and took a drink of her beer. "I'm not afraid of anything."

"Yeah, I'm gonna have to call bullshit again." Lisa snorted. "Your ex did a number on you, and now you can't see a world where love and military SpecOps exist in the same place."

"Yeah, well, I'm not sure it can. Did you see how Martell reacted to the mission? He was scared out of his mind, and rightly so. But worse, he pulled back, didn't talk to anyone, and didn't say goodbye when he left. Don't blame me that I haven't reached out because he sure as hell hasn't, either."

"You can't solve anything if you don't talk to him, Wizard." Lisa leveled her with a pointed look. "You really should read some of those military romances I keep telling you about. They might give you some insight."

Hermione groaned. "You know those things are fantasy, right?"

"Oh, my glory, are you a fiction snob?" Lisa's eyes opened wide in mock-shock. "Of course, I know they're fantasy. I was in the Army, remember? But one thing romance authors get right is relationships, and they show how to work through problems that seem insurmountable. Of course, it means the characters have to stop being whiny babies and *talk* to each other like adults." Lisa shook her head. "I can't believe you actually insulted me about romance novels."

Hermione sighed. "Sorry. I didn't mean to."

"Yes, you did. But take it from me, they're worth the read when the shit hits the fan. Life might suck, but everything works out in the stories. You could learn a lot from them, including how to heal from the bullshit of your past." She sipped her tea again, getting a faraway look on her face.

Hermione tipped her head. "If they're so great, why haven't you found your...what do you call it? Happily-ever-after?"

Lisa sighed and cradled the mug between her hands. "Because she died and it was too late by the time I was ready to make my move." She met Hermione's gaze. "Don't be like me. Learn from my mistakes and talk to Chester. It'll be worth it, believe me."

She clapped Hermoine on the shoulder. "Matter of fact, I'm gonna go find a book boyfriend right now, I think."

"I'm sorry, Dunwoody—"

"Don't worry about it, Wizard." She shot Hermione a smile that didn't reach her eyes and disappeared inside.

"Fuck." She hadn't meant to hurt her teammate. She knew Lisa hadn't had an easy time of it with love despite her model's face, but out of respect, she hadn't pried.

Maybe I should have. Except she'd never been very touchy-feely before or after her failed marriage. *I can hear Dunwoody say it's a mistake many beginners often make as if I've never loved.*

But had she? Had Hermione actually loved for real? Her ex had been a controlling misogynist, and a narcissist. She didn't think it had been possible to love him even if she had. Instead, she'd been in love with the idea of him and their marriage until it became clear it wasn't what she really wanted. Him *or* the marriage.

Chester, on the other hand, was kind, funny, generous, ridiculously smart, and yet attentive to her as a lover. Granted, she hadn't known him long, but he carried none of the energy her ex had. And she liked being with him, even when all they did was watch TV or go for a run.

She propped her beer against her knee and stared blindly out at the dark, rainy yard. *Shit,* am *I afraid of trying anything long-term with Chester?*

They'd solved the domestic terrorists hunting him down, so he was free to resume his life, just like her. But the life she'd been living seemed dark and colorless after spending the last few weeks with Chester. Technically, nothing stopped either of them from connecting.

Except you haven't made a move since he left.

Hermione groaned and rubbed her face with her hands. She should take her ass to bed. Or better yet, take her ass to *his* bed and apologize for being such a wuss. Would Chester accept her apology?

She scowled. *Won't know if you don't try. Woman up and get it done, Wilcox!*

Sighing at her inner drill sergeant, she unfolded herself from the chair and grabbed her beer bottle. She couldn't do anything that night, but she'd text him in the morning and see if they could meet up to talk.

She grimaced as she headed inside the Cabin. She hated the phrase 'we need to talk,' but she *wanted* to talk to Chester. She wanted a real chance with him, and she wanted back in his bed. Could he handle being with a woman who regularly went out on dangerous missions?

Won't know until you ask.

Damn drill sergeant. Hermione tossed her beer bottle in the trash and headed to her room for rack time. She almost stopped at Dunwoody's room to apologize and ask for one of the romance books Lisa had been touting, but decided against it and let herself into her room.

What she needed was a plan of action, a way to approach Martell with the best possible outcome.

Which is what, exactly?

She undressed and crawled into bed, fluffing the pillow and shoving a hand under it as she let her mind go over everything. What exactly did she want?

I want Chester.

Why? She let the question sift through her mind, stirring up reactions and explanations. Why did she want him? Because he reminded her how to relax and have fun. He made her feel good, both in and out of bed, and he didn't pressure her to be anything other than what she was.

Except he freaked out when he realized I do this shit all the time.

Yeah, but maybe there was a way around it. Maybe they could be a couple if they talked it out. Which wouldn't happen *unless* she messaged him.

First, a text. She sat up and grabbed her phone, finding Chester's contact information. The last text she'd sent him had been over two weeks ago asking if he preferred trout to salmon for lunch.

Taking a deep breath, she tapped out a new text.

> Hey, Dr. Martell. I found something of yours here at the Cabin. Can we meet up tomorrow so I can bring it to you?

She stared at the words for a few minutes, debating if it was a good way to start the communication. While it was true Chester had snagged her heart, she didn't think he'd find it amusing when she showed up and told him that. The 'Dr. Martell' seemed too formal and the rest of the text felt dismissive of all they'd shared. She slowly deleted the text and bit her bottom lip in thought.

What do you want him to do? It wasn't a simple question. Kiss her? Hug her? Run his hands over her body? Wrestle her to the bed forever and ever, over and over?

All of the above?

She never thought she'd go for a man who spent all his time with poisonous animals and toxic substances, but Chester Martell had continually lit her fire over the weeks she'd spent with him. She'd pictured spending time with the scientist in inappropriate ways while they'd been together, and it hadn't changed just because they were apart.

Which we'll be forever if I don't actually text something intelligible.

She took a deep breath and started typing.

> Hey, Chester. I'm sorry I haven't reached out sooner. There was a lot going on and by the time I woke up, you'd left the Cabin. I also noticed you pulled back a bit on the ride home from the research campus, and I wasn't sure if you wanted to hear from me again.

Hermione clenched her jaw and stared at the bathroom door of her room, trying to sort out her thoughts. What could she tell him that made sense after two weeks of silence?

Dunwoody would say stop being a chickenshit and be honest.

She tapped her chin with one finger, going over the words in her head before typing again.

> TBH I was afraid you wouldn't want to hear from me at all after everything that happened. It got really intense there at the end, and I got all caught up with the feds. But Dunwoody called me a chickenshit for not reaching out, and she's not wrong. So here I am, asking if we can meet up for coffee in Broken Pass at The Bearded Walrus coffee shop some time? I'd like to see you if you have time. Text or call me.

She nodded sharply and put the phone down. There. She'd womaned up and made the first move. Now all she had to do was wait. And hope he didn't ignore her.

Chester read the text for the thousandth time after he parked his car in the diagonal parking spots on Main Street in front of The Bearded Walrus coffee shop. He didn't know why the proprietors named it for a sea creature when they were located in the intermountain west, but the logo was cute with a tusked walrus holding a large, steaming mug with a look of satisfaction on its face.

He couldn't argue with that. Coffee, either iced or hot, brought him satisfaction.

Most of the time.

It hadn't worked for the past several weeks. Nothing had been very satisfying after the clean-up of the Broken Pass Research Center by SWAT and the FBI. He'd been debriefed three different times, by different FBI agents, all trying to determine if he'd been in cahoots with Avery Gentry. All the answers he gave were the same. No, no, and no. On top of that, he'd accepted a mandatory counseling session with a local psychologist to deal with his memories and fears and anxiety, mostly stemming from old beat-up pickup trucks and dark places.

Dr. Hembry said he might be experiencing some PTSD from the traumatic events in the underground and had promised to recommend his lab get moved to the ground floor instead of the basement. Chester was glad he was given mandatory leave to take some time to reassess. Did he want to go back to work at Broken Pass Research Center, or did he need to look for a different duty station? Did he want to stay in Broken Pass, Montana or move somewhere busier, like Seattle or Portland or hell, even Missoula?

He didn't have any answers, and it left him feeling aimless and untethered. He used to feel like he was doing the world a favor, helping find affordable and easy solutions to toxic problems. He'd wanted to make the world a better, safer, and healthier place. It never occurred to him that anyone would use his skills and knowledge to hurt others.

Not that my skills hurt others, but they were used to protect terrorists.

The anger surged, and he had to force his hands to release his steering wheel while he took some calming breaths. Fury raced through his mind at Avery, at all Avery's thugs, and at the audacity to use his skills to protect the few while hurting thousands. It offended Chester in every way.

Breathe, just breathe. That asshole's dead and his creepy buddies failed.

It didn't make him less angry, but at least the Sirens and the FBI had stopped them.

He took a few more deep breaths before he raised his gaze to The Bearded Walrus. Speaking of Sirens, he'd agreed to meet with Hermione to talk. A new surge of unease flooded through him. She'd said Dunwoody called her a chickenshit, but Hermione wasn't the only one.

After the debriefing, and Chester managed to get some downtime, he hadn't had the energy to seek Hermione out. He rationalized it by telling himself he didn't have a phone or her number, and once he got a new phone, that she probably didn't want to hear from a guy she'd had to rescue, twice, and she'd probably moved on. He tried to do the same, getting back into the rhythms of his little life. But everything was familiar and yet empty, and he couldn't focus on his usual pleasures.

He went to his therapy sessions, talked about his fears, and tried going running a few times to excise Hermione from his mind. Unfortunately, the beat-up pickup trucks gave him anxiety so bad he seriously considering buying a treadmill so he didn't have to be outside, and Hermione was never far from his thoughts.

The anxiety was better now that he'd been in therapy and had some tricks to use when it assailed him. And Hermione had finally texted. He'd been both relieved and nervous when he saw her text. It had been a couple of weeks and he had no idea where they stood considering his disappearing act while she slept. But he had to talk to her about what had happened, about who they were to each other, and where they would take their relationship.

If there is an actual relationship. What if she's meeting me just to let me down easy?

His gut clenched with the idea. Over the time he'd been back at home, his life had seemed...uninspiring, ordinary, drab. At first, he'd thought it was just because he'd experienced an extraordinary event and a quiet life after that would seem boring. But as the days passed, he realized what he missed wasn't the stress or the threat of capture. He missed Hermione.

He missed her confident snark, her dry humor, the way her eyes lit up when he undressed. He missed the quiet moments in the evening, watching the summer rainstorms roll across the valley.

I want more of that.

He missed her, and despite her dangerous job, he wanted to be around her, sharing their experiences of the day, watching weapon-making shows, and yes, fucking into the night.

Was that love? He had no idea, but he wanted to see if they could be something together. Friends with benefits? Long-term lovers? Maybe even a real relationship. Now that he'd started therapy, he could see how the intensity of their meeting influenced their connection, but the quiet moments at the Cabin deepened it to something worth working on.

If she feels the same. Glory, he hoped she did because he wanted more.

He groaned and forced himself to get out of his new car. The Eagle Militia had destroyed his old one, but the insurance had bought him a newer model electric vehicle, and it still had the new-car smell. He took a deep breath, locked the vehicle, and headed for the door to the coffee shop. Nothing would be resolved if he didn't at least go inside. He pulled open the door and stepped inside, scanning the interior for Hermione.

Chester found her at a table with clear views of all the exits and just a wall behind her. Her gaze periodically scanned the room until it met his, and it hit him in the chest with the force of a thrown brick. She was so damn beautiful and strong, though she looked a little uncertain. He raised his hand in a wave and pointed to the counter. She nodded, and he quickly ordered something hot despite the warmth of the day outside.

You got this. Don't fuck it up. Listen to her and try not to jump to conclusions.

His sisters' voices crowded into his head, and he tried not to grimace at the barista as she handed him his chai. Chester brought it to her table and sat down, trying to figure out what to say. He gave her a nervous smile.

"Hi."

She nodded. "Hey."

"How've you been?"

Ugh. Small talk. He'd sucked at it before he met her, and it hadn't improved with the time.

She didn't say anything for a few moments and her eyes narrowed, but then she nodded. "I haven't been great. You?"

He let out the breath he hadn't known he was holding. "I've been working it through, though the last few weeks have kinda sucked. It's been rough."

Her expression softened. "I can imagine. I'm sure the memories weren't too good."

"No. I get nightmares sometimes, but my therapist says it's my mind trying to expunge the sharpness of the memories so they become duller and I can heal from them." He sipped his chai to coat his suddenly dry throat. "I still don't like running near roads or old pickup trucks. They're triggering." He grimaced. "But I've been working on it. How have you been?"

"Good. Same old, same old. Contracts to fulfill, missions to complete." Her voice matched the vague descriptions as she turned her to-go cup around and around in her hands.

"Yeah." He nodded, rubbing his own cup with his thumb before screwing up his courage and meeting her green hazel gaze. "I wanted to thank you for your text. It was good to hear from you. I'm sorry I didn't get in touch. Between losing my phone in the research center and returning the burner phone you gave me, I didn't actually have your number. And as the days went on without contact, I wasn't sure you would welcome it." He grimaced again as her eyebrow went up. "Yeah, stupid, I know. My sisters pretty much said the same thing."

"You talked to your sisters about me?"

He nodded. "Yeah. I needed someone to bounce ideas off, and like you, I was too chickenshit to do more than realize I couldn't contact you. I've missed you, though."

"Did you? Miss me, really?" Both eyebrows went up.

He nodded. "I did. Particularly the days immediately after we got back from..." He trailed off and glanced around before lowering his voice. "That thing in the place with that guy."

She barked a laugh as her face split into a wide grin. "Oh yes, the thing in the place with that guy. That's a great way to describe it. You're learning fast, doc."

He snorted, some more tension bleeding away. "Yeah, well, the FBI made it very clear I wasn't supposed to talk about it with anyone other than those involved or my therapist." He rubbed the back of his neck. "But I really wanted to talk to you."

She raised her eyebrows again. "About the thing in the place with the guy?"

He shrugged one shoulder. "About that, and about the time we spent together, and about...well, what might come after. Maybe?"

She sighed and ran her fingers over the edge of the table. "Do you really want something to come after? The impression I got in the van after our escapade was that you were freaked out by what happened."

He gritted his teeth against throwing his hands up and demanding to know who wouldn't be.

Don't fuck it up. Listen to her and try not to jump to conclusions.

Vivian's voice repeated in his head, and he nodded. "I was. I'd never experienced anything like that and having someone's... having someone get shot right next to me was scary. And then I started thinking about your job, about what you do and how dangerous it is. You put yourself in those situations all the time. It's your *job*, and that scared me even more. So yeah, I completely freaked out."

She sighed. "It makes sense, but you have to know, Chester, I'm not going to stop doing what I do, even if it freaks you out. It's part of who I am, and I'm good at it."

"I know. And I won't ask you to stop what you do."

"I think I hear a 'but' coming." She crossed her arms over her chest as she sat back.

"No, no 'but.' I won't ask you to stop being the amazing warrior woman that you are. I only ask you don't resent me for worrying or being unnerved by your profession. I *can't* do what you do." He gave her a sad half smile. "I'm a nerd, remember? Part of the Nerd Herd? I study, watch, learn, read, analyze, and report. That's it. That's my life, and it used to make me happy doing only those things."

"Now I definitely hear a 'but' coming."

He snorted with a smile. "*But* then I met you, and you made my life extraordinary. You knocked me out of my routine and gave my life vibrancy."

"That wasn't me, that was a traumatic event in a local place with a bunch of guys." She smirked, though it didn't reach her eyes. "Speaking of which, how is Tessa Barton doing?"

He blinked and reorganized his thoughts at her subject change. "She's doing a lot better. They managed to get the artery tied off and saved her leg. Her wife and daughter were very grateful. They said I saved her life." He shrugged. "I'm just glad she's okay."

"You did save her life. Without the tourniquet, she would've bled out and no one could've helped her."

He scoffed. "That was mostly you. The superglue and tourniquet were all your ideas. I just followed directions."

"Hey, don't sell yourself short, doc. Following directions is the only reason the Army works." Hermione gave a little smile before she grabbed her coffee and leaned forward. "Listen, Chester, I'm not very good at this. In fact, you could say I suck at it. But spending my time with you while at the Cabin was the best in my life, and I want the chance to have more time with you, despite my job. Hell, despite *your* job."

"My job? What worries you about my job?"

"Are you kidding?" She raised her eyebrows. "You work with some of the most toxic substances known in the world. One mistake, one little scratch of a needle, and you're dead in minutes. I might work with bullets and knives, but there's hope of healing from both. Some of those snake venoms will kill you just by looking at them."

She reached across the table to grasp his hand. "That said, I still had the best time with you while you stayed at the Cabin. I'd like more of that, actually."

She looked so earnest, and some of his unease melted away. Maybe they could find their way back to what they'd shared at the Cabin.

"Really?" When she nodded, he squeezed her hand back. "It was the best time for me, too, even if a deranged terrorist wanted to kidnap me. Helluva time to start a relationship... you know, if that's what it was—is." He rubbed the back of his neck, trying to find intelligent words. "But do you really want to be with a nerdy researcher whose idea of an adventure is going running on a rainy and windy day? I'm not very adventurous overall. I don't have a T-type personality or the abilities of the special operators you know. I might not be exciting enough for you."

She nodded slowly, a smirk curling her lips. "Yeah, see, T-type personalities are exhausting, and dating men in the SpecOps community is a little like those black and white spies in *Mad Magazine* from back in the day. No one can talk about anything, you're always gone, and there's too much crap to process." She grimaced. "Is it bad that I'd rather have someone I know will be at home waiting for me?"

Chester snorted. "You mean like a househusband or boy back home?"

She shrugged, her cheeks turning pink. "Yeah, maybe, kinda? I mean, it would be nice to know there's someone waiting for me when we're done with a mission. Not that you'd be pining or waiting by the phone like some sort of 1950's style housewife. But someone happy to see me when I get home."

"You could get a dog." He smirked to show he was kidding.

"Yeah, I could. But I'd much rather have someone who I can show my appreciation." She tilted her head. "Besides, who'd take care of the mutt while I was gone? At least with a hot boyfriend, he can entertain and feed himself." She grinned.

He laughed. "Yeah, I'm pretty good at both things. Can't vouch for laundry or folding a fitted sheet, but the rest of my skills are pretty solid." Then her words caught up with him. "Wait, did you just call me hot?"

A hint of pink touched her cheeks. "Yeah. I've always found you sexy. Even when you were doing your antidote thing. *Especially* then." She raised her chin. "And I've got the sheets and laundry covered." Her grin mellowed until it faded entirely. "But I'm serious about the appreciation bit. I really want to be with you, Chester. I want the chance. We're different enough that we'd have things to talk about, but we have lots in common. Like watching Making Weapons 101 and going for early morning runs. Do you think you can be with someone who periodically saves the world, but still likes to come home to a good cock ride?"

Chester blinked, and his attention sharpened on her. "Wait, what? Did you say 'cock ride'?"

She smirked. "Yup."

He chuckled, but his mind went back over their predicament. Could he handle having a wife who regularly put herself in harm's way to save others, while he stayed home and studied venom?

Whoa, wait. Wife? Putting the cart before the horse a bit there, aren't you?

Maybe, but when he truly took time to think about living with or without Hermione, he'd choose with every time. The idea of being alone with just his work again was so repugnant, he didn't even want to consider it. That was a cold and gray life, and he'd spent too much time in the fiery light of Hermione's presence to return there.

Not that I'm ready for a wife, but working on long-term-girl-friend would be fine.

"Okay, I really like that cock ride idea." He met her gaze and gave her a matching smirk. "And I'd really like more time with you to see if we can be a couple when we're not in a highly stressful situation." He took a breath and ran his thumbs over his cup. "It's going to take me a little bit to get used to the idea of you going out to save the world as your day job. But I wouldn't change you if I could because you're the woman I'm attracted to as you are. If you're okay with dating a member of the Nerd Herd, who doesn't know much about weapons other than knives—from watching Making Weapons 101—"

"Yes, I'm more than okay with that." Her smirk widened into a brilliant grin as she reached out to grasp his hand on the table. "I'm not leaving Montana for a while—the Cabin is our home base, but also, I have some mandatory downtime coming to me. I could either spend it with you at your place, or you could come back to the Cabin and hang out there, too. Lots of room there." She squeezed his hand. "Please just tell me we have a chance at success."

"I'd say we're sitting at about eighty-eight percent where we are right now." He squeezed back. "But that number rises to about ninety-eight percent if you let me tell you a secret."

She raised her eyebrows, though her smile didn't change. "Secret? What secret?"

It's now or never.

He took a deep breath and hoped he wouldn't scare her away. After making sure no one was watching them, he leaned forward and lowered his voice.

"The secret that I'm in love with you."

Her eyes widened and her smile froze, and so did the breath in his chest.

Oh fuck, she looks like a deer in headlights.

Chester swallowed hard and forced himself to take a breath in as quietly as possible. Any wrong move would get an equal and opposite reaction, to mangle one of Newton's laws. He tried not to fidget or worry while he waited for Hermione to say something. Would she laugh at him? No, that wasn't her style. But she might let him down gently, saying she wasn't there yet. Maybe she'd tell him they could work up to those sorts of feelings for her. She'd seemed interested in them having a chance at a relationship, but maybe love was a bit too much too soon.

Not for me.

"You're in love with me?"

Did she sound panicked? Or was he projecting his own fears and insecurities onto her? He swallowed hard and nodded.

"Yup. Have been for a while, though I can't pinpoint when it happened." He sat back and gripped his chai cup to keep from fidgeting. "I know we didn't talk about love or anything, but I saw your text and thought—"

"Thank fuck." She let her breath out and her shoulders relaxed. "Me, too, doc. It took Dunwoody to bitch-slap the daylights outta me so I could realize it, but yeah, me too."

"You...too, what?" His thoughts whirled in a maelstrom of surprise and hope, but too incoherent to decipher.

"I'm in love with you, too." She gave him a sheepish smile. "Dunwoody says I have to work on my communication because you can't read my mind. It's a guy thing."

Chester blinked then barked a laugh. "A guy thing? That I can't read your mind?"

"Yup."

He grinned. "That's very true. I don't think I'd even want to try."

"So, what are we going to do?" Hermione rolled her lips inward in an uncharacteristically unsure expression.

"About that? About reading your mind?"

She snorted. "No, I've got that part covered. I meant about you and me. What are we going to do from here?"

"Oh." Chester picked up his cup to sip his chai, only to find it empty. He set the cup down and met her gaze. "How about we start with regular dates?"

"You mean like dinner or lunch?"

He couldn't help the heat rising to his cheeks. "No, I meant more like Netflix & chill, possibly naked."

Her grin bloomed big and bold. "I'd say that's a perfect start. Your place or mine?"

"Yours. You have a better theatre system."

She narrowed her eyes. "True, but there's no way we can be naked while watching. Too many roommates and no good bed there."

"Yes, but the bedroom isn't far…" He waggled his eyebrows. "What do you think? My TV is only a forty-inch, nothing compared to your big screen."

"You know what they say—size really does matter." She grinned as he laughed. "But that forty incher is in a place where there's no other people around. And it's a lot closer than the Cabin, which is a half-hour away. Besides, privacy does come at a premium at the Cabin."

Chester sighed and nodded. "I know. But my apartment is just…empty. I mean, it's a place to sleep and shower, but there isn't much life there. After all the time we spent at the Cabin, it started to feel more like a home to me than my own place." He shrugged. "It's ridiculous, I know, but that's the way it is." He met her gaze again. "I missed being with you."

"Yeah, see, I missed being with you, too." She ducked her head a little and grimaced. "So, if you could handle some good-natured ribbing from the ladies, would you like to come over to my place?"

His heart leapt with hope. "Yeah, I'd like that a lot. When's a good time?"

"Right now?" She grinned when he blinked. "Okay, I guess I could let you pack a bag so you could spend the night. Or several nights. Or maybe even a month or two."

Excitement bubbled up in his chest. "I, uh, I could probably pack for that long. I mean, they only gave me a few weeks off to recuperate, but the commute to the Cabin isn't too bad. You know, if I stay longer than my time off."

"Tell you what. I'll follow you back to your place and help you pack as much or as little as you like, and we'll go from there, yeah?" She grabbed their cups and tossed them in the nearest trash before she turned back to him. "You and I can figure it out as we go. Sound fair?"

"Yes, ma'am. That's more than fair." He nodded and followed her back out to the street. He desperately wanted to spend more time with Hermione, but she wasn't wrong about the privacy and the roommates. "Hey, wait."

They stopped beside his little Prius and he rubbed the back of his neck with sudden unease. "Given what you and your colleagues do, and that the Cabin is your HQ, is it okay that I stay there? I mean, don't you sometimes have to bring your clients there?"

She smiled and shook her head. "Nope. You're the first. Most of our clients aren't located close. We go all over. You just happened to be local. As for if it's okay, technically it's my house, so I can have anyone I want to stay over for as long as I want. But I'll definitely tell my team that you're staying for the foreseeable future."

"And they'll be okay with that?"

Hermione snorted ruefully. "I suspect Dunwoody will throw a damn party about it. She keeps telling me I should read some of her romance books, and she'll say you coming to stay is the beginning of the happily-ever-after that's the goal of the stories."

He laughed. "You don't believe in the happily-ever-after?"

She tilted her head and narrowed her eyes thoughtfully. "I dunno. I used to think it was silly storytelling. But after being around you, there might be some truth to it. Jury's still out."

He pushed his glasses up his nose and straightened his shoulders. "Maybe I'll just have to prove it to you."

"Prove? How are you gonna do that, doc?" She gave him a half-smirk as the sun glinted off her hair.

He loved it when she called him that. "Let's look at it like a scientific experiment. We know that we were very compatible while together before."

"Yeah, but there were extenuating circumstances."

"True, but that's just one of the variables in this experiment. The thing with the guys in the place isn't a usual event, right?"

She nodded slowly. "Right."

"So, we know that we worked well together, and were compatible sexually despite the extenuating circumstances, perhaps we could remove those circumstances from the experiment and test for compatibility then." He reached into his car and pulled out a little notebook. "We could make a list of all the variables and put them to the test."

"Uh-huh..." Hermione tapped her chin. "I think you're onto something. Let's go to your place and pack up a few of your things so you'll be comfortable during this experiment. Then we'll go back to the Cabin and make that list."

"I recall one of the stipulations was nakedness." He smirked.

"True, and I'm totally good with that, doc." She matched his smirk. "But remember, I do have a whole team of roommates, and while I love those women, I'm not into sharing you with them. I'm just not that kind of girl."

"I suppose we wouldn't want to introduce too many new variables at once until we've established a control sample." He leaned closer to her and lowered his voice. "I'm not that kind of guy, either. I'm only willing to get naked for you."

Hermione nodded sharply. "Good thing. Dunwoody can have her book boyfriends. I prefer the real thing. So, let's get your stuff and get back to the Cabin. I'm in the mood for some experimenting."

She winked, and his cock hardened in his pants. Holy fuck, she was sexy. He scrambled to get into the driver's seat as quickly as possible. He'd never been so excited to pack his shit as he was at that moment. His cock reminded him he was probably going to get laid, but more important than that, he was going to get more time with Hermione, and just the opportunity made the packing worth it.

Chapter Twenty-One

Hermione tried to rein in her excitement, but her inner teenaged girl bounced around like she was going on her first date. Chester had agreed to come back to the Cabin and stay a while. True, he wanted to make a list of all the ways they were compatible to prove happily-ever-after actually existed, but she'd take him any way she could get him.

He'd lit up like a candelabra when he told her they'd make it an experiment, and she swore she'd make every effort to get him to do that again. Something about his excitement enhanced hers, and she couldn't wait to get him home alone.

Home. That word had so many meanings. But the last couple of weeks, the Cabin hadn't felt the same. *That's because he wasn't there.*

When had it only been home while he'd shared the bathroom?

It didn't matter now. He was coming back to stay for a while.

If I have anything to say about it, it'll be forever.

They parked their respective vehicles in front of a decent apartment building with three stories and balconies at each window. Chester exited his Prius and headed up to the second floor. Hermione followed, keeping an eye on anyone watching his place too closely. She didn't see anyone, and by the time she got to his place, he'd left the door open and rustling sounds came from the bedroom.

She scoped out the living room and found his place surprisingly sparse.

Damn, it's like he's in the military or something.

"Hey, doc?"

"Yes?" Chester's voice came from the bedroom, but he didn't step out.

"How long you been livin' here?"

She took in the worn couch, the aforementioned forty-inch TV, and an old fiberboard coffee table.

"Four years, why?" He came out of the bedroom and ducked into the bathroom.

"Huh. It's kinda empty, isn't it?" She noted all the dishes were cleaned and put away in the kitchen, the counters free of debris or appliances.

He appeared and shrugged with a smile. "It was really just a place to sleep and store stuff. I didn't spend all that much time here."

"Yeah, I can tell. Anything I can help you with? Like your running or workout gear? Your computer, phone, chargers, tablets, stuff like that?"

"Yeah, here." He came out and handed her a laptop bag with laptop, tablet, and their respective chargers. "I'm almost all packed with the things I need for a couple of days. Plus condoms and lube." A blush made his cheeks turn pink.

She grinned. "How many condoms you got, doc?"

The blush deepened. "Two boxes."

"Nice." She nodded. "You almost done packing? I think it's time to get back to the Cabin and work on that list of yours."

"Of *ours*. This is *our* experiment. And I foresee us having a lot of tests to get the results we want." The blush still stained his cheeks, but his eyes glittered with excitement.

"Right. Are you ready? I'd like to get going on this experimentation." She held her hand out so he'd precede her out the door.

"Yup. Let me get my bags."

"Bags? Plural?"

"Well... I wanted to be sure I had enough of my things...you know, in case I stay for more than just a couple of days." He paused in front of his bedroom. "Am I overstepping?"

"Nope, I'm good with that. I'm just surprised because this is an experiment after all. It could have...unexpected results." She bit her lip. "I mean, you did say only a couple days."

"Yeah, but we already have some preliminary findings from earlier that will help us refine our current efforts." He came out carrying two duffel bags and a backpack over his shoulder. "Right?"

"Right. Come on, doc. Let's get going. I'd like to get at least one experimental session in before it's time to be social with the rest of the team." She took a duffel bag along with the laptop bag and stepped out of the apartment, scanning the surroundings as she waited for him to lock up.

No one suspicious was about, and the only moving vehicles were leaving the complex. She followed Chester down to the parking lot and helped him load his things into his vehicle. She set the duffel bags into the back of her vehicle, but let him keep his backpack and his laptop bag in his.

"All right, I'll follow you as far as the turn off to the Cabin. I'll call you on the way to make sure we're in constant contact."

He frowned. "Do we need to be in constant contact now that the Eagle Militia has been arrested by the FBI?"

"There might not be a known threat to your well-being, but it'll make me feel better until we get to the Cabin and I can teach you a little about defensive driving. Okay?"

He looked at her for a few moments before he nodded. "Okay, Wizard."

She snorted. "Good. Let's get going. I'll call you." She closed his door and tapped the roof before heading for her own SUV.

She didn't remember much about the drive to the Cabin, but she and Chester talked on the phone about random things until the turnoff came into view. She sped around him to get the gate open and let the rest of the Sirens know he'd be staying with them for a while.

"Define a 'while,' Wizard." Mo sounded amused.

"I'll let you know. Wizard out." She wasn't ready to let the ladies get into her business quite yet.

Hell, I don't even know the answer.

A little spike of fear zipped up her back at the thought that things might not work out.

Shut it, Wilcox. No use sabotaging the mission before it's started.

She kept her eye on the rearview mirror as she drove through the gate to make sure Chester followed her without problems. Again, she didn't expect any issues, but she couldn't turn off her situational awareness. She didn't relax until they reached the garage and pulled into the relative darkness of the space.

Hermione closed the garage door before she let Chester out of his vehicle. Then she helped him gather his things.

"Ready?"

"Yes, ma'am. But I do have one question." He shouldered his pack before he took one of the duffel bags while she took the other.

"And that is?" She held the door to the kitchen open.

"Am I staying in the room I had before, or am I staying in your quarters?"

"I'd like the answer to that question, too, Wizard." Staff Sergeant Marisol Gomez nodded to them as they crossed through the open space behind the island.

"That's need to know, Gomez, and you don't." Hermione raised her chin as she sailed through.

"I beg to differ, Wizard. I gotta know if I have to set up a new room with sheets and shit." Gomez followed them into the main foyer of the Cabin, her expression mulish.

"If I might put in a request." Chester pulled their attention to him as they all came to a halt.

"Yes?" Hermione raised her eyebrows.

"Perhaps it would be easier at this juncture to share a room and tomorrow we can make other arrangements if needs be. What do you think?"

Gomez switched her gaze between the two of them and grinned. "That's an excellent solution, Dr. Martell. Wizard, you just let me know if you need any changes, yeah?"

Hermione refused to blush or give Gomez anything to gossip about so she nodded curtly and spun on her heel, leading the way up to her room. She heard Chester thanking Gomez behind her, but she was done worrying about what the others thought about him staying in her quarters. He was hers and she was going to take advantage of his proximity.

"Where should I put my things?" Chester closed the door of her room and set his pack and laptop bag on the floor.

She dropped the duffels on the floor and grabbed him, pushing him up against the closed door. She angled her head to take his lips in a desperate kiss she'd been dreaming of for days.

Chester moaned and opened his mouth to accept her tongue. He gave as good as he got, wrapping his arms around her and feasting on her lips. Hermione couldn't get enough of his taste, and her pussy grew wet with arousal at each swipe of his tongue against hers.

"Good glory, doc." She pulled back and rested her forehead against his, breathing hard. "I've missed that so much."

"Oh good. Me, too." He nodded, depositing little kisses on her cheeks and forehead, wherever he could reach. "Can we go to the bed, though? My knees are getting weak, and my cock is trying to break through my zipper."

She laughed. "I don't think I've ever heard a guy admit that, but I totally understand what you're talking about." She backed up. "Come on, doc. Let's go to bed."

"Wait, do me a favor first." He pulled his shirt over his head and kicked off his shoes.

"What's that?" She raised an eyebrow as she watched his beautiful, fit body appear.

"Strip for me?" His cheeks grew pink again. "I'd like to watch you undress, please."

"Now you're talking." She grinned. "But you first. Get naked and then I will. I can't guarantee I'll be as good as the strippers in the local strip joints, but I'll do what I can."

"Yes, ma'am." He unzipped his jeans and pushed them off his hips. His underwear went with them, and his hard shaft sprang free. He dropped his clothes and crawled onto the bed, flipping over onto his back. "All right, I'm ready."

"Yes, you definitely are." She nodded to his straining cock. "I'm looking forward to enjoying that again." She turned her back and pulled off her boots before looking over her shoulder. "Ready for the rest?"

"Yes, ma'am." He licked his lips and grasped his shaft, stroking slowly.

Her pussy clenched with the need to feel his hard flesh between her nether lips, and she took a deep breath before reaching behind herself to grasp the zipper on her red bustier top. She pulled it down slowly and let the top fall off her shoulders.

He gasped. "No bra?"

"Not in this kind of top." She extended her arm and dropped the shirt on the floor. "But I don't really need one. You ready for more?"

"Oh glory, yes."

He sounded desperate, and she swallowed her laugh. She unzipped her ripped jeans and tucked her thumbs into the waistband, snagging her underwear as she shimmied the cloth off her ass. She bent in half, giving him a full view of her cheeks and thighs as she stepped out of the jeans.

"Shit oh dear, Hermione."

She kicked the clothes away and turned around slowly, letting him get a good look at all the marks on her body. She'd covered a lot of her scars with ink—mostly flowers or mandalas—but a few showed despite the decoration. She hoped he wasn't disappointed with what he saw.

Don't be ridiculous. He's seen you naked before.

"You're so fuckin' beautiful." Chester's voice held a note of awe, and he let his gaze caress her limited curves. "Do I get to touch while I look at all your sexiness?"

She laughed as she sauntered to the bed, stopping beside it with one hand on her hip. "You want to touch this, Chester?"

"Yes, ma'am." He licked his lips, and her pussy clenched again in anticipation.

"Good, because I've missed sucking on your cock, and I need it now."

She crawled over his body until she crouched with her breasts hanging over his groin. His dick flexed under her and made her mouth water. She scooted backwards and settled onto her knees as she lowered her head.

"I'm gonna enjoy this."

She slid her lips over the taut head of his cock, and he hissed as his hands fisted in the bedcovers. She swallowed her smile as she let his hard flesh slide deeper into her mouth until it hit the back of her throat. She massaged it with her tongue, enjoying the tangy tastes of his precum coating her palate.

Damn, I forgot how delicious he tastes.

She hummed as she pulled back, laving the stiff flesh as she held it up with her free hand. Chester moaned and rocked his hips, chasing the heat of her mouth. She flashed him a grin before she engulfed his shaft again, this time scraping her teeth against the edge of the head.

"Oh, fuck, Hermione." He thrust into her mouth as if he couldn't hold still. "Your mouth is divine. Suck my dick so hard."

Not the most romantic thing a man had ever said to her, but it turned her on and made her pussy clench with erotic need. She tightened her grip on his shaft as she sucked it down, making sure her tongue still laved the taut skin. He groaned as she raked her teeth over the head again and she let her fingers trail down over his balls. The skin tightened up, and he gasped as she stroked them.

"Oh, glory, Hermione. If you keep…" He gasped again as she squeezed his dick in her fist. "If you keep going, I'm going to blow."

She pulled back off his cock and tilted her head. "As much as I'd love to see you lose control from sucking you off, I don't want the party to end quite so soon."

"Good, 'cause I was going to suggest we change it up a little." He sat up. "I've missed your pussy on my face."

Hermione grinned. "Have you?" She lifted her head from his cock and trailed her fingers up his belly to his chest, gently plucking his nipple. "Do you want it right now?"

"Yes, ma'am."

"All right then."

She took her time to kiss him as her breasts brushed his chest and he grasped her head, turning his to make sure he could get his tongue deeper into her mouth. She moaned and her pussy clenched with arousal before she pulled back and looked him in the eyes.

"Time to eat pussy, doc."

She crawled up to straddle his head, and he groaned with pleasure.

"Oh, fuck yeah." He grasped her hips and drew her vulva down to his mouth with an avaricious grin. "Let me lick this sweet pussy."

The first swipe of his tongue against her nether lips had her throwing back her head and gripping the headboard to keep from falling. Chester's hands on her hips kept her in place as he feasted on her sensitive flesh like a starving man.

He pushed his tongue between her folds and licked her leisurely, tasting and touching every surface. The pleasure ramped up and Hermione closed her eyes, reveling in his deft caresses. Each swipe of his tongue between her folds sent electric shocks of ecstasy through her, increasing her arousal.

She ground her hips on his face, trying to get closer to his clever tongue. She needed more. The hot, slick slide pushed her arousal higher until she was whimpering in time with his strokes. Sensation swamped her mind, making her feel everything as he feasted on her tender flesh.

"Oh, glory, doc. Yes, yes. It feels so good."

She rocked on his face, trying to find the sweet spot where his touches would send her over the edge. He slid his hand away from her hip and inserted a finger into her cleft while he tugged her clit into his mouth.

"Fuck yeah, Chester."

She moaned as she rocked on his finger, and he sucked harder on her clit. She whimpered, her hands tightening on the headboard as her mind swam with the rising tide of sensation. When Chester added another finger and used his tongue to flick her clit, it was all over.

Her mind shot out among the stars as her orgasm exploded through her. She cried out her pleasure as he pumped his fingers in and out of her grasping channel and sucked on her clit in the same rhythm. She let go as the pleasure swept her away, and only her grip on the headboard kept her upright.

When she finally came back to the bedroom, she slumped enough to look down at Chester, and he smirked up at her like the cat who'd stolen the canary.

"Holy fuck, that was amazing."

"I'm glad you liked it."

"'Like it' is an understatement."

She scooted back until she straddled his hips again. She leaned in and kissed him, enjoying the taste of her cum on his lips. He moaned as she reached down and stroked his straining cock.

"But I need more."

"Well then, my sexy warrior woman, take my cock and give yourself more." He grasped her hips and rocked his, letting his cock caress her clit.

"Oh glory, yes. I want your cock so much." But she lifted away and gave him a smirk. "Where'd you put the condoms?"

He groaned but reached over to the drawer in the bedside table. "Right here."

"Good man." She grinned as she pulled it out and took out several of the foil packets before ripping one off. "I like a man who plans for the best, doc."

He shook his head as she smoothed the latex down his shaft. "I learned from the best."

She didn't hesitate to position herself over his shaft and sink down on him. Her slick pussy slid down his cock without resistance, and he filled her up completely. She paused once he sat balls-deep and savored the fullness of him inside her.

"Holy fuck, Hermione. You're so perfectly tight."

"Oh yeah? I hope you like it because you feel fuckin' amazing in my pussy." She slowly lifted off him and he made a sound of protest, but she quickly sank back down, and they both moaned. "Don't you worry, doc. I'm not getting off this ride until we're both satisfied."

He grinned until she started to move in slow, deep thrusts, taking her time to drag his cock across all the sensitive flesh between her legs. Every slide in hit her g-spot, and every slide out stroked her clit, stoking her arousal.

She gazed down at Chester, enjoying the hardness of his cock and watching his features tighten as his arousal built. A new feeling filled her along with the erotic pleasure—a feeling of tenderness as she rocked on his hard shaft. She wanted this connection to last. Oh sure, the sex was exquisite, but she wanted the happily-ever-after Dunwoody talked about. Hermione wanted it in real life with Chester.

"Fuck yeah, Hermione, ride me hard." Chester gritted his teeth in a grimace of concentration as he rocked with her. "You feel so fuckin' good."

"Damn straight." She clenched her inner muscles around him, and they both moaned. "I'm gonna ride this hard cock of yours real slow until we can't hold back. You with me, doc?"

"Fuck yeah."

He lifted his hips and drove his cock deeper, making her damn near swallow her tongue. She lost all coherence except the need to ride, slow and deep, to make the pleasure exquisite. Despite her singular focus on reaching her release, the tenderness built with her arousal, weaving through it as if one couldn't be without the other.

She wanted to come, and the way he moved beneath her ensured it would happen, but she also wanted him to come with her, find that deep pleasure of connection. She stared into his eyes as her orgasm neared, trying to convey all she felt beside the pleasure.

I love you. She said the words in her head, amazed that it was true. She did love Chester Martell for all his quirkiness, for his determination to save the world one venomous critter at a time. She might have rescued him in the Broken Pass Research Center, but he was as much her hero as she was his.

As it should be.

The thought shoved her over the precipice of ecstasy, and she flew with a shout. "Yeeessssss! Fuck yes!"

"Aw yeah, come for me, Hermione." Chester bucked under her, driving her higher into her bliss. "Fuck yeah, yeah, yeeeaaaaah-hhh..."

His cock hardened even more inside her before hard jets of hot cum filled her as he gripped her hips tight. She tried to keep him in focus, but the pleasure overwhelmed all her senses and she let herself fall into it.

When she came back to herself, Chester had his hands still holding her hips, his eyes closed and a satisfied smile on his face. Hermione couldn't help her laugh, surprised at how relaxed and joyful she sounded. He opened his eyes and looked up at her.

"You look happy."

A slow smile curled her lips. "That's because I am."

"Good."

She took a deep breath before she climbed off his softening cock. "Let me clean us up."

He frowned. "Oh no, I can do that."

She shook her head as she pulled the condom off him, careful to keep the contents inside. "I got this. Besides, you have to tabulate our results."

He blinked. "Results?"

She nodded as she retreated to the bathroom to throw away the condom and grab a washcloth full of warm water. She wiped herself down before rinsing and bringing it back to him. He still lay with his beautiful body exposed as he puzzled over what she'd said. She settled on the bed and carefully cleaned his genitals with loving strokes as she waited for his mind to catch up.

She tossed the washcloth back into the bathroom to deal with later and crawled into the bed beside him. He'd pulled the covers over his body, but his chest remained exposed with one hand behind his head. She settled with her head on his shoulder as she wrapped an arm around his belly, and let out a sigh of contentment.

"That's a good sound."

"Yup." She smiled though she didn't look up at him. "Did you finish tabulating the results?"

He chuckled. "I did."

"And what have you concluded?"

"We've verified that outside circumstances, whether chaotic or calm, don't have any influence on our sexual compatibility."

She bit back a laugh. He sounded so serious. "I would agree."

"I also think that it's too early to draw any long-term conclusions."

Hermione froze then lifted herself to look down at him. "What do you mean?"

She expected his expression to be wrinkled in thought, but he wore a thoughtful smile.

"An N of one is a poor sample size. I think we need to continue the experiment."

"Oh, I'm all for continuing. And I agree we need to verify the results, over and over."

She bit her bottom lip as she studied his features. She loved his two-tone brown eyes and the scruff coming in. She loved the abraded feeling of what that scruff had done to her inner thighs, and the tight hold he'd had on her hips. She also loved his analytical mind and his kindness, generosity, and determination to help others.

Chester's forehead wrinkled as he frowned a little. "What?"

"Stay."

His expression smoothed into a smile. "So, you'd count our experiment a success?"

"Yes, sir. Don't you?" She trailed her fingers over his chest.

"Mmm." He hummed as he narrowed his eyes. "I think it was a good first attempt, but more sessions are required to see if we can duplicate the results. Maybe adding different variables."

She raised her eyebrows. "Different variables? Like what?"

He shrugged. "Like reverse cowgirl, mutual masturbation, and doggy style, for starters."

Hermione threw her head back and laughed. "Hell yeah, doc. I think you're right. We definitely have to add those parameters to our next experiments. But don't forget the list."

A wide grin stretched his lips. "Ah yes, the list, of all the variables that we need to introduce, and the other list that we'll build over time."

She frowned a moment. "Which list is that?"

"The one where we'll record all the ways we're compatible, both in bed and out, and why happily-ever-after is scientifically proven." He pulled away a moment to grab his tablet and bring it back to the bed. "If you want, you could use some of Dunwoody's instruction manuals to see if we've used all the suggestions documented in them."

Hermione blinked. *Instruction manuals?* Her eyes widened. "You mean her romance novels?"

Chester grinned as he typed something into his tablet. "Yup. It sounds to me as if the authors have a lot of experience and we should see if we can duplicate their results, to make our experiments scientifically viable. Don't you think?"

She laughed again and pushed the tablet aside. "Yes, I definitely think so. I love you, Chester."

His eyes widened, and he stared at her in wonder. "You love me, a certified member of the Nerd Herd?"

"Yes, I love the way your mind works, and I'll do my best to keep up so you'll never get bored." She leaned down to kiss his lips, enjoying the feeling of his chest hair on her breasts.

His eyes sparkled when she pulled back. "I'll never get bored, Hermione. Because I love you, too. My beautiful warrior woman who can outrun, outfight, and outdrive me."

She snorted. "I gotta be good at something." She grinned. "I'll always use those skills to protect you, especially if you stay here with me. Please, stay." She bit her lip in unusual vulnerability.

"You really want me here with you?"

"Yes." She didn't bother to elaborate because it was the simple truth.

"Okay, Hermione."

Her eyes widened. "Okay?"

"Yup. I'll stay here, with you, for as long as you want me."

She threw herself into his arms and hugged him tight. "I want you. I want to continue our experiments and scientifically prove happily-ever-after."

He laughed and hugged her back. "Perfect. Want to start on the next one?"

She pulled back and tilted her head. "What do you have in mind?"

"Well, we could add the meal and movie variables, and see how that goes."

Hermione grinned. "Hmm, maybe we should start with the shower variable first."

"Hell yeah." He slid out of bed and tugged on her hand. "Let's start that experiment right now. I'm a big fan of testing."

"Wait." She tugged back at the threshold of the bathroom. "I want to test one more thing."

"Oh yeah?" He tilted his head as he led her into the bathroom and started the shower with his free hand. "What's that?"

"Do you think we could use these experiments to test the theory of forever?"

Chester stopped and gave her his full attention. "Forever, as it pertains to happily-ever-after?"

She bit her lip. "Yeah."

He pulled her to his chest and wrapped his arms around her. "Hell yeah. I definitely want to test with the expectation of forever." He brushed his lips across hers. "I love you, Hermione."

"I love you, too, Chester. Please stay forever."

"That's my intention and expectation. Let's compile the results of this current experiment to support the theory that happily-ever-after exists."

He dragged her into the shower and proceeded to reinforce that happily-ever-after did indeed exist.

THE END

About Siobhan Muir

S iobhan Muir lives in Cheyenne, Wyoming, with her husband, two daughters, a house panther, and a very old dog. When not writing, she can be found looking down a microscope at fossil fox teeth, pursuing her other love, paleontology. An avid reader of science fiction/fantasy, her husband gave her a paranormal romance for Christmas one year, and she was hooked for good.

In previous lives, Siobhan has been an actor at the Colorado Renaissance Festival, a field geologist in the Aleutian Islands, and restored inter-planetary imagery at the USGS. She's hiked to the top of Mount St. Helens and to the bottom of Meteor Crater.

Siobhan writes kick-ass adventure with hot sex for men and women to enjoy. She believes in happily ever after, redemption, and communication, all of which you will find in her paranormal and dauntless romance stories.

Connect with Siobhan online at:
https://siobhanmuir.com/
Facebook
Instagram
Siobhan's Blog
Ko-fi

Tumblr

MeWe

BlueSky

Patreon

YouTube

Or sign up for her newsletter to get excerpts and cover reveals and other fun extras.

NEWSLETTER

Other Books by Siobhan Muir

Her Devoted Vampire
The Sorceress of Song and Flame
Mr. Fixit's Billionaire
Fossil Beds Bed & Breakfast
The Dreadstone King

Bad Boys of Beta Squad Series
Bronco's Rough Ride
The Navy's Ghost
Rimshot's Hard Target
Bam-Bam's Inked Hart
Deli's Take Out

Callowwood Pack Series
Queen Bitch of the Callowwood Pack
The Callowwood Canine Caper

Cloudburst Colorado Series
A Hell Hound's Fire
The Beltane Witch
Christmas I.C.E. Magic
Cloudburst Ice Magic
Cloudburst Coffee & Spa
Courting the Dragon Widow

SIOBHAN MUIR

The Samhain Soldier

Concrete Angels MC Series
My Forever Cocky Biker Encounter
Dude With a Cool Car
Angel Ink
The Concrete Angel
Running From the Texas Millionaire

Elemental Hearts Series
Wildfire's Heart
A Timeless Heart

Rifts Series
Take the Reins
A Centaur's Solstice Wish
In Death's Shadow

Silver State Mysteries Series
Second Chance Succubus

Sirens, Inc. Series
The Siren and the Scientist

Summit Springs Sapphic Romance
Broken Chains
In Plain Sight

Triple Star Ranch Series

Rope a Falling Star

Star Light, Star Bright

Star Spangled Banner

Ultimate Recon Series

Darwin's Evolution

Warbler Peninsula Series

Order of the Dragon

The Valkyrie's Sword

Burning Yuletide

The Ivory Road Serial

A Walk in the Sand

Outback Dreams

A Dance Between Worlds

The Karobis Calls

Coming Soon

The Siren and the Drag Queen (Sirens, Inc. #2)

The Siren Queen (Sirens, Inc. Novella)